Yuri and Gregor left the room and got back in the car. "How will we get on the Air Force base?" Yuri asked.

"That is easy. You are a lieutenant (JG) naval officer. I'm a petty officer, first class, your driver."

"Surely it can't be that easy. We will have to show official papers, orders, identification?"

"If asked, you have official papers. But the question is almost never asked. On this car there is a sticker for the military base. The car was liberated from a military person on temporary deployment. It has a decal appropriate for getting on base. The guard waves everyone in with the decal—without checking papers or ID cards. After we are finished with the car, it will be left in the same location it was taken from. No one will ever know it was used."

"It is unbelievable that American security is this lax."

"Believe it." Gregor smirked as he put the car in reverse. The American idiom rolled easily off his tongue, pushed along by his gravelly voice. "In the United States, if you look like you know what you are doing, almost anything is yours for the taking."

THE TAKING
OF THE
KING

NELSON BLISH

JOVE BOOKS, NEW YORK

THE BERKLEY PUBLISHING GROUP
Published by the Penguin Group
Penguin Group (USA) Inc.
375 Hudson Street, New York, New York 10014, USA
Penguin Group (Canada), 90 Eglinton Avenue East, Suite 700, Toronto, Ontario M4P 2Y3, Canada
(a division of Pearson Penguin Canada Inc.)
Penguin Books Ltd., 80 Strand, London WC2R 0RL, England
Penguin Group Ireland, 25 St. Stephen's Green, Dublin 2, Ireland (a division of Penguin Books Ltd.)
Penguin Group (Australia), 250 Camberwell Road, Camberwell, Victoria 3124, Australia
(a division of Pearson Australia Group Pty. Ltd.)
Penguin Books India Pvt. Ltd., 11 Community Centre, Panchsheel Park, New Delhi—110 017, India
Penguin Group (NZ), Cnr. Airborne and Rosedale Roads, Albany, Auckland 1310, New Zealand
(a division of Pearson New Zealand Ltd.)
Penguin Books (South Africa) (Pty.) Ltd., 24 Sturdee Avenue, Rosebank, Johannesburg 2196,
South Africa

Penguin Books Ltd., Registered Offices: 80 Strand, London WC2R 0RL, England

THE TAKING OF THE KING

A Jove Book / published by arrangement with the author.

PRINTING HISTORY
Jove mass-market edition / May 2006

Copyright © 2006 by Nelson Blish.
Cover design by George Long.
Cover illustration by Chris Moore.
Text design by Kristin del Rosario.

ISBN: 0-515-14052-X

JOVE®
Jove Books are published by The Berkley Publishing Group,
a division of Penguin Group (USA) Inc.,
375 Hudson Street, New York, New York 10014.
JOVE is a registered trademark of Penguin Group (USA) Inc.
The "J" design is a trademark belonging to Penguin Group (USA) Inc.

PRINTED IN THE UNITED STATES OF AMERICA

10 9 8 7 6 5 4 3 2 1

FOR
Joyce, for instilling the joy of reading
and
Sharon, for always believing

ACKNOWLEDGMENTS

The author gratefully acknowledges the help he received from a number of individuals in the writing of this novel. Some read a chapter or helped with strategy, but all provided enthusiastic support. In no particular order, those giving of their time and energy include Laura and Scott Hunt, Shelby and Lieutenant Commander Jeff Edwards, Roxanne and Edwin Stern, Bonnie and Major Jay Blish, Wendy Buskop, Corrine Chorney, Phillip Tomasso, Gretchen Heyer, Ray Hays, Glen Smith, Tara Piccone, and Commander Steve Mamikonian. Sharon Stiller did much of the heavy lifting, reading the entire manuscript and providing detailed comments for revision. In particular, I would like to thank my agent, Bob Mecoy, and my editor, Tom Colgan. Without both of them, the manuscript would have gathered dust rather than readers.

FOREWORD

IT was a time of turmoil. After a rapid succession of leaders, the Soviet Union had fallen apart. It was uncertain which of the remaining states would be nuclear powers, which ones would own the military assets within their borders, and which ones would be relegated to Third World status. There was a possibility of war between the new republics and a probability of conflict with the United States. An edge in weapons technology might be the difference between survival of the new Russian Republic and annihilation. The world was a powder keg, and there was electricity in the air.

1. SENIOR CHIEF JOSHUA CLARK

Charleston

HE woke to dreamlike silence, his bunk tilted in a head-down position. The submarine often made depth changes during the night, so there was nothing much to worry about, and he wasn't worried, not really. The angle seemed steeper than usual, but with the bunks oriented fore and aft, there was no danger of falling out of bed. He looked at the bottom of the bunk above him in the nearly complete darkness, a few inches above his face, unable to go back to sleep. A wormlike worry nibbled at his mind.

The hull creaked loudly, like a large, metal door with arthritic hinges. He felt fear, like a butterfly, flutter across his belly. There was really no reason for concern, since the cylindrical hull of the submarine expanded and contracted with changes in depth, due to changes in water pressure outside of the ship. Still, the hull didn't groan like that except on large depth changes, the deep dives. It wouldn't hurt to check the control room and see what was going on.

He pushed back the tan curtain that gave him some small privacy from his shipmates and swung his body out of the bunk, leading with his legs. He slipped on his one-piece coveralls in the dark. His feet found his shoes by instinct. Reaching back into his cubby, he turned on his bunk light and checked the rack above and the rack below. Both empty. His roommates must be on watch.

Clark looked in the crew's mess out of force of habit. Empty. Not unusual this time of night. The middle of the night was the only time you could find this complex piece of underwater machinery almost deserted, except for a few critical watches like maneuvering, to operate the reactor, and control, to steer the ship and maintain depth. Everyone else was safe in their bunks below.

He walked forward, down the dimly lit passageway, literally downhill, since the ship still had a down angle on. He felt a sense of urgency but couldn't seem to force his way forward any faster. The air itself seemed to hold him back, like some viscous fluid dampening his stride. The ship's hull creaked again like fingernails on a blackboard, and then quieted with a loud pop. It was not the hull that creaked, of course, but the structural framework attached to the inside of the hull, shifting and adjusting to the change in diameter of the submarine as the ocean compressed it at the deeper depth. The knowledge brought scant comfort. It was a disconcerting noise inside the otherwise quiet sub.

He rapidly climbed the ladder to the operations compartment, upper level, and entered the control room. Control was rigged for red. The effect was eerie, like a half-forgotten dream, but necessary during night hours to ensure that the officer of the deck would have his eyes adapted for night vision if the ship had to surface unexpectedly. He walked over to one of the depth gauges. Nothing unusual, normal cruising depth. He tapped the gauge out of force of habit. The pointer dropped down to near the maximum end of the scale. There was a sharp pain in his stomach, fear, like acid eating his insides. The gauge had been stuck! Not only had they exceeded their maximum operating depth, they were close to crush depth, the depth the submarine would crumple inward like a beer can squeezed in a belligerent fist.

He turned to shout a warning, but his breath froze in his throat. The control room was empty. They had all abandoned ship without him. He sprinted toward the ladder to the escape trunk. As he started up the ladder, he saw the massive support frame twist, and the hull plates, inches-thick slabs of high-strength steel, sag inward like wet cardboard, ripping at the seams. He tried to scream as the ice-cold water hit him like a steel hammer and knocked him from the ladder.

JOSHUA Clark kicked his feet reflexively and surfaced through many layers of sleep. His eyes opened like curtains being drawn up on a stage. There was no transition from sleeping to being awake. He woke like a cat, poised and alert. He breathed deeply, consciously slowing his heart.

Sarah filled his field of view as she filled his life. The back of her head partially obscured the translucent curtains on the bedroom window. The curtains moved softly with the early morning breeze, which carried the light, pungent smell of damp pine needles. Even in the early spring she insisted on keeping the window open, if only a little.

He looked at the slice of gray white, early morning Charleston sky visible through the window. *Perfect weather. Perfect weather, that is, for Charleston, the underbelly of the world.* He thought it fondly. The soggy weather and the smell from the pulp mill became as familiar as your own sweatshirt after a two-mile jog. Not pleasant, but not unpleasant, a fact of life, a reminder of reality. The smell was more an amalgamation of memories than a sensory characteristic that stood alone in and of itself.

He lightly kissed the back of Sarah's head as she lay on her side in front of him, careful not to wake her. He breathed deeply, catching the fragrance of her hair. There was the faint odor of whatever perfume she had been using recently. She switched so often it was hard to associate any particular fragrance with her. Most of all the scent was of Sarah, something natural and magic folded in the artificial smell, like cinnamon or cedar shavings, fresh air and sunshine. She added something to the perfume that made it smell better on her body than it would straight up, out of the bottle.

He put his hand on her waist and ran it lightly over her hips, silky nightgown on satin skin. She put her hand on his, light bronze on a deep brown, and held it to her stomach.

"You rascal," he said. "How long have you been awake?"

"Awhile. You were starting to toss. Dreaming again?"

He tightened his arm and pulled her back closer to his belly, until they were nestled like two spoons. "Must have been," he said in a neutral voice. The terror of the dream was fading fast. The rush of icy water, cold enough to stop your heart, now seemed unreal, a fragment of a movie half-remembered. The unspoken dream dissipated before he was out of bed. There was no need to alarm Sarah; she would worry enough of her own accord while he was out at sea.

"Hey, you sound sad," he said, changing the subject. "Why so sad so early?"

"It's almost time for you to leave for patrol again. You'll be gone three months, Josh. Three months is almost forever."

"Three months is nothing. I could do three months standing on my head."

He brushed his hand across her breasts. Her nipples hardened under his hand, flower buds swelling beneath his palm. She put her hand behind her and ran it over his hard, heavily muscled leg. Runner's legs. She slipped her hand between them and drew her fingers across his jockey shorts, stretched tight by his stiffened penis.

"Nicole will be one year old, and you won't even be here," she said.

He kissed her shoulder. "Baby's still asleep."

"Oh really?" Her voice rose at the end. She knew her lines. She had played this game before.

His hand brushed her belly and followed seamless contours to thigh and rising hip. "So the alarm hasn't gone off yet," he said.

"Yeah?"

"So I've got the time." Her perfume was making him feel intoxicated. His fingers walked her nightgown hem up around her hips. No panties.

"It sounds like you got the notion, too."

"Well, you know, three months is a long time."

"Oh, Josh," she turned to face him, took him in her arms. "Three months is forever."

2. A MATTER OF TIMING

Offshore, Rota, Spain

THE seagulls wheeled and banked, riding the brisk, chill breeze. They squealed and squawked at each other, always keeping a sharp, weathered eye on the ship below. A seaman came on deck and dumped some scraps over the side. The gulls were on the treasure trove of trash before the seaman had turned his back. They fought for the meager scraps of food discarded by the crew, fierce in their battle for survival.

The spy ship, thinly disguised as a Russian trawler, cruised in lazy circles in the bright, cold, springtime sun. It was just outside Spanish territorial waters. A light breeze capped the higher waves with foam. Inside the ship, technicians, insulated from the day, huddled like moles, monitoring sonar screens, radarscopes, and electromagnetic radiation detectors. The electronic equipment in the "fishing vessel" was as sophisticated as any modern warship. Its sensors searched the airwaves for bits and pieces of electronic information carelessly discarded by the ships in port, scraps that would be hungrily analyzed by other molelike men in Moscow.

The ship was an AGI. The Russians called it *sudno svgazy*, a communications vessel. It carried a crew of more than one hundred men and women and displaced over five thousand tons. Even before the Soviet Union had dissolved into ethnic nation states, both the Soviets and the Americans had given up pretending that these intelligence-gathering ships were fishing vessels. There was peace between Russia and the United States, but old habits die hard. The United States still operated a formidable fleet of warships, and the Russians still followed them like pilot fish, spying when they could, and gathering scraps of information that might later be stitched together.

The radar operator bent over a display panel, his face bathed in green light, and marked a contact on the glass screen with a grease pencil. He called to the watch supervisor, "Radar contact departing the harbor."

The supervisor, Boris Sokolov, scratched the stubble on his cheek, groaned, and then stood. He leaned over the operator's shoulder to peer at the scope. "Very well, designate the contact Bravo One." His voice was as rough as his face. It had been a long watch.

He stepped back to the supervisor's console, looked at his wristwatch, and wrote in the contact information log, "28 March, 1027 a.m., Bravo 1."

"Do you have a turn count on him?" he said to the sonar operator. The turn count was based on a sound pulse picked up on sonar, like a fast-paced metronome, each time a propeller passed a certain part of the ship's hull. The number of propeller blades, which was known for each ship type, was divided into the pulse rate to calculate speed of the contact.

The sonar operator said, "The sound profile signature

indicates it's a submarine. No clear reading on propeller rpm yet. It's similar to the sonar readings on the American submarine that pulled in two weeks ago."

Boris sat forward suddenly. His forehead creased, pulling his unkept curly hair closer to his bushy eyebrows. There was something important about that submarine contact, but what? He leaned back in his chair and thought, never an easy matter for him. Should he wake the Bear? He put his arm up to scratch the back of his head to help his thoughts but quickly put it down as the stale smell of his sweat reached him. The captain had left instructions to be called about any important contact. The trouble was that the captain's idea of what was important changed from day to day and mood to mood.

He sighed as he picked up the phone at the supervisor's station. He pressed the intercom button, waited.

"*Da,*" came the sleepy voice at the other end of the line. Boris knew the cause: too much vodka and too much sleep in the middle of the day. Boris rubbed his palm across the bristles on his face.

"Captain, the new American submarine is under way." He kept his voice respectful, hiding his fear of his captain.

"Their new ship, the *Martin Luther King*? You have positive identification?" The sleepy undertones in the captain's voice were suddenly gone.

"No sir, but the radar profile is small. It would have to be a fishing boat or the conning tower of a sub. Also, the turn count is garbled, as if there were some type of masking of the sound. It is similar to the sonar signature we obtained when the submarine arrived two weeks ago."

"Prepare a message to Moscow, for immediate transmission, reporting that the new U.S. submarine is under way. I will be right down. Do we have one of our subs on station to establish trail?"

"No submarine available in the local operating area, sir." Boris cringed in his seat. Surely he would be blamed for this, also. "I'll have the message coded and ready for your signature," he added, hoping to change the course of the conversation.

"You've done well." The phone went dead.

Boris breathed a sigh of relief as he returned the phone to the cradle. The Bear did not eat him for being aroused. In fact, the captain was pleased. This American submarine must be important.

He let his mind wander back to Katerina, which was where he had started when the submarine intruded. She would be getting off cooking duty in the galley about now. Katerina would be tired after work, but perhaps she could be persuaded. The Americans only now were discovering the advantages of mixed male and female crews. And they thought they were so technically advanced.

He laced his hands behind his head, contemplating Katerina's ample breasts. He quickly dropped his arms, covering the damp spots at their base. Perhaps a shower first would help his cause.

Off the Coast of Sicily

THE black freighter plowed doggedly through the choppy Mediterranean swells. She pushed her way through them, her matronly bow shoving the waves aside rather than cleaving them neatly like a man of war or riding placidly over them like a pleasure boat. An occasional wave washed over her thick bow, surged along her deck, and sluiced out through her rusty scuppers.

She was a workhorse. At over thirty-seven thousand tons' displacement, she was a type referred to as a RO/RO, roll-on/roll-off. Cars, trucks, or tanks could be driven into her hold for transport. Both types of missions, civilian and military, were incorporated into her design. Even without the white, blue, and red horizontal stripes

on the flag at her mast, she would have been readily iden-
tifiable as a ship of the Russian Republic by the Cyrillic
letters on her bow.

On the bridge, Seaman First Class Aleksander
Akhromeev hugged a cup of strong black tea between his
hands. The second cup of the morning watch was always
the best. With the first cup, he was still too much asleep to
appreciate it. He took a sip from the steaming mug, savoring the bittersweet taste of the tea, warming his stomach and his hands. He hunched his shoulders to pull his
head deeper into the funnel formed by the turned-up collar of his woolen coat.

Thank God the radar was working. He looked out the
bridge window. It was too cold to stand the lookout watch
outside on the bridge wings. They were in the Straits of
Sicily where the island of Sicily thrust itself toward
Tunisia. Although there was very little ship traffic, the
captain would surely post the lookout watch outside if the
radar were out. It was bad enough being a messenger and
having to go out and make inspections around the unprotected upper deck in this cold. With the wind whipping
spray in your face, it could turn your eyebrows to icicles.
It would be even worse standing lookout on the unprotected bridge wings.

Still, Aleksander thought, it was better to be a messenger on a freighter than being back in the motherland
plowing frozen earth. Other citizens were not so lucky. It
was good to have a job of any kind in this newly "free"
society. It was increasingly apparent that *free* might mean
free to stay home because there was no work.

A periscope broached the surface two hundred meters
off the starboard bow, the mottled gray shaft nearly invisible against the gray green waves. Sunlight glinted off its
face as it swung through a 360-degree arc. The reflected
light struck Aleksander a glancing blow. A second

periscope appeared immediately behind the first, trailing in its U-shaped wake. He tightened his grip on the mug of tea as he slopped the hot liquid on his hands and shoes. He opened his mouth, but no words came out. A submarine this close to the ship was dangerous!

"Submarine!" he shouted when his voice returned, pointing, momentarily forgetting his training. Heads turned toward him, rather than the sub. "Submarine off the starboard bow," he said on his second attempt, his voice loud but calm, making his report short and precise, as he had been taught.

Naval Operations Center, Moscow

AN enlisted watch stander in the Naval Operations Center in Moscow received the report of the submarine sighting by the freighter. The position of the unknown contact was plotted by other men on the situation map along with the time and the date of the sighting.

It was perpetual twilight in the operations center. There were no windows in the two-foot-thick concrete walls, a feature that conserved heat and preserved secrets but killed men's souls. Clocks at one end of the room showed the time in London, New York, Tokyo, and Moscow. Somewhere the sun was shining, but here it was only a dim memory.

Ivan Ogarkov, the night watch officer, compared the double fore-and-aft mast configuration of the contact to configurations of American submarines listed in *Jane's Fighting Ships. Jane's* had more secret, accurate information on both American and Russian ships than either the CIA or KGB—or AFB, it was hard to unlearn old acronyms—or both together could gather, or at least more than either would admit. Jane's *would be the place to see some state secrets, not the AFB,* Ivan thought. He looked around to see if someone was reading his subversive thoughts as he thumbed through the thick book. *Although there are probably no secrets worth selling at this point.* He smiled. The AFB was giving tours of Lubyanka, the old political prison, if the tourist had enough money.

He found the correct page. The contact was an American submarine, the USS *Martin Luther King. Jane's* identified it as the inexpensive follow-on to the Seawolf class. The project was previously code-named Centurian by the Americans. This information was also included in *Jane's.*

Ivan reviewed the night orders. There was a section pertaining to sightings of the new King submarine class. He ran the end of his pencil through a short list of telephone numbers, picked up the phone, and dialed.

"Da." The voice on the phone was cautious, noncommittal, and neutral.

"Colonel Borzov, this is the intelligence watch officer. We have had a sighting on an American King-class submarine at a position just south of Italy."

"Impossible. Recheck your information. I'll be right there, but this can't be right." The voice on the phone was irritable. The watch officer hung up the phone and blew air silently out through pursed lips, an extended sigh to try to relieve the sudden tension that had seized him. Now he would be raked over the coals if he was wrong, and he was only doing the job he had been ordered to do.

Fifteen minutes later, Colonel Borzov arrived and went straight to the situation board. He removed his coat while he walked. Borzov looked at the position of the newly reported contact and handed his coat and gloves to the watch officer without looking at him. He stalked to the previously marked position of the *King* near Rota, Spain, where the trawler had reported a submarine contact leaving port. He examined the mark, one fist on his hip, his other cupping his chin.

The watch officer motioned to an enlisted man and handed off the colonel's coat and gloves, resisting the temptation to throw them on the floor. He caught up with the colonel. "Is there some problem, Colonel Borzov?" He tried to keep the anger from his voice, but it colored the emphasis of all his words. Why should this rude Ukrainian colonel doubt his work? The accent was not so great, but you could tell Borzov was from the Ukraine. He couldn't hide it if he tried. The hard *g* sound became a softer *h*.

"Yes, there is a problem," Borzov snapped, momentarily looking up at the taller watch officer, then back to the map. "This is a sighting of an American King-type submarine." He pointed to the position plotted near Spain. "It is the only one of its class. It was sighted departing Rota yesterday by our spy ship.

"If this is a King-class submarine," he said, thumping his finger on the clear, Plexiglas board near the marker south of Italy, "it's the same submarine. Look at it, almost one thousand nautical miles in less than twenty-four hours! Do you know how fast a submarine would have to travel to move between these points in that amount of time?"

The watch officer's face turned red, but he said nothing.

"Of course, you don't know. You didn't make the calculations. You sat on your thumb, waiting for someone to come and tell you what to do!" Borzov's voice deepened as he turned up the volume.

"At this position in the Mediterranean, the speed of the *King* would be nearly fifty knots. Fifty knots is impossible for a missile submarine, even one carrying the smaller cruise missiles. That far exceeds the capabilities of any submarine except our Alpha class, and the Alpha is noisy. This submarine, the *King*, became invisible on sonar as soon as it submerged."

"But Colonel," the watch officer said, changing tack,

his voice placating. "How could it be wrong? All Russian merchant ships have an intelligence-gathering mission. And all have naval sailors aboard in addition to the merchant seamen. I think it is unlikely they would make a mistake."

Borzov ignored the answer. "Reverify the position of all submarine contacts, French, British, American, our own. We will eliminate the possibility of this being any other submarine. After all other possibilities have been discounted, we will then consider the impossible.

"Bring me the report on the sighting and the dossier on the freighter commander." Borzov snapped his fingers as the watch officer searched frantically in his pockets for paper and pencil.

"Request a detailed follow-up report from the freighter that reported the submarine periscopes," Borzov continued. "Light conditions, sea conditions, etc., everything in great detail. Now, move!" He barked the last. Anyone in operations who hadn't heard the dressing down before now would have had to be deaf to miss the finale. Ivan snapped to attention and saluted. He moved away briskly to carry out the orders.

Colonel Borzov ran his hand through his close-cropped gray hair. The Americans appeared to have incorporated some major technological change in this new submarine. Despite the inept watch officer, the report was probably true. The Americans continued to spend money on research and development despite *perestroika*. Russia, meanwhile, wasted time and money arguing about who was in charge. Still, Russia would have to have this new technology despite the fools in the government.

Russia, or perhaps the Ukraine. He looked carefully around the room at the military men working at maps and computer displays. There was opportunity here for an officer prepared to take a chance.

3. FLYAWAY

Charleston

SENIOR Chief Joshua Clark was the first to arrive for the muster. He liked getting in early. It gave him a few minutes to relax, to get organized. To think. He also liked setting a good example for the troops.

He stood in front of the barracks across from the FBM Training Center. The rising sun touched his face but brought little warmth. The crisp cold made pockets of tears at the corners of his eyes, and the frost-covered grass crunched under his feet when he moved.

Joshua Clark thought about how much he loved the Navy. Of course, you could never tell that to the troops. They weren't really happy unless they had something to bitch about, and that was usually the Navy. If the truth be known, a lot of them liked it, too, but they would never admit it.

He pulled the collar of his peacoat up around his ears and thought that the only thing missing was a cup of strong, black coffee. Coffee was available on the quarter-deck at the FBM Training Center, but he didn't want to be inside on such a beautiful morning, and drinking coffee outdoors would have been unmilitary. It would have felt almost as uncomfortable as being outdoors without your cap, uncovered. He knew he had been in the Navy too long when he discovered how he was uneasy going out-side without a hat, even in civilian clothes. It was not quite as embarrassing as going to work without your trousers (talk about being out of uniform) but close.

The other members of the crew arrived in ones and twos. Machinist Mate Second Class Scott Palmer had his wife drop him off half a block down the street so the rest of the crew wouldn't be able to watch him say good-bye. Joshua Clark could see him kiss his wife good-bye, even from here, and imagined him blushing as he did so. Six foot two and 220 pounds, his shipmates called him Hon-eybear because of his shy, easygoing nature.

During the last few minutes before expiration of lib-erty, the pace of arrivals quickened. Those who had come early stood back from the curb and heckled the late ar-rivals as they kissed their wives and girlfriends.

"Hot damn!"

"Give her one for me!"

Clark smiled. Most of them were college age, and the excitement running through the crowd was the same as you would find at a pep rally before a football game. He couldn't fault them for their youth and envied them their enthusiasm. He had said his good-byes at home and driven himself in. Sarah could pick up the car later if she needed it, but it was the old one and would keep just fine in the off-crew lot until he returned. Good-byes were for home. They were personal. Not meant for sharing, not even with ship-mates.

Machinist Mate First Class Mark Gates was one of the

last to arrive. He pulled his car directly up in front of the formation. The rest of the men were already falling in by division for muster. As he got out of the driver's side, his wife, Jane, got out of the passenger side. Coming together near the front of the car, Gates picked her up off the ground and gave her a kiss, which lasted forever. He slid both hands down to her bottom, which was covered, barely, by tight-fitting, faded blue jeans. Some of his shipmates cheered him on as he set her down. He raised his hat in greeting, cheering at himself. Sweet Jane, as she was called by most of her friends, not to be outdone, curtsied to the crew.

Clark turned to find that the ship's yeoman had come up beside him with a nonrated seaman.

"Senior Chief, this is Bill Wilson. He reported aboard yesterday and was assigned to your division. He's striking for auxiliaryman."

Wilson stood several inches taller than Senior Chief Clark and was built like a block. Straight, sandy-colored hair spilled out around the white circular cap pushed down tightly on his head. His pinkish freckled face had a permanent sunburned look.

Clark noted his hair was a little longer than regulation as he unconsciously inspected the new man. "Welcome aboard, Wilson." Joshua held out his hand. He would have plenty of time to work on Wilson's appearance.

"Hello," Wilson said, his voice a slow drawl. He slowly slid his hands into his pockets, letting his eyes slide away from Joshua's coffee-colored face.

"OK." Joshua pulled his hand back. "Fall in," he said with more emphasis. He pointed with his thumb over his shoulder, and his jaw muscles tightened.

"Thank you, Yeo," Clark said to the yeoman, dismissing him.

The yeoman's face turned red with embarrassment as

he watched the senior chief and Wilson. He left without a word, but Clark knew it would be gossip for the next several days. Joshua rubbed his hands briskly, scraping off the cold, washing his hands in the air.

The executive officer ordered the crew to fall in. Clark could feel the blood rushing up under his light-brown cheeks as he came to attention. Racial prejudice was still common enough that he shouldn't have been surprised, but he was. He was surprised, angry, and at the same time disappointed with himself for being angry. *It is going to be a long patrol,* he thought.

The executive officer stood in front of the assembled crew. He looked to his right, looked to his left, and called in a large, parade-ground voice, "USS *Martin Luther King*, ah-ten-hut!" The syllable *hut* echoed off the building walls.

Clark put Wilson out of his mind. The executive officer was a Naval Academy graduate, but the way he gave orders, he could have come from West Point. "Attention" didn't carry very well, so it became "ah-ten-hut," which easily reached the troops in the last rank. When he ordered, "Department heads, report," he made the *t* at the end sound like a gunshot.

The department heads sounded off in turn. "Engineering department, all men present and accounted for, sir." Reports by the weapons department, operations department, and supply department followed in order. Each saluted the XO as he made his report. The XO returned the salute, his fingers and thumb lined up with his forearm, the tip of his fingers touching his right eyebrow.

Good turnout, Clark thought, as he listened to the reports. Only one man was absent. On a deployment like this, there were usually several people who decided they just could not leave their sweet young brides at home alone for three months. The troops put it more bluntly: his wife was going to be getting pregnant, and he wanted to be there for the conception. Part of the reason for the good turnout was due to the deployment to Spain with a refit in Rota. There weren't many opportunities to get a trip to Europe as the Navy shrank in size.

"Stand at ease," the XO said. A ripple went through the ranks as the men relaxed.

"Men, as you know, all deployments of U.S. nuclear-powered submarines are important. The job you are doing is important to the national defense. I emphasize *defense*."

Clark was distracted by the word *defense* every time he heard it. The business of the Department of Defense was war, despite the name. The United States was first in war, first in peace, and best in public relations.

"You are part of the U.S. nuclear strategic deterrence force," the XO continued, unmindful of Clark's wayward thoughts. "While you are on patrol, your very presence, submerged and undetected, makes it less likely that the Russians, China, North Korea, or anyone else is going to start a war. They know if they launch their missiles, they have no way of knocking us out because we are essentially undetectable. They also know that we will certainly launch our missiles on their cities and other strategic targets." The XO slowly turned his head right and left, pacing his words as he spoke.

The XO put his hand up. "The Soviet Union no longer exists, and all the new republics that used to be part of the Soviet Union want to be our friends. But they still have hundreds of missiles and nuclear warheads that we know nothing about. The next guy in the saddle in Russia after Yeltsin may not like us as much as this one pretends to."

Clark had a sudden urge to scratch, which had nothing to do with talk of missiles and warheads. He gritted his teeth. He wouldn't do that in front of the troops, even if the XO went on forever, and it was starting to look like he might. This XO loved to give a speech.

"This particular deployment is also significant for an-

other reason. The *King* is the first of a new class of submarines designed to carry forty-eight cruise missiles, in
addition to torpedoes. It is not really a missile boat in the
technical sense of the word, since it does not carry intercontinental ballistic missiles, but it is also more than a
fast-attack submarine.

"With the shorter range of the cruise missile, we have
to be closer to our targets in Europe and Asia when we
launch. This means that during transit from the United
States to places where the submarines are in range of the
target, we will not be doing our job. Therefore, these new
boats are being staffed with Blue and Gold crews, just
like the Trident submarines. To increase the time within
range of target, the United States is considering making
deployments out of advance sites like we used to do with
the old Polaris boats. Two sites are being considered:
Holy Loch, Scotland, and Rota, Spain."

Clark couldn't help feeling cynical. Using a Blue crew
and a Gold crew was also a damn good way to justify
keeping extra Navy men on active duty while Congress
cut the defense budget.

"Those of you who have been in the Navy a long time
might remember that Polaris submarines used to make
regular patrols out of Spain. However, the Spanish asked
us to leave in no uncertain terms. To put it more explic-
itly, they kicked our butts out of their country." A few
chuckles came from the crew. The executive officer liked
to throw in some earthy language once in a while to show
he was not a stuffed shirt. He reminded Clark of one of
his uncles who made everyone feel embarrassed when he
cussed, trying to be one of the boys.

"It started off with removing the nuclear submarines
from Rota, but at that time it didn't matter, since the
range on our intercontinental ballistic missiles had increased to the point where we were in range of targets al-

most as soon as we left the United States. The Spanish then followed up by requiring that our F-16 fighter squadrons be removed from Tarrejon."

Clark flexed his knees to keep the circulation going. The XO was in a talkative mood today. You would think he was running for office, the way he gave a speech every time he had more than three people together.

"The *King* is the first U.S. nuclear submarine to be allowed to make patrols out of Rota, Spain, in a long time, and it is only on a trial basis. I guess they decided the dollars sailors spend in town were worth the extra political heat the government will take by allowing U.S. troops on Spanish soil." The XO paused; more laughter from the crew on cue.

"So I want all of you to be on your best behavior when you are on liberty in Rota. There will be a lot of hard work, but there will be time for play after hours. Remember, you are ambassadors of the United States, and whether we're allowed to continue to deploy out of bases in Spain depends in large part on your conduct. That's all I've got. There will be more briefings on this after we reach the ship, but it can't be emphasized enough. The buses will be along in a few minutes to take us to the airport."

Clark relaxed as the XO wrapped up. It was just the right amount of God, motherhood, and apple pie. It might have been pompous spoken by someone else, but the XO really believed what he was saying. He was quite good about putting things in perspective. Giving the troops an overall picture of what was required and why made them feel the job was important, and it would make them work harder to get it done. Many other officers just assumed everyone knew what was going on.

Charleston

SARAH Clark drove north out of Charleston on Interstate 26. It was almost like driving out of the twilight zone, she thought. The fog—Clark would have called it smog—outside of the city had been burned off by the sunlight. It was springtime in Charleston. The sunlight took the chill out of the air and warmed the spirit as much as the body. The heat that would come with summer was still a long way off. Some brief, pristine days to lift the spirit before the summer flogged the body with heat and humidity.

Sections of pine forest appeared more frequently as Sarah distanced herself from the city. Significant patches of green broke the monotony of suburbia. They passed unnoticed as Sarah put her mind in cruise control and drove mostly by reflex. Clark insisted on saying good-bye at home and would never approve of her following him down to the MAC terminal to see him off, like some of the wives and girlfriends did. With the military fetish for being ready to go long before the scheduled flight time, and the predictable, typical, interminable delay in takeoff time, there was usually a one- or two-hour wait at the terminal before the crew boarded. After two hours of saying good-bye, the parting was usually not so much sweet sorrow as unmitigated relief.

She turned off at the airport exit and followed the cloverleaf back around through 270 degrees and up over the interstate. She passed the Ramada Inn, currently one of the hotter nightspots in town. The clubs on the Air Force base, less than a mile away, were very nice, but some of the men felt they had to get completely off the base to have a good time, even if it was just outside the gate. The greener pastures factor was also involved. The best nightclub was always just over the next hill or just down the road. Also, many of the civilian ladies probably felt more comfortable going to a nightclub off base, even if all they

were doing was trying to meet some eligible tech sergeant or Navy chief.

The road from the interstate ended at the perimeter
road. Turning right, she paralleled the chain-link perimeter fence to an area stripped bare by the large number of
cars that had parked there watching flight operations.
Pulling in, she settled down for a long wait. She was surprised to notice a red Toyota parked at the other side of
the clearing. The girl sitting on the hood of the car in blue
jeans and a short leather jacket looked familiar. It was unusual to have anyone else out here on a weekday morning. On a weekend you could find several civilians
rubbernecking, watching the planes take off and land, especially when the C-5s were flying, but during the week
everyone had something better to do.

The woman half turned, looking out from long hair
that spilled across her face. *Why, that's Jane Gates,*
Sarah thought with a small intake of breath as she recognized her.

Jane pushed herself off the bumper of the car and put
her hands in her coat pockets as she walked over across
the red clay soil, crunchy with early morning frost. Sarah
rolled down her window. Jane put her hand on the door
and leaned down to look in.

"Hello, Mrs. Clark. I don't know if you remember me.
I'm Jane Gates. We met at one of the division parties."

"Sure, I remember. The A Division is not so big that I
can't remember all the men and their wives. Not like
when Joshua taught at Sub School. There were just too
many there to try to remember them all. And once you
got to know one group, they graduated and were replaced
by another." She stopped, felt like she was babbling.

"Well, we were only at that one party, and I wasn't really sure if you remembered who I was." She looked
down, like she was deciding whether to go on. "How is
your little girl?"

"She is doing just fine." Sarah gripped the wheel, feeling nervous and not sure why. "I left her with a sitter today. At her age, she has too much energy and requires too much of my attention for me to work up a good depression if she came out here with me.

"Well, I guess you came to see the plane off," Sarah said.

"Yes, I heard that you could watch the takeoffs from the perimeter road," Jane said, turning to look at the ten-foot-high chain-link fence that marked the edge of government property. "I didn't really want to go over to the terminal. I probably made enough of a fool of myself when I dropped Mark off this morning.

"Say," Jane said turning back to Sarah. She put her hands into her coat pockets. "I saw you at the Market Place while the ship was on sound trials, but you were with some friends. I wanted to come over to say hello but didn't want to interrupt."

"I remember. It was just a couple of neighbors. You should have come over."

"You looked busy, and I wasn't even sure if you'd remember me. And, anyway, I was with someone," Jane said, punctuating her sentences with puffs of frosty breath.

"That was Alex Pendergast, wasn't it? Alex and Joshua were together at Prototype."

Jane looked down. "Yeah, I thought you did. Look, Alex and I were just having something to eat."

Sarah was silent, not sure what she should say.

"What I mean," Jane continued, "is that some people might get the wrong impression if Alex and I had lunch together while the Gold crew was out and, the way some wives talk, they would make something out of it even if there was nothing to make out of it."

Sarah put her hand on Jane's hand as it rested at the edge of the window. "Some people haven't got anything better to talk about than other people, Jane, but I like to think I'm not one of those."

Jane took Sarah's hand in both hers. "Thanks, Sarah," she said, her voice suddenly enthusiastic. She wiped away some moisture that had collected at the edge of her eye with her fingers. She squeezed Sarah's hand again and said, "Thank you."

"Well, I guess I'd better be going," Jane said, standing, shifting around restlessly. "It's a little cold out here."

"Aren't you going to stay for the takeoff?" Sarah said.

"I get awfully restless. I don't know if I can sit still that long," she wiped at the corner of her eye again with her sleeve. "Besides, I've got a little bit of a cold, sniffles, or spring flu, or something. I think I'll get on the road." She gave a half wave without looking back and walked around the front of the car, headed back toward the Toyota.

Sarah watched her go, feeling sad. It didn't take long to work up a depression today.

Moscow

COLONEL Borzov waited in the anteroom outside the admiral's office. He understood the power game and had played it many times himself. Keep the subordinate waiting. Establish proper pecking order.

By conscious effort, Borzov kept himself from tapping his fingers on the arm of the chair. No sense letting his irritation show, even though the sergeant manning the reception desk was the only other person in the room.

A light blinked on the phone on the sergeant's desk and he picked it up. "He will see you now," the sergeant said as he stood and opened the door to the interior office.

Borzov marched into the room and stopped a few paces in front of the desk. The room was luxurious. It was paneled in a highly polished walnut up to the twelve-foot ceilings and was big enough to house a family of ten.

"Colonel Borzov reporting as ordered, sir," he said, saluting.

The admiral continued to write, not looking up from his desk. Borzov completed his salute and remained standing at attention. *The game continues,* he thought, watching the man at the desk.

Admiral Oiktor Tikhonov was an old man in a uniform, a military bureaucrat. The white fringe of hair around the balding head and pudgy face didn't fool Borzov; Tikhonov was a powerful, ruthless man who had chosen the military road to the top.

"Colonel Borzov, explain your plan to me again," Tikhonov said, finally putting his pen down and looking up.

He was not asked to sit; it was a bad sign. Admiral Tikhonov was not a friend, but they had worked together before. The admiral was keeping the relation as formal as possible. Borzov wondered if the office was monitored electronically.

"Admiral, the Americans have developed technology that enables their new submarine, the USS *King*, to achieve speeds in excess of fifty knots. As you are aware, that speed is much higher than the speed of any of our ships except the Alpha class, which is much smaller. A breakthrough like this will give the Americans a great advantage in combat at sea."

Tikhonov rested his chin on his fingertips, staring at Borzov. Silent. Borzov felt a drop of perspiration run down his back, even though the room wasn't excessively hot.

"It is vital that Russia have this information," Borzov continued, trying to fill the silence.

"Why?"

"Pardon me, Admiral?" Borzov leaned forward.

"Why is it vital that Russia have information on how

the Americans have achieved fifty knots submerged in a large submarine?" Tiknohov raised his voice and clipped each word, as if speaking to a slow child. "We are at peace with the United States," he continued in a more normal tone. "Yeltsin has said so. What of *perestroika*? Why spend more money on hardware to keep up with the Americans when our leader has chosen peace?"

"Admiral, peace does not mean that we should be unprepared. The present leader"—he emphasized *present*—"has chosen to put the ship of state on a course toward peace. What if the next premier wishes to alter course? We can't wait until the shooting starts to develop the technology to win the war."

The admiral held up his hand to silence Borzov. "We don't discuss the leader of the country here. Things have not changed so much. Continue. Tell me about your plan."

Borzov resisted the temptation to shift back and forth on his feet. "The new technology will take too long to develop. It would be best to take the technology from the Americans. The easiest way to steal the technology would be to steal the submarine," Borzov said, spreading his hands.

"Wouldn't the Americans notice that their submarine was gone?" the admiral asked with a smile.

That must be the way the cat smiles before he eats the canary, Borzov thought. "Of course, Comrade Admiral, but they would not know what happened to it. They would think that it had been lost at sea. They might even think we sank their submarine, but they would never imagi—" Borzov stopped as he realized he had lost Tikhonov's attention. "What is it, sir?" Borzov asked, as Tikhonov rolled his eyes and glared at him.

"Why can't you learn, Colonel? You speak Russian well, even for a Ukrainian. *Tovarisch*—comrade—is no longer a fashionable word. *Citizen* is what we call each other now. But for me, Admiral is sufficient.

"What is the plan, Colonel?" Tikhonov sat back in his chair, obviously struggling to get his temper under control. "How do you propose to accomplish this magic trick?"

Borzov struggled to keep his voice from shaking as he spoke. All of this was covered in his report. Didn't the admiral read the report? Unless there was more going on here than he thought. "The plan is simple. The American submarines require a certain number of officers and men on board for normal operations. If we remove one of their men before patrol, preferably an officer, they will have to bring in a replacement from the States. The new man will be a stranger to the crew. It will be easy to replace the newly assigned officer with one of our operatives.

"At a predetermined time, our operative will eliminate the crew and surface the ship." He made himself slow down. If he talked too fast, he would appear to be eager and wouldn't be persuasive. "Units of our fleet will be standing by and will put a new crew on board and sail the ship into a secret location, where it will be disassembled."

"By 'eliminate the crew,' you mean kill them?"

"It is necessary, Admiral. When the Americans captured the German U-boat in World War II, they took the captured crew belowdecks so they would think the U-boat had sunk. The crew had opened the sea valves before they abandoned ship. The Americans then went aboard the submarine and saved it. Half of the value of having the boat was in keeping the knowledge that it had been captured from the Germans. The Americans and the Allies not only learned technology about U-boat design but also learned the German cryptographic codes and operational plans. If the Germans knew the submarine had been captured and not sunk, they would have changed codes. There was no way to keep such a secret if the German crew knew the boat had not sunk.

"Likewise, when we capture the American submarine, we will get operational plans, codes, and of course technology. It will be the greatest covert operation of the century," Borzov said, his voice rising. "Also, to avoid adverse world opinion, we cannot let it be known we have the ship. Besides, the fools in power would probably give the ship back."

Tikhonov slammed the desk with his hand. "Silence. You overstep your limits. I will not have you speak of the members of government in this fashion. Even Ukrainians should know better. Regardless of the current open policy in this country, you are a member of the military."

Borzov felt the blood rush to his face. Many of the Russians looked down on those born in other republics, even when the Soviet Union was intact. It had become worse after the breakup.

The admiral rose and waved the back of his hand toward the door. "You may proceed with your plan. You will speak to no one of this but me. I will give personal approval of all actions. For the sake of your career, you will do well to make sure the plan succeeds.

"Dismissed." The admiral motioned with his head toward the door.

Borzov saluted, turned on his heel, and marched out. He barley noticed the sergeant coming to attention as he passed through the outer office. He closed the door to the reception room behind him.

The meeting probably had not been taped, he decided. The admiral would not want a record of the conversation. That did not give him any comfort. No one would know of this operation but him and the admiral. Was the admiral putting himself in a position to deny giving permission if the mission failed? Probably so, but there was nothing to be done about it. If the mission succeeded, the admiral would also take the credit. If it failed . . . Best not to think of that.

The admiral's contempt for him as a Ukrainian still smarted. Perhaps this plan could be turned to his own advantage, something that would put Tikhonov and the Russians in their place.

4. MOSCOW AND POCATELLO

Moscow

KOMSOMOLSKAYA Pravda lay spread on the floor at their feet. The cups of hot tea were just warm enough to take the chill off their hands, but his nose was still cold. Illya sat beside Yuri on the small, threadbare sofa with her feet tucked up under her. Yuri leaned against her for support and body warmth. He could feel the heat of her through her thick wool sweater. He knew there was nothing else under the sweater but Illya, which made him even warmer.

Yuri slowly stretched his legs. He was enjoying one of those rare moments in a personal relationship without any feeling of urgency that something was waiting to be done, without feeling a need to talk, merely taking comfort in each other's company.

He could see a McDonald's advertisement on one of the pages of *Komsomolskaya Pravda*. The hamburgers cost as much as a worker made in a day, and people still stood in line to buy them. This was free enterprise? *Pere-*

stroika! Next they would be advertising American Cadillacs, which no one had the money to buy either.

The sofa faced the only window in the small apartment, which had frosted up near the bottom corners from the moisture in the room and then frozen. Outside, a light snow was falling from an overcast sky. Yuri wondered if it would ever quit snowing. As the last of winter hammered the city, it was hard to remember Moscow without snow. He pulled Illya closer to him. The plain, concrete walls of the apartment not only didn't stop the cold, they didn't even slow it down much.

Yuri was shaken out of his subversive thoughts about the climate by a heavy knock on the door. Illya jumped, and Yuri was startled by the sudden sound. Yuri delayed getting up, tempted not to answer the door at all. Illya looked up at him, watching him for a clue as to how she should react. There was no second knock after a proper interval, but a floorboard creaked, indicating someone was still outside the door. Yuri patted Illya on her leg, gave her a smile, and got up to answer the door.

The man at the door was a mountain. Yuri took an involuntary step backward. All he could think of was a line from a movie he'd seen as a child, "There's a giant on the beach." He knew exactly how the Lilliputians felt. The behemoth was at least two meters tall and looked to be more than one hundred kilos in weight, but with heavy winter clothing it was hard to tell exactly. Tufts of hair accentuated small ears, which looked like they were glued to the large, fat head. A wool cap strained to cover a scalp that was mostly bald.

The giant spoke. "Captain-Lieutenant Yuri Amelko, you are to come with me." He waited with an air of authority as if a negative reply was clearly impossible, similar to not answering the door when he knocked.

"By whose order?"

"By order of the state, Citizen," he said with a smile.

Yuri hesitated, and the mountain said, "You will come," with a confident emphasis on the *will* that Yuri could not mistake.

"You have identification, of course?"

The giant didn't move. Yuri faced him squarely. Reluctantly, the giant removed a paper from his pocket and handed it to Yuri. Yuri passed over the name, Gregor Kostikov. It was the *Argentsto Federalnoe Bezopastnost*, AFB, printed next to the name that gave his heart an extra kick. It was the same, old *Komitet Gosudarstvennoi Bezopasnosti*, the Committee for State Security, the KGB, with a new name. It was old trash in a new package. But, even in the new Russian Republic, the KGB, or AFB, still could strike fear in the soul.

"I will get my coat," Yuri said, trying to push the door shut.

"Good," Gregor said, putting his foot against the door to keep it from closing. Yuri and Gregor locked eyes for a moment, but Yuri blinked first. As he turned away, Gregor stepped into the room and closed the door behind him.

Yuri gathered his coat and a hat and returned to where Illya stood by the sofa, holding her book. He took her hand and looked into her eyes.

"Yuri?" she said.

He could see all the questions in her eyes, but he had nothing to say that would reassure her. He raised his shoulders and squeezed her hand. He put more confidence into his smile than he actually felt. Their hands parted, and Yuri turned, walked out the door, and closed it behind him.

Yuri walked down the narrow stairway to the first floor in silence. Gregor followed.

"Here," said Gregor, grabbing Yuri's arm and pointing to a black sedan parked outside the door. Yuri pulled hard on the car door to get it past the dirty snow that banked the curb.

Gregor got into the car, taking more than his half of the small front seat. "I am Gregor," he announced, forgetting Yuri had just looked at his identification. Yuri looked at him, but now it was Yuri's turn to be silent. He might have to go with this man, but he didn't have to make little conversation.

"That's the best part of it," said Gregor as he started the car.

Yuri didn't answer. If this clown wanted to talk, he could talk to himself. Yuri looked out the window as Gregor maneuvered the car away from the curb. The pedestrians leaned into the wind.

Gregor laughed, a deep-throated, unpleasant sound, and continued. "The knock on the door; night is better, of course. You will come with me," he said, making his voice threatening. "Some of them scream at you, not too loudly, of course. They always hope the neighbors won't hear, but they do. Some of them beg and cry. Some of them offer you anything not to take them, especially the women." Gregor looked over from his driving, a twisted smile on his heavyset face.

Yuri returned his gaze and said, "Where are we going?"

Gregor's smile hardened. He returned his attention to his driving.

THE briefing room looked much the same as government briefing rooms the world over. The walls were a nondescript shade of beige and looked as though they had received a coat of paint once every ten years, whether they needed it or not, one coat on top of another. Rusty metal fasteners held the hard wooden chairs together. The chairs were as stiff and unyielding as stone virgins and looked as if they could easily break your back if you sat upon them in any other position than rigid and erect. The only indication that this might be a briefing room in Russia as opposed to any other nation was the coldness that permeated the place.

Yuri knew some of the men present from the naval service. Although some were in civilian clothes, he suspected that all were military personnel from their posture, their self-assured manner.

A man in an admiral's uniform of the Voyenno Morskoy Flot, VMF, military Maritime Fleet entered from a door to the left of a podium at the front of the room. He was followed by an AFB colonel. Yuri sat upright in his chair, then stood to attention along with the others in the room.

Yuri recognized Admiral Oiktor Tikhonov at once. After Admiral Gorshkov, Tikhonov had changed the Soviet Navy more then any other individual. If Admiral Gorshkov could rightfully be called the Father of the Soviet Navy, then certainly Tikhonov was the midwife of the Russian Navy. While Gorshkov had brought the Soviet Navy from a small coastal defense force into an organization that was equal or greater in numbers to any maritime force in the world, Tikhonov had made the Russian Navy a technologically sophisticated fighting machine, and was struggling to continue improvements with the shrinking budget in the new Russian Republic.

Tikhonov was also astute enough to have picked the right contacts and made the transition to the Russian Navy without losing power or losing his head. Yuri had seen the admiral before, but never this close. A briefing by Tikhonov was important.

The admiral walked to the center of the room. "Be seated.

"Your presence here is a matter of national security.

What you hear will be considered top secret. It will not be discussed with anyone outside this room.

"The Russian Navy has made many significant advances, both in number of ships and in technology, compared to Western navies. However, our intelligence gathering service indicates that the Americans have made a technological breakthrough in the area of submarines. There have been confirmed reports of an American submarine achieving speeds in excess of fifty knots submerged. As naval officers, I'm sure you are all aware of the significance of that achievement."

A ripple of noise passed through the room as the men turned to look at each other. Of course they knew. Most ships were able to make only thirty knots maximum.

Tikhonov held his hand up for silence. "As you know, the Russian Federation has a submarine capable of this speed, the one known to the Americans as the Alpha class." Yuri smiled.

"However," Tikhonov continued. "The Alpha is a small, high-powered sub. Very noisy compared to other submarines. The American submarine is much larger. We believe it is a missile boat.

"Russia and the United States are at peace, but we must not fall behind technologically. Our scientists are studying the data but have little to work on. An alternate means of obtaining the information is necessary, thus making it available for our own use. We will obtain this information through covert operations."

Tikhonov looked at each of them and drew out the pause. Yuri saw that Tikhonov had much practice leading groups of people where he wanted them to go.

"You have all been carefully selected. Because of your background, both naval and civilian, you may be of use in this operation. You are all as of this moment on temporary assignment to the AFB." Tikhonov waved his hand toward the colonel. "Colonel Borzov will brief you on further aspects of this operation." He glanced at Borzov briefly as he walked past him.

The men came to attention as the admiral left. Colonel Borzov stepped to the center in front of the podium. "Seats, Citizens."

Yuri saw Borzov glance at the door through which Tikhonov had departed and smile. Something about the admiral's participation in briefing the operation had pleased Borzov. Borzov turned his attention to the men in the room. He watched them in silence for a moment, hands behind his back.

"Obtaining intelligence data about U.S. submarines in the conventional manner is close to impossible." Borzov faced the group with his feet apart, relaxed.

"The background investigations for men selected to serve on those ships is extensive. Friends and acquaintances from childhood to present are questioned. Thus there is almost no possibility of infiltrating one of our people into the crew of a submarine." He punctuated each point with his finger.

"After the Walker brothers spy network was exposed, the opportunity to turn an American to our cause was diminished. The chance of infiltrating our personnel into the workforce of a shipyard constructing those nuclear submarines is almost as small as getting someone on the crew, and the time to gather the necessary information would be too long.

"There is another alternative." Colonel Borzov paused. He ran his hand through his close-cropped gray hair as he looked at several of the men in turn. Yuri wasn't surprised that most of them looked away. The KGB, or AFB, still carried much power in Russia, and it was always better not to be noticed.

"You are that alternative," Borzov said. "One of you will be aboard that submarine."

As the colonel paused, Yuri looked at those around

him. Everyone had their complete attention focused on Colonel Borzov, sitting forward in their chairs. Was he the only one with questions?

"Excuse me, Colonel," Yuri said, standing to get the colonel's attention. "You just said it was impossible to infiltrate the crew of a U.S. nuclear submarine, so how will you get us aboard? Also, what good would it do to get us aboard? We are sailors, not spies."

All heads turned toward Yuri with various expressions of surprise, as if the wall had spoken. The room was silent as they waited for lightning to strike down this person who questioned an AFB colonel.

The colonel drew out the silence, waiting for Yuri to drop his eyes. Yuri continued to meet his gaze. Giving up, Borzov said, "That is not what I said. It would be almost impossible to integrate a man into the crew of an American submarine. The emphasis is on the word *almost*. There is a way. However, only the one selected for this duty will receive all the details.

"As for the rest of your question, you were selected because of your experience as sailors and your ability to speak English fluently. It is easier to make sailors into spies than to make spies into sailors. In particular, you were selected because you are submarine sailors. When you finish here, you will be American submarine sailors."

Pocatello

NEIL Thomas finished a chapter of his book, *Flight of the Intruder*, as the bus neared the city limits of Pocatello. One of the least appreciated benefits of working at the nuclear test facility in Idaho was the opportunity to get in two hours of reading each day. Students weren't allowed to drive their cars to the site, and classified study material was not allowed off site, so the alternative choice was a novel or two a month. An hour drive into the desert in the morning and an hour drive back at night was recreation time for readers.

Of course, there was always the possibility of getting stuck next to a talker. Neil looked around at the other riders. He tried to avoid those who loved the sound of their own voices and required only that you nod your head once in awhile. Even though it was a monologue, they still demanded some eye contact to assure themselves their audience had not escaped. There were also the sleepers, but they were rather sedate, and the poker players kept to the back of the bus and were relatively quiet.

Thomas looked over at the sleeping passenger next to him. He could have been a lumberjack with his tan skin and his red plaid wool shirt, but Thomas knew he was one of the maintenance workers. The site maintenance workers usually were in plaids or hunting jackets, ready to go out and shoot something during their time off. The students mostly wore button-down casual shirts and could be distinguished as military by their clothes and short hair just as surely as if they had put on uniforms.

He tucked the paperback book into the pocket of his coat as he got off the bus. That was another of his requirements for bus ride reading; it had to be light reading. Not only to take the mind off the heavy reading required all day—nuclear physics, chemistry, and the like—but it had to be really light. It had to fit in his pocket or runner's belt pack and not be so heavy as to throw off his stride.

He got off at the first stop as usual and started jogging. Any farther along the route, and he would have to backtrack and crisscross to get in a good twenty minutes. He started off slow to warm up, not much more than a shuffle. It wasn't really cold, but the moisture in his breath was starting to freeze on his mustache.

After a few minutes, he put on a little speed. A few sprints and then time to warm down as he crossed the "trees": Cedar Street, Poplar, Walnut, Maple, Elm, Oak. A couple of dogs barked as he passed their houses, but none were loose. He avoided streets with loose dogs; as fast as he was, the dogs were faster. When the house was in sight, he walked the last block to cool down.

The front door had a solid sound as he closed it behind him. The small, yellow brick rental house was well-built if nothing else.

"Neil?"

"It's me, Dee." Neil said, rubbing his hands together to warm them.

"You're home early." Dee's voice came from somewhere in the back of the house.

"A little. The bus was ahead of schedule. Where are you?" he said, hanging up his coat in the foyer closet.

"Down here in the basement doing laundry."

He went through the living room, barely seeing the faded carpets, through the small kitchen with its sad old appliances, and down the wooden stairs to the basement. The basement was bare except for the washer and dryer, which came with the house. There were a few dust bunnies cowering in the corners, but not even very many of those. They hadn't been married long enough to accumulate a basement full of useless treasures, things too valuable to throw away but no longer useful. The dust balls came with the house.

Dee stood with her back to him, folding sheets as she took them out of the dryer. He put his hands on her shoulders and tried to turn her around.

She shrugged him off and said in her little-girl voice, "Later, I'm busy."

"Hey," he said, persisting. "We received our submarine assignments today." He slipped his arms around her waist, hugging her to him.

"Did you get Charleston?" she said, turning, tilting her face up to him, smiling and happy. At five feet three inches, she was just short enough to make him feel tall from his vantage point of five foot seven.

"No." He knew she wasn't going to like this.

"No?" Her voice held a hint of a quiver.

"No."

"Where are we going?"

"San Diego."

"San Diego? But that's on the West Coast."

"Last time I checked it was." He tried for humor.

"But we'll never get to see our families," she said, and her eyes started to fill with tears. She meant her family, but he let it go.

She let him pull her against his chest. The sheet was now hanging loosely from her hands, which hung at her sides. The tears ran silently down her cheeks.

"Don't cry, Dee. My class standing at Nuclear Power School was just above the bottom and in the middle at Prototype. With that kind of score you have to go where they tell you to go, not where you want to go. I suppose I could have studied harder, but we partied a little too much instead. Trips to Napa Valley wineries. Hell, we were on our honeymoon. Besides . . ." He shrugged. "There was nothing out of Charleston in this group anyway." He kept his arms around her waist.

"Did you get a boomer?"

"No. Missile boats don't make patrols out of San Diego. We got an old fast-attack, the *Pintado*."

"You don't care where they send you, do you?" She tried to push him away, but he held her tighter. "They could send you to hell, and you wouldn't care. You would just go flaccidly along, going where they tell you, doing what they tell you. Not happy, not sad, just limply going along. Don't you care about anything?"

She probably meant *placidly*, but he wasn't about to correct her. He knew how angry she could get when he contradicted her about grammar, and he wasn't about to subject himself to that. This wasn't the time to correct her grammar.

"I care about you," he said, watching the snow fall out of the gray Pocatello sky through the small basement window above her head.

5. TURNOVER AND TRAINING

Rota, Spain

JUST enough spray was coming over the bow to flavor the air. You could tell by the smell you were at sea, even if you closed your eyes. It wasn't often that a submarine sailor actually got to see the sea or smell it or taste it or feel it on his face. Usually the only contact with seawater in a submarine was the ever-present puddle in the bilge, and that was mixed with diesel fuel or lube oil.

Lieutenant Paul Jones leaned a little farther over the side, his hip on the rail and his hands in his pocket. He breathed deeply as if savoring some elusive perfume. The wind in his face and the deep-throated growl of the diesel was exhilarating.

He looked at the khaki-clad officers and the enlisted men in their blue dungarees huddled behind the low superstructure of the tug, keeping out of the relative wind and chatting. Talking to each other would be their main entertainment for the next three months while submerged on patrol, and here they were, missing an early morning ocean cruise and one of the last chances to see sun and blue sky for a long time. He looked forward again, past the tug's bow, shielding his eyes from the sun's glare, searching for the submarine.

"Good morning, Mr. Jones."

Jones turned to find that Senior Chief Clark had approached. "Good morning, Senior Chief. How are you this morning?"

"Fine, thank you, sir, and you?"

"Outstanding. Just trying to catch a glimpse of the submarine," Jones said, looking forward again. "Should be coming in sight soon. It's amazing how fast these ocean tugs move. We must be going twenty knots."

Clark took his pipe out of his mouth and looked over the side and back along the smooth wake behind the flat stern of the tug. "Could be."

After a pause appropriate for a change of subject, Clark said, "We've got a small personnel problem this morning, but with your permission, I'd like to handle it myself." Clark kept his feet spread to compensate for the motion of the tug, which rolled slowly, side to side, as it took the long swells on the port quarter.

Jones looked back at Clark, waited for him to continue.

"Gates and Davis didn't make it back from liberty last night in time to catch the tug this morning," Clark said. "I caught them coming up the gangway to the tender this morning about fifteen minutes before the tug was getting under way. They had had more than a few, and they looked pretty bad, so I told them to get below, keep out of sight, and I would take care of them when I got back."

"I don't mind you handling the discipline problems, Senior Chief," Jones said, leaning back against the rail to brace himself. "But we have to observe the operation of a lot of equipment before crew turnover, and we have a short time to do it. I'll be in the control room observing the diving evolutions and assisting the XO, and there is just no way you can do everything yourself. The check-off list for Auxiliary Division is just too long."

"Yes sir, that's why I brought Honeybear with me. I stopped by crew's mess, and he was up, shaved, and showered, and was getting breakfast." Clark reached over and grabbed the rail as a particularly high wave caused the tug to jerk to the side as it rounded the top.

"Honeybear is not that far along in his qualifications. Will he be much help to you?" Jones leaned hard against the rail to keep his balance.

"I'll use him to observe the hydraulic pumps and accumulators. He's checked out on those, I signed him off on the systems myself during the shakedown cruise. I'll observe the oxygen generators and other atmosphere equipment and use him on the trim and drain pump and maybe some of the hull valve evolutions."

"That sounds like it might work out. Those two probably deserve to be written up, much as I dislike the paperwork associated with a captain's mast." Jones and Clark both ducked as spray from another high roller carried across the fantail and wet their faces.

"Well, sir, you're the boss," said Clark, wiping his face with a handkerchief. "But here are my thoughts on that. If you write them up, they'll get a bad mark on their records, the captain will slap their hands, probably restrict them to the ship for a while, and the whole thing will leave a bitter taste in everyone's mouth." Clark put the damp handkerchief back in his pocket. "They'll resent being disciplined, the captain and the XO will resent having the extra chore of holding a captain's mast during refit, and you'll resent the paperwork. Worst of all, any chance of a promotion for either of them will go right down the tubes. They're both pretty good sailors. I would hate to ruin their careers for one screwup.

"On the other hand," Clark continued, "if you let me handle it, I'm going to give them some unofficial restriction and work their asses off." Clark held the bowl of the pipe in his hand and used the stem to punctuate his points. "The ship will get a good deal because I'll get a lot of scraping and painting out of them in the bilge, and our divisional spaces will look a lot nicer. They will have learned their lesson because I am going to work them hard. Yet they won't resent it, because they will feel that they are getting away with something."

"Good. Do it that way," Jones said, putting his hands on his hips as he reached his decision.

"Yes, sir." Clark saluted, and Jones returned the salute.

Jones watched Clark walk to the other side of the ship and start talking to the other chiefs. *Clark really does run the division,* he thought. *If he were a little bit better at paperwork, I wouldn't have anything to do. But, then again, he probably is a little bit better at paperwork and just wants me to have something to do so I feel useful.* It was not the first time he had seen some of the more experienced chiefs training their division officers as well as training the men. But Senior Chief Clark did it so subtly, you were never really sure. Jones looked forward again as the tug slowed to come alongside the submarine.

SENIOR Chief Clark looked back at Lieutenant Jones as he lounged against the rail of the tug, watching the submarine. *Good officer,* he thought. One who could let a chief petty officer run the division without trying to supervise every little detail, and yet still capable of making a decision when a decision was necessary. Of course, it didn't hurt that Jones had been an enlisted man himself at one time. He had taken a test, gone off to college on one of the Navy educational programs, and come back an officer.

Checking the operation of all equipment was an important part of crew turnover. When the Gold crew took over from the Blue crew, all the equipment throughout the ship would have to be inspected by the oncoming crew under operational conditions. All deficiencies would be noted and repairs made during refit. There would be no surprises. A Division had a lot of equipment and some extra A-gang bodies on board today would have helped. Clark clamped the pipe stem firmly in his teeth. Gates and Davis would sure as hell wish they had not come back drunk by the time refit was over.

The tug slowed as it drew abreast of the *King*. It lowered the bow, which it had carried in a vertical position, to the short, flat section of the deck of the submarine, aft the sail. The flat area formed by the missile hatches seemed almost made for an evolution like this.

The short length of the cruise missile ship made it look squatty and misshapen compared to the sixteen missile Poseidon boats. The comparison with the even bigger Trident was worse. Joshua shook his head as he looked at what he could see of the 380-foot length of the hull and wondered again how 102 enlisted men and officers would make a hundred-day submerged patrol in a submarine that size, let alone twenty-one days of refit. The *King* sure looked pint size compared to other subs.

As the last of the officers crossed the brow and disappeared down the hatch into the submarine, the chiefs and enlisted men started crossing over. Senior Chief Clark put his unlit pipe back into the pocket of his green foul weather jacket and zipped it closed. "I guess we're ready, Honeybear. Let's go."

Clark stepped easily on the gangway between the two ships and started across. He held the rope rail that stretched between the ships on one side of the gangway loosely in his hand as his body easily adapted to the swaying motion of the two ships plowing through the chop at one-third speed. As he neared the other ship, he looked back at Honeybear, slowly maneuvering his way across the gangway, holding on to the single rope with both hands.

Honeybear reached the submarine, took a deep breath, and said, "Now I know why I'm a submariner and not a surface skimmer."

"You and me both," said Joshua, patting him on the back. He turned and started down the ladder to machinery one.

"Well, here they are," said a voice from below. "I'm halfway through my checkoff, and you are just barely getting here. I guess you'll just have to take my word that everything in that first half worked out."

"Pendergast, how are you?" Clark said to the first class petty officer standing beside the ladder.

"Fine, Senior Chief, welcome aboard." Pendergast sat perched on one of the sheet metal storage lockers at the bottom of the ladder. "Here's your checkoff sheet," he said handing a clipboard to Clark. "I had it, you've got it. If you have any questions, you know my mailing address."

Clark ignored his banter, looking at the information on the sheets on the clipboard. "Where is Chief Olley?"

"He's got the dive, so I'm going to be going through the A Division sections with you. On the ride back, after sea trials, he'll see if he can get relieved and sit down with you and review any discrepancies.

"Where's Gates?" Pendergast said, looking up at the hatch as if he expected Gates to appear momentarily. "I thought he was going to be your atmosphere control petty officer this run. Why isn't he out here checking out the equipment with you?"

"I'm going to watch that part of the evolution myself," Clark said, continuing to flip pages on the board. "I'll use Petty Officer Palmer for some of the other evolutions."

"Well, Gates did come with you, didn't he?" The rise in pitch in Pendergast's voice was almost imperceptible.

"Yes, he'll be making the patrol with us." Clark gave Pendergast a long, penetrating look. Honeybear stood in back of Clark, shifting from foot to foot and trying to look inconspicuous, waiting for the senior chief to tell him what to do first.

"Sarah said she ran into you at the Market Place Restaurant while the Gold crew was running sonar tests at Tongue of the Ocean," Clark said. He tucked the clipboard under his arm, giving his full attention to Pendergast.

Pendergast held Senior Chief Clark's eyes for a moment and then looked down. "Yeah, I remember. She was with a group of friends." Clark could barely hear his voice.

"Well, sooner started, sooner finished," Pendergast said loudly, changing the subject, smiling again. "We may as well start with machinery one so you can observe the atmosphere equipment." He jumped down from the top of the storage cabinet. "I'll get permission from the bridge to shut everything down, and we'll restart them one at a time. After we shut down the oxygen generators, we'll leave them off, since we won't need them during refit.

"Honeybear can go back to the drain pump." Pendergast looked at Clark for approval. "If that's OK with you."

Clark nodded.

Pendergast continued, "When he's ready, he can have the watch stander get permission to pump. Then he can start on the hydraulics, unless you want him to do something else. By then we should be ready for the submerged evolutions."

Russia

"**THE** lecture today will be on general background information," the instructor said.

Yuri sat in the first row of desks with a pad of paper and pencil in front of him, trying to stay awake. He had eaten too much lunch, and the room was too warm. The food at the compound was American, and there was always too much of it.

There were only eleven students, including Yuri, left in the program from the initial group of eighteen. The ones who were gone had disappeared like ships in the night. The instructors gave no explanations, and the students didn't ask questions. Everything was very secretive, and the students were encouraged to keep to themselves.

"Up to today you have been given the chemistry and physics and electrical courses that an officer in the United States Navy would receive in preparation for assignment to a nuclear-powered submarine." The instructor was conducting the course in English. All instruction was in English. Yuri was starting to think in English.

"Much of this has been review, since you are already knowledgeable in the operation of submarine power plants, although some material has been directed specifically to differences between the U.S. Navy nuclear power plants and Soviet nuclear power plants. Excuse me, Russian nuclear power plants."

The lecturer was a middle-aged man with glasses and long, sandy-colored hair going gray. He stood facing the group as he talked, making a tent with his hands, fingers spread. He tapped the fingertips of one hand against the fingertips of the other and balanced forward on the balls of his feet. His green plaid sports coat and brown tie contrasted sharply with the uniforms of his audience, uniforms of U.S. naval officers.

"Today you will be given a general outline of the geographic locations associated with each part of the U.S. Navy nuclear power pipeline, names of places that would be familiar to a student actually taking the course." His hair had slowly fallen across his forehead over his glasses. He combed it back with his fingers.

"The first part of the U.S. training program is Nuclear Power School. There are two Nuclear Power Schools currently operating. One is located at Orlando, Florida, and one is at Mare Island, California. At these two locations, the officer is given basic chemistry, physics, electrical, and mechanical courses, specifically oriented toward nuclear power plant operation." He wrote "Mare Island" and "Orlando" on the blackboard as he talked.

The instructor began pacing. Three steps to the left, reverse direction, three steps to the right, reverse direction. His tapping fingertips kept pace with his steps. Four taps per step, nonstop talking. Yuri watched, fascinated by the dancelike routine, forgetting to take notes.

"This basic Nuclear Power School lasts six months. On completion, the officer is sent to a Nuclear Prototype School for six months." He stopped pacing long enough to write "6 months" on the board.

"The Prototypes are land-based, operating nuclear power plants used for testing design concepts and training. They are the prototype of power plants that were later used in the fleet. Prototypes currently operational are located at Schenectady, New York, and Idaho Falls, Idaho. One that was located in Connecticut has been shut down." He again pushed back his hair, which had crept down across his glasses.

"After Prototype, the officers are assigned to Submarine School for a three-month period at New London, Connecticut. This course is designed to familiarize officers with submarine concepts and submarine weapons systems. This is the basic submarine course. At some later date in the officers' career, they are assigned to a more detailed advanced submarine course.

"You," the instructor said, pointing to a student to Yuri's left, whose head had nodded down and snapped back up several times. "Where in New London is the Sub School located?"

"Sir," the student said standing to attention beside his desk. "The American Submarine School is located on the naval base in New London just a short distance uphill from the Navy Exchange."

"No, no, no!" The instructor said, throwing a piece of chalk at the student. The chalk bounced off the student's arm as he threw up his hands to protect his face. "What is this 'American' Submarine School! You are a United States naval officer; you would say 'Sub School' not 'the American Submarine School.'

"And while the Submarine School is located on the Navy base, the Navy base in not located in New London at all! It is in Groton, Connecticut, across the river from New London. You did not adequately study your briefing materials. Be seated." He waved the back of his hand at the student.

"You," he said pointing at Yuri. "Where did you live when you were at Prototype?" Yuri came to attention beside his desk.

"Pocatello, sir."

"Pocatello! That's a longer bus ride to the test site than from Idaho Falls. Why did you live in Pocatello?"

"Because I wanted to."

"Excellent answer!" the instructor said loudly. He pointed at Yuri and looked around the room. "The rest of you take note. That is an answer that can't be challenged."

The instructor clapped his hands and smiled. "Very good; be seated." He dismissed Yuri with a wave of the back of his hand.

"There are other reasons that you could have come up with after reading the briefing papers. The University of Idaho is in Pocatello, and you thought you might have time for a football game or a basketball game. Or you had friends there. But all of those are subject to challenge, such as 'Where did your friends live?' Or 'What was your friend's name?' Or 'I didn't know you were a basketball fan. What do you think of the Bullets?' That's just one more area for you to slip up on. If you are not familiar with a certain area, be as vague as possible without arousing suspicion.

"This information may save your life, so pay attention. If you need something to help focus your concentration, you may consider that Gregor will be conducting your hand-to-hand combat class this afternoon." He tossed a piece of chalk up and down as he talked, searching for another target. His other hand rested in the pocket of his sports coat.

"Those of you who have met Gregor can understand why you want to be on your toes. When Gregor runs the class, there are always bruises and sometimes broken bones."

A ripple ran through the room as the men shifted in their seats.

The instructor smiled. "Good, I see that you are completely awake. Now we can continue. Where can I get a pizza in Groton?" He looked around the room.

YURI sat cross-legged on the gray, cotton-covered mats, in a line abreast of the other students. The musty smell of the mats betrayed the years of dust and sweat that had collected in them. That smell could never be completely beaten out by the bodies that were pounded on the mats on a regular basis as the students slammed each other to the floor.

Yuri looked down the row at the other candidates for the mission. Dressed in their heavy cotton gi, the group could have been a karate class anywhere in the world. He was only half glad to be among those remaining. He liked the challenge but would not be unhappy to be among those who had been dropped. There hadn't been any chance to see Illya since being dragged into the program by Gregor.

At least the hand-to-hand combat classes were a good opportunity to relax, despite the hard exercise and sore muscles that often resulted. Yuri liked exercise, both the thrill of the competition, facing someone else in simulated combat, and the chance to keep athletically fit. He was proud of his athletic body. Though he was only 1.8 meters tall, it was all hard muscle. Illya used to kid him about being addicted to exercise and told her friends he was all twisted steel and sex appeal. Every day, without fail, he would do at least one hundred sit-ups, fifty in the morning and fifty in the evening. His size was only average, but good conditioning and prior experience gave him an edge in class.

Yuri matched himself mentally against his fellow students. They all had a good knowledge of English and experience in submarines. That was why they had been selected. Yet he was the only one who had martial arts training. He could tell by looking at them in class, the way they moved, that this was their first exposure to unarmed combat. Although some were picking it up quickly, they were like beginning dancers counting steps rather than feeling the music. He saw no reason to bring his prior training to anyone's attention. That would draw unnecessary attention to himself, and in Russia, keeping a low profile was still a healthy habit. He used just enough skill to win the practice matches but was careful not to show off.

The hand-to-hand combat classes always brought back pleasant memories. They reminded him of the karate classes he had taken as a youth when his father was stationed at the Soviet embassy in Washington, D.C. In some ways, the Americans were crazy, rushing from fad to fad like a herd of animals, but the health and sports fad, which had dominated America for the past several decades, was quite beneficial. Without the brief period in America, Yuri would not have developed the skill and interest that he had in the martial arts.

Gregor entered the instruction room. The students stood and formally bowed. Gregor returned the bow.

"Sit," Gregor said. He had a malevolent gleam in his eyes.

Gregor's gi fit him like a tent. His head poked obscenely though the neck opening, and the tufts of hair around his ears emphasized the baldness of his head. His neck was short and as wide as his head. He looked overweight, but he was massive and solid, not flabby.

"I am your instructor today. Up until now, you have learned the basic moves of hand-to-hand combat, how to defend yourself from blows with a club, and how to unbalance your opponent and turn his movement to your advantage.

"We do not teach you to be fighters. You do not have what it takes to be fighters." His voice showed his contempt for them. "We teach you enough so that you won't be a pushover for anyone who surprises you and hits you with a wrench. If you are attacked, I hope you will unpleasantly surprise them and possibly disable them." Gregor's face twisted into a grimace that he probably thought was a smile.

"You have learned the basic movements, you have practiced them. Now I will test you. The marks here will be a nice bruise or broken bone for those who fail. Those of you who fail badly will not go on the mission. Think ahead; expect the unexpected.

"You," Gregor said, pointing his stubby finger at one of the students. The student selected was a large Armenian, large, that is, in comparison to other people and the rest of the students in the class, but still smaller than Gregor. Yuri felt some momentary respect. At least Gregor had chosen the largest student in the class to practice on.

Gregor picked up a wooden baton that was wrapped with heavy foam rubber at one end. The student faced him. "Here you have one advantage over real life," Gregor said facing the students. "You know I am going to strike you with the club, and you know the club is padded so it probably won't kill you. Also, you have had some time to think about your defensive moves."

Gregor swung the club toward the student without any preamble, in a large circular arc parallel to the floor. To his credit, the Armenian was not completely surprised by the move. He pivoted toward Gregor and slashed downward with both hands at Gregor's arm.

Yuri watched with surprise as Gregor let the arm with the club bend at the elbow before he was struck by the student's two-handed slash. The student's hands, rather than one hitting at the wrist and one at the biceps, hit together near the crook of the elbow, without the leverage that the defensive move would otherwise have had.

Gregor followed through with his forearm carrying the club over the student's head rather than being stopped by the defensive blow. Reversing the direction of his club, he cracked the student sharply on the back of the head. The blow brought the student to his knees. He fell into a crouched position, hands on the floor.

Gregor put his foot on the student's ribs and pushed him over. Yuri felt the blood rush to his face with a sudden flush of anger. Not only had Gregor hit the student, which was not proper, he had struck him much harder than necessary in a practice situation. Then he kicked him when he was down. Kicking an opponent when he was down, especially a student, was an outrage.

"Return to your place," he said to the Armenian. "You're next," Gregor said, pointing to another student.

The students shifted restlessly, as if a wind had rustled down their ranks. It appeared that Gregor was going to beat them up one at a time.

The student chosen took his place in front of Gregor. He never took his eyes off Gregor.

"I see I have your attention now. Good. You expect your opponent to hit you with the club, but he does the unexpected. He takes you by the throat instead." Gregor said, dropping the club and grabbing the student by the throat. Gregor's muscles stood out as he squeezed. The student instinctively grabbed Gregor's hands.

"You are still somewhat surprised." Gregor laughed. "You were thinking of a move, a defense against the club, so you hesitate rather than starting your defensive move for the choke," Gregor said, applying more pressure to the student's neck.

The student turned toward his left, raising his arm over his head. As he did this, Gregor brought the student closer and lifted him off his feet.

"Good, you remembered the defense against the front choke," Gregor said almost conversationally. He wasn't even exerting himself. "Twist, raise your arm high, and bring it down across the choker's hand. Once again you are surprised. You are off your feet. You have nothing to push against." The student's face was turning purple, and he started clawing at Gregor's hands.

"Do something. Clawing at the hands is not effective. See, my fingers are on your Adam's apple. With my thumbs, I could crush your windpipe." Gregor looked like he would enjoy doing just that.

Yuri jumped up, unable to hold back his anger. "You took an unfair advantage. You know the simple defenses planned by the students, and you thwart the defenses. These would work against a civilian or one in the field. You know the defense in advance and do not allow the student to use it."

Gregor dropped the student. The student fell to his knees, gasping for breath.

"Ah, one with courage. Yuri Amelko, our friend from the Ukraine. Well, you are next, Yuri Amelko. Now you know that I know your defensive moves and will thwart them. Now we will see how you will use your knowledge."

Gregor picked up the wooden baton again. "Now we will see if courage helps you defend yourself," he said, looking at the class.

As the gasping student crawled back to his place, Yuri moved to a position in front of Gregor. He never let his eyes leave Gregor's face, even as he gave him a half bow. As Gregor stepped closer, he could smell Gregor's pungent, stale, animal-like order.

Gregor suddenly stepped toward Yuri, bringing the club all the way up from the floor, behind him, up over his head, in a vertical arc aimed at Yuri's head. Yuri had half expected this move. His defense, of course, would be to use the two-hand block, hands crossed at the wrist over his head, catching the baton near the wrists, twist to the side, follow through, and bring the assailant's arm up behind him. Instead, Yuri ignored the baton completely and stepped forward, toward Gregor, hitting him in the solar plexus with a closed fist. His instructor in the United States had been a member of the Professional Karate Association. He taught the traditional style, but he also taught the way karate could be used to win, not just an athletic competition with rules, but a street fight.

Gregor grunted and doubled over. Yuri was so close that the baton didn't hit him. Instead, Gregor's arm glanced off his shoulder. Gregor stepped back, holding his chest. His smile was frightening. The blow should have incapacitated him. Yuri's hand hurt like he had hit a frozen slab of meat.

"Aha, you know some of the martial arts. Now we will see how—"

Yuri didn't wait for him to finish his sentence. He kicked Gregor's feet out from under him with a foot sweep, counting on the fact that Gregor's speech center was engaged. This would give him an extra fraction of a second before Gregor could react. Gregor came down hard, like a mountain. Wasting no time, Yuri dropped down and brought his knee sharply into the heavy, meaty part of Gregor's upper leg, not hard enough to do any permanent damage, but hard enough to bruise the muscle so that walking would be difficult for several days. Yuri wanted to continue, but instead he stood back. There was complete silence in the instruction room.

Gregor got to his feet and stumbled, having obvious difficulty standing. He started to advance on Yuri and thought better of it. "The class has ended," he growled, a scowl on his face. He turned and limped from the room.

6. HOME FRONT

Charleston

THE dress felt uncomfortable. Not that it looked bad; the synthetic, poly-something fabric clung to the breasts and legs and probably looked very provocative. And the wine color of the dress contrasted nicely with her black hair. *It's just that this dress isn't Jane Gates,* she thought, running her hand across the fabric as it lay on her legs, smoothing an imaginary wrinkle. It was someone else, but Alex had said one time he liked women in dresses rather than jeans.

That was another thing: dressing to please men. That wasn't Jane Gates. *Mark never cares what I wear, but husbands are like that; after a while they stop noticing you, taking you for granted.* Anyway, jeans just felt so much more comfortable. Not that the dress was physically restraining, it was more psychologically restraining. You had to sit quietly. Just like at Sunday socials as a little girl.

She took a Marlboro from her purse and recrossed her

legs for the tenth time in an hour, and still no one had come through the customs gate. She sat apart from the other people in the terminal. The wives, sweethearts, mothers, fathers, all chattering like birds in their excitement. The crew had split after the new construction period, which wasn't that long ago. The sound trials, missile test firings, and torpedo certification were all that had transpired between the end of the yard period and now. Still, the Blue crew dependents seemed like strangers. But then most of the Gold crew were strangers also. She hadn't cared much about meeting anyone after Mark brought Alex home to dinner that night.

That night had been magic. Alex had touched her hand almost casually, but it was like having static electricity run between them, and she could see that it had affected him the same way. The whole time the three of them had kept talking as if nothing were happening. Of course, for Mark, nothing was happening, just a friend from the ship he had brought home for dinner who seemed to be getting along well with the wife.

When Mark had gone out to mix another round of drinks, Alex had lightly touched the back of her neck. He asked if he was bothering her. She had said no so fast, he hadn't really finished the question. And probably a little too loudly, too. She had worried that Mark would hear her in the kitchen, but he hadn't.

After that it was only a question of time. Soon they were going out to the state park together when Alex would get off early after a duty day. They would park the car at the edge of the road and climb the wooded hills with a blanket under Alex's arm. She always worried that a tour bus would come by and they would be the topic of idle speculation by some strangers, not that it would matter. Or they would meet at night. She would use a shopping trip to the mall as an excuse, and they would park out behind the Baptist church just like a couple of teenagers. She often worried that they would be caught, but most of the time she didn't care if they were, and sometimes she wished they would be.

The pair of navy blue trousers that appeared in front of her brought her back from her daydream. She looked up at Alex. He took the cigarette out of her hand and put it into the ashtray beside her. He took both of her hands in his and stepped back. She stood, their eyes never leaving each other. He brushed the side of her cheek with the backs of his fingers.

She wanted to grab him and squeeze him, and couldn't catch her breath, and felt like butterflies were running across her stomach. She closed her eyes as he kissed her lightly on the lips. He put his arms around her and squeezed, tightly now, no longer quite so gentle. She shivered as he kissed her again, noticing in a detached fashion that her toes were several inches off the floor.

"I didn't think you'd come to the airport," he said. "Although I'm glad you did. It's very public." He nervously looked around. There wasn't anyone near them in the smoking section, and the others in the terminal were involved with each other or rapidly heading for the exits.

"I know, but I couldn't wait to see you." She stood on her toes and pressed her head against his chest. The scent of him was wool and a hint of English Leather.

"Oh, Alex," she said, leaning back to look up at him. "I've got ten thousand things to tell you and can't think of a single thing to say or what to say first. It all seemed so important a few minutes ago and now seems so unimportant."

He laughed. "Well, I've never known a woman to be at a loss for words for long, so while you pause, let me suggest dinner for two and perhaps some champagne to celebrate my coming home. Afterwards, maybe a game of Scrabble."

She laughed. "I've got an after-dinner game in mind,

and it's not Scrabble. In fact, I don't know if it can wait until after dinner. We might have to skip dessert."

He laughed. "I've already decided on what's for dessert. Perhaps who is for dessert would be more correct. Come on." They started for the car arm over shoulder, arm around waist.

"YOU just can't beat the Market Place for dinner," Alex said, one hand on his stomach.

"I heard that the Navy serves the best food in the world," Jane said, leaning forward, putting both her hands on his as it lay on the table.

She pulled on his finger, running her fingers up and down its length. When she finished with one finger, she moved to the next. She played with his fingers whenever she started to get excited and Alex wasn't sure if it was because she was aroused or if it was causing her excitement.

"The Navy serves better food than the rest of the military, and the submarine service eats better than the rest of the Navy. But even submarines don't get Chateaubriand. Of course, the candlelight and the wine, maybe even the company, improves the flavor."

Jane moved her leg over so that her ankle touched Alex's ankle underneath the table. She ran her foot up and down his calf. "You're just saying that because it is true.

"I talked to Sarah Clark," she said.

"That's nice." Alex released her hand and took a drink of his wine and looked around the restaurant, trying not to appear interested.

"Hey, I just wanted to see if she noticed us. Do you remember when we saw her when the boat was out for sound trials? We were having lunch."

"Of course, I remember. You were so nervous you were almost sick."

"Well, anyway, she did notice us," Jane said, running a finger around the lip of her wineglass. "But, I don't think she'll say anything. She seems like a real nice person, a very warm person." She stuck her finger into the red wine and then ran her finger over Alex's lips.

Alex took her hand and sucked the wine off her finger. Smiling, he put her hand back on the table. He leaned back in his chair and hooked his other arm over the back, watching Jane. "She said something to Joshua."

"What!"

"She said something to her husband, Joshua Clark, about bumping into me. He knows that much anyway."

"Why do you say that? What did he tell you?"

"Josh didn't say anything about you being there. He isn't the kind of guy to gossip. I can't image him saying, 'I hear you're seeing Mark Gates's wife,' even if he knew it was true. It's just that when Mark's name came up, the way he looked at me, I felt like he probably knew something. It's one of those things that you know, that you're one hundred percent sure of, without having it spelled out."

Jane pulled her hand away from Alex. She put both her hands on the table edge with her arms straight as if pushing back from the table. She was staring at the table, not seeing it.

"I'll have to tell Mark."

"What do you mean, you'll have to tell Mark?" he said loudly. He looked around to see if the other diners were listening and lowered his voice. "That's stupid. Why would you have to tell Mark? Just because Sarah Clark saw us having lunch together? That's crazy."

"I can't have him finding out that his wife is seeing another man from someone else. If he has to find out, he should find out from me." She whispered loudly. "That's the only fair thing to do."

"But he doesn't have to find out." He realized he was whispering and continued in a normal voice. "No one knows anything. You're going overboard on this. There has always been a chance that someone would find out. Even coming to the airport to meet me was taking a chance someone would recognize you. Having dinner at a restaurant is taking a chance. Hell, having an affair is taking a chance. But we haven't been found out yet. We may never be caught."

"You may be right that he doesn't know yet, but he would find out sooner or later." Her hair swirled back and forth across her face as she shook her head. "Rather than take a chance on him finding out from someone else, I'm going to tell him when he gets back."

"Damn," Alex said, thumping the table with his fingertip, visibly restraining himself from pounding the table. He put his hand to his chin, watching Jane, and thought for a moment. "Well, then we'll get married."

"Oh, no," Jane said, surprised. "I don't want to marry you. I mean, I don't know if I want to marry you. I don't think I want to marry you."

"Well then, why are you telling Mark if we can't be together?"

"I've just explained: I don't know. I have to."

"What a hell of a homecoming," Alex said, throwing his napkin on the table, his voice getting louder again.

"Oh, Alex," Jane said taking his hand in both of hers and kissing his fingertips. "I'm sorry to have upset you. I didn't mean for it to turn out like this. Just let me think it through for a while."

He let his breath out slowly and gulped the last of his wine. "OK."

Moscow

ILLYA kept bounding ahead of him and then turning back to hurry Yuri along. Yuri laughed as she tugged at his hand.

She was like a child, so full of energy that she just could not get the world to go fast enough to keep up with her.

"Let's sit here," said Yuri, stopping at the first bench they came to, a tired old contraption made of weathered wood, partially covered with chipped green paint.

"Not there," she said returning to take his arm. "Everyone who comes into the park will pass right by here. How can we be alone sitting right at the edge of the path?"

"We can't be alone in the park. If we wanted to be alone, we should have stayed in the flat."

Illya ignored him. Yuri knew she saw through his quiet complaint.

Yuri looked at the patches of snow still on the ground, only half covering the brown, stunted grass between the naked trees. It was cold, but spring was in the air, and he was happy to be with Illya. This was the first break from the intensive training program, and it was long overdue.

"This way," she said pulling at his arm like a puppy straining at the leash, leading him off the path. "There's a bench back by those trees. I've seen it before."

"But that spot is very secluded. Someone may attack me and molest me," said Yuri.

"Only if you're very lucky." She laughed.

"Ha! You do have ulterior motives then."

"My motive is to stuff you so full of food that no one else will look at you; that is, if you haven't already eaten all the picnic." Yuri pretended to hide the basket behind his back.

"You're too late. I already saw you with your hand in the hamper," Illya said.

She took the basket from him as they reached the bench. She spread the napkin that was covering the food on the bench, and set out their meal. Yuri sat on the bench and watched as Illya arranged the food on the cloth between them. It wouldn't do to eat anything until Illya had it all set out just right. It was a little like a tea party for dolls, but nothing she did could displease Yuri today.

"This seems so bourgeois, having a picnic in the park. We could eat at home, and we wouldn't have to sit out in the cold." Yuri tried to make his voice stern.

"This will warm you," Illya said, pouring some vodka into glasses for them. "If you're still cold, I'll keep you warm," she said, taking his hand. "Besides, bourgeois is what everyone wants to be now.

"Here's to us," she said and touched her glass to his.

He put his hand over her glass as she started to raise it to her mouth. He leaned forward and kissed her. He kept his eyes open, looking at her closed eyes and long, dark eyelashes. After their lips parted, he rested his forehead against hers for a moment longer, savoring the aroma and warmth that their breaths made mixing together. Her hair fell forward, surrounding their faces, making a private world for them.

"That will warm me more than vodka, I think," he said. He touched his glass to hers and drank it down.

"Well, let's have some food," Illya said with renewed energy after the moment of quiet. We have bread, cheese, and sausage, and even some little pastries."

"You are a wonder. Where did you get all this food? Did you steal from the store? Won't your boss catch you?"

"And be shot by a firing squad? Of course not. And who would fend off the women if I were not around to take care of you? I just do my job like any good Russian and am justly rewarded. When the boss tells me to type a letter, I type a letter. When the boss tells me to take dictation, I sit on his lap and take dictation."

Yuri choked on the piece of bread he was eating. As Yuri coughed, Illya pounded him on the back, laughing. He struggled to regain his breath and motioned for more vodka. Taking a drink, he said, "If I thought that fat old store manager even thought about having you sit on his lap, it would be my patriotic duty to break both his legs."

"Well, of course, he thinks about it." Illya sighed, rolling her eyes. "He's a man. Why do you think he gives me this extra food? But as far as actually asking me, he has not yet been so foolish." She took a bite of the black bread and washed it down with vodka.

"He had better think twice about taking food," Yuri said. "Even though *glasnost* has arrived, people can still be shot for corruption. The KGB is still around, even if they call themselves something else."

"If there is corruption," Illya said with a slight edge to her voice, "That's his problem. Where he gets the food, I don't know, and I don't want to know. I'm doing nothing wrong. But let's talk of something else," she said in a softer voice. "Will you think of me while you're gone?"

"Of course I will," he said. He leaned across the im- provised table setting that separated them, putting one hand behind her neck. He pulled her head against his.

"How long will you be gone?" she asked.

"Two months, if everything goes well."

"Well, tell me about it. Don't make me pry everything out of you."

He put down his food, leaned forward, and looked into her eyes, but didn't say anything.

"Oh," she said, pulling away from him. She stood, turn- ing her back to him. "You always insist on having secrets."

He stood, took her shoulders, and turned her around. "We've been through this. You know I can't tell you. It would be dangerous for you to know, and it would endan- ger others, me included. It's not my secret to tell, it's a state secret."

Relenting, she put her arms around him and hugged him tightly. He tilted her chin up with his finger and said, "You're just excited because it's springtime. You're like a little flower bursting with energy, running out to picnics and pushing seeds into flowerpots. I've been on submarine cruises before that have lasted longer. One or two months is nothing to get upset about."

"But always before I've had some idea where you're going," she said. "This time I don't know, and it's something to do with the horrible man, Gregor. He frightens me."

"Now, that is something that bothers me," said Yuri, his face creased into a frown. "Not Gregor, but the KGB—excuse me, AFB—involvement in all of this. The GRU should be handling this operation, especially outside Russia. Military operations should be handled by military intelligence, the GRU, not the AFB."

"You shouldn't be telling me this," she said with a smile. "It will be dangerous to people, including me."

"You're right, but this bothers—"

She stopped him with a kiss. It was a long, lingering kiss. When she stopped kissing him, he stared blankly at her for a few moments.

"Sometimes when I'm with you," he said, "my mind just seems to go blank. There's just you, and the rest of the world is a little bit fuzzy around the edges."

Her breath had grown shorter. He unbuttoned her coat while he talked and put his hands around her waist underneath the coat. He could feel the warmth of her body through her sweater and skirt where her stomach and hips pressed against him. She pulled him close with an almost imperceptible shudder. He knew she was becoming aroused. It was like her body had gone into overdrive and been flooded with adrenaline when she shivered like that. He slipped his hands under her sweater, under her blouse, and ran them up her naked back, her beautiful, naked back.

"Perhaps you would like to take some dictation now," he said.

"I have something more interesting than dictation in mind," she said, unbuttoning his shirt and running her hands against his bare chest.

"We can't make love in the park, Illya," he said, as she nibbled his lower lip.

"I don't believe you," she said as she unbuttoned his trousers.

Yuri wondered if she had planned this all along. He used to think men were in charge of lovemaking, but they weren't. He wrapped his long overcoat around them both. This was one argument he was happy to lose.

7. SETUP

Rota, Spain

"LIBERTY went down two hours ago, Gates, what are you still doing on the ship?" Clark said as Gates and Honeybear came through the hatch into machinery one. He put his black plastic government-issue ballpoint pen down.

"Well, Senior Chief, you know chow is free if I eat in the crew's mess. If I go out in town, I have to pay for dinner myself. That means less to spend on beer and ladies."

"What do you mean, ladies?" Clark said, turning his writing tablet facedown and taking his pipe out of his pocket. "You're a married man, Gates."

"That's only half right, Senior Chief," Gates said with a broad smile. "In Charleston, I'm a married man. In Rota, Spain, I'm a sailor.

"Request permission to go ashore," Gates said, giving Clark a mock salute.

"Have you finished painting the trim pump?" Clark leaned back against the bulkhead and put his feet up on the metal desk as he lit his pipe.

"Senior Chief, I have painted every A Division bilge and every A Division piece of equipment on the ship. I have painted just about everything on this U.S. Navy submarine that doesn't move. If Lieutenant Jones had stood still long enough, I would have painted him, too. Now, may I leave the ship? I promise never to fuck up again." He raised his hand, palm out, like he was taking an oath.

Clark tilted his head down to hide his smile. Looking up, he took his pipe out of his mouth and carefully examined it. The slightly sweet scent of the tobacco permeated the air. "I guess you can. Just don't lead Honeybear astray."

Honeybear blushed and looked down. "Nah, Senior Chief. I'm just going into town for a couple of beers. We thought you might want to go with us."

"Well, thank you anyway, but I'm going to stay and watch the *Star Trek VI* rerun on the mess deck and write a letter home. Be back before morning quarters," Clark said. He gave Gates a hard look before putting his pipe back in his mouth and returning to his paperwork.

"OK, then," Gates said. He pushed his neatly combed hair back along both sides. "Catch you later." He pointed at Clark with his index finger and winked.

"Come on, Honeybear, we'd better get going before somebody else gets it first," Gates said as he started forward, stooping to pass through the watertight door into the missile compartment.

"Wait up," Honeybear said. He ducked his head and climbed through the watertight door after Gates. Gates had turned to the starboard and was halfway through the missile compartment, accelerating rapidly. His footsteps echoed on the metal deck plates. Honeybear hustled to catch up.

"Would you mind if we stopped by crew's berthing to see if Wilson wants to go to town with us?" Honeybear said, slightly winded, as he caught up with Gates. Honeybear was big but soft. Not obese, but wrapped in a layer of baby fat that some men never lose, until one day they shrivel up and turn into old men.

"Sure, that would be fine. You know where he bunks? Go ahead and lead the way," Gates stepped aside, shaking his head, to let Honeybear go first.

Honeybear took the lead and proceeded through the forward, watertight door between the missile compartment and the operations compartment. He climbed down the ladder to the lower level of the darkened berthing compartment and headed for the port side, outboard.

Stopping at the tier of bunks near the crew's head, he squatted down by the lowest bunk of three that were stacked one over the other. He knocked on the metal rim of the bunk and waited until the privacy curtain was pulled back. Wilson, in undershorts and T-shirt, had one elbow propped on a pillow. An automotive magazine was spread out in front of him on the bunk. The small, fluorescent light over his pillow gave the coffin-like space a clinical look.

"Gates and I thought you might want to go out in town and have a beer with us."

Wilson looked at Gates, then back again to Honeybear. "Sure, sounds good. You have time to wait while I put on some clothes and wash my face?"

Honeybear turned to Gates, who was leaning on the middle-level bunk looking bored.

"That OK with you?"

"Sure." Gates shrugged. "Why don't we wait in the crew's mess. I'll buy you a cup of coffee."

"Put a hustle on, Bill," Honeybear said in his slow drawl as he turned to follow Gates. "We'll wait for you in the crew's mess."

They retraced their steps and took the ladder up one deck to the crew's mess. Honeybear drew a mug of coffee from the ten-gallon stainless steel urn. The other urn chuffed slowly as it came up to speed.

Gates stirred powdered cream into his coffee. "Why didn't you ask him earlier? Then we wouldn't have had to wait while he got ready."

"Couldn't ask him earlier until we saw whether Senior Chief wanted to go into town with us."

"Why is that? Everybody gets along with Chief Josh."

"Almost everybody," Honeybear said in his slow drawl. "Wilson is from Alabama, and Chief Josh is just a little black, if you hadn't noticed."

"Bullshit," Gates said, taking his turn at the coffeepot. "Senior Chief is bronze, not black. I've seen people with a darker suntan than that. Besides, he's the best chief on the boat."

Gates made a face as he took a drink of the coffee. "I think the Blue Crew put a sneaker in the coffeepot again."

"Naw, we cleaned both pots after turnover. They're not going to pull that trick on us again," Honeybear said.

"Anyway," Honeybear continued, "Wilson has been told since he was a pup that blacks are inferior to whites, and now here he is working for one, and he just can't seem to adjust."

Honeybear reached into the galley refrigerator, grabbed a can of whipped cream, and squirted a large gob in his coffee cup.

Gates looked ill. "You ain't going to drink that shit, are you? That's disgusting."

Honeybear ignored him. "So anyway, he can't keep how he feels under his hat, and none of the other guys in the division will go out in town with him. They feel they have to choose between him and Senior Chief."

"Well, Honeybear, you ol' pushover. Always looking out for everyone. You must be striking for social director this cruise," Gates said. He grabbed Honeybear by the back of the neck and shook him playfully.

Dear Sarah,
I enjoyed talking to you last week. I think Nicole recognized my voice when you put her on the phone. I only wish these international calls were not quite so expensive and we could talk more frequently, although that might prove frustrating and make me feel more, rather than less, lonely.

The refit is proceeding well, despite the fact that we sometimes find two problems for every one we correct. We are, however, working our way through the refit package. Thank goodness we're a nonnuclear division. The nukes, as usual, are working their tails off. In addition, they have the ORSE at the end of this patrol, so that's an extra burden for them. You remember I mentioned that the ORSE exam is the operational reactor safeguard exam that the nukes have every patrol. They have done everything except polish the reactor (and it glows in the dark anyway).

I have let Mark Gates off restriction. He didn't enjoy the extra duty, but it was probably one of the better things that happened to the division. I got the bilge areas painted, and that wouldn't have gotten done, since the equipment overhaul takes priority. He never complained about being on restriction, and quite wisely, since I told him I talked Lieutenant Jones out of giving him a captain's mast instead. He went into town tonight with the Bear, which is good. Honeybear will keep an eye on him and keep him from getting into too much trouble. Although if the truth be known, I think his devil-may-care attitude is just show for the rest of us. He is acting out the part that he thinks a sailor should play. He really is a happy guy. One of the few completely happy people I have ever met.

In addition to everything else, the electricians are working overtime with the tech reps, fine-tuning their new toy, a piece of secret equipment. I feel I have almost said too much even saying "secret equipment," but I haven't given anything away. Mainly because I don't know anything. Still, it's good no one censors our mail these days.

One of the few thorns in my side on this refit is Bill Wilson, the new man who reported aboard right before we left. He is a real, live, dyed-in-the-wool redneck racist. In fact, he is a stereotype of a Southern bigot, or better yet, a caricature. I would sit him down and try to explain it to him, but he is such a slow thinker he probably wouldn't even know what a caricature is. (I guess I am doing some stereotyping now.)

In some ways, Wilson reminds me of the little, white-haired Southern ladies I mowed lawns for in high school. They were so nice and refined. You can probably remember two or three right off the top of your head. They would no more say "damn" than forget to go to church on Sunday. But yet they could "nigger this" and "nigger that" with the best of them without batting an eye. But, they never meant anything by it. It was just the way they were brought up.

Now, Wilson is one-third their age, and he really does mean something by it. Although he has never said the word, and he better not say it when I'm around, that is how he thinks of me. It is not just the way he was brought up, although that's part of it. He really believes it. And on top of everything else, he doesn't seem to get along well with anyone else in the division. In fact, he gets along so poorly I'm worried already about him being able to get anyone to help him with checkouts

on required systems. Then if I can't qualify him as
an auxiliaryman, I'll wind up feeling guilty and
wonder if I gave him every chance or bilged him
out because I didn't like him.

Well, enough of that. I didn't mean to burden
you with my problems. Sure do miss my two ladies.
I'll give you a call same time next week.

Love,
Josh

The visibility in the bar was worse than outside under
the streetlights. A few blue neon signs here and there
around the bar advertised Miller, Bud, and the local brew,
and provided enough light to count money as the American sailors turned over their paychecks a little at a time to
the bartender.

There were never any Spaniards in the Rota bars,
Lieutenant Paul Jones thought, looking around. The bartender might be Spanish—at least this one certainly
looked Spanish—but the patrons were always American
sailors or the Navy town camp followers. That part had
not changed much from the days when the Polaris subs
used to make patrols out of here.

Jones took a drink of his sangria and looked again at
the two women seated halfway across the nearly deserted
room. *Those two are probably Australian,* he thought,
judging by their accents. For some reason, this year, a lot
of Down Under women seem to be turning up in Rota.
The two women spoke in low, conversational tones and
laughed at some private joke as they glanced his way.

He sighed as he took another swig. He had no moral
objection to chasing skirts, but most of the time it was unproductive. It was usually a lot of work with no reward.

Jones turned his attention to the only other person at
the bar. *Definitely not Spanish,* he thought, looking at the
large man sitting against one wall. *Spaniards don't grow*

that big. Also, the slightly baldish head with the fringe of
hair around the ears was not typical of Spanish types.
Among all the problems Spaniards may have, a receding
hairline was not one. The giveaway, however, was the
ruddy complexion. He was probably from a Northern Eu-
ropean country.

Jones poured the last of the sangria from the pitcher
into his glass and took a long drink. One of the nicest
things about Spain was the sangria. He munched a few
pieces of the fresh-cut fruit floating around the top. Also,
not very expensive. If you are going to poison yourself
after a hard day's work, best not to spend a fortune doing
it. Jones finished the last of his glass, pushed his chair
back from the table, and slowly stood up.

Better not overdo it, he thought, as he steadied himself
against the edge of the table. Tomorrow would be the operational test of the overhauled oxygen generator, and it
would not do to have a wine headache while having to sit
through that.

Gregor, sitting against the wall, waited until Jones was
completely out the door of the small bar. He took a small
transmitter from his coat pocket and keyed a button on it.
He followed Jones out.

Down the street from the bar a small alley led from
dim light to greater darkness. A transceiver tucked in the
pocket of a nondescript man dressed in civilian clothes,
emitted a beep. The man quickly lay down on the littered
floor of the alley. He held his stomach, moaned, and
rolled slowly back and forth.

Lieutenant Jones stopped as he came abreast of the
alley.

"Are you OK?" he called looking at the man lying on
the ground some fifteen feet inside the poorly lit alley.

"Help me," the man replied in English.

Jones was undecided. He didn't have time to get involved with a drunk, but the man spoke English. It might

be a shipmate. He stepped into the alley and knelt beside the man. The man continued to moan, clutching his stomach.

"Are you OK?" There wasn't anything visibly wrong with the man. Jones pulled the man's hands away from his stomach.

Gregor stepped into the alley. Several quick steps, and he was behind Jones. Jones turned his head to see who had entered the alley. The man on the ground suddenly grabbed Jones by his jacket lapels and held him in position. Gregor stooped down and seized Jones by his jacket collar. Grasping the seat of Jones's trousers, he lifted him off the ground. Jones's feet pedaled futilely nearly a foot above the ground as he twisted left and right in an attempt to reach behind him. Gregor lowered his left hand, which was on Jones's collar, so that his body was parallel to the ground. He took several quick steps toward the wall on his left, pivoting and transferring his forward motion to Jones as he neared the wall.

Jones became aware that time had stepped down to half time, to one-quarter time, to one-eighth time. The world had slipped into slow motion. He saw that the cobblestones were set with sand rather than mortar. The tops of the stones were slightly rounded and polished. The light from the far-off streetlamps made the cobblestones seem to glisten in the cold, crisp night air.

The air was rich, full of subtle odors he had never noticed before. The smell of ripe banana was layered on the scent of horses. He never knew 'til now he could identify a horse with his nose alone.

Each heartbeat seemed like distant, far-off thunder, and each beat was slower than the last one. The reverberations seemed to last forever. The little life he had left played out *ritardando*. He could hear distant, far-off voices. "I'll Always Love You" came faintly from a distant bar. Somewhere people laughed. Time stood still.

He thought of Celia.

His head struck the wall at nearly twenty-five feet per second.

SENIOR Chief Clark stepped out of the chief's quarters with his pipe in his hand. He dug through the pockets of his khaki shirt for tobacco in an absentminded fashion as he stepped across the passageway and into the crew's mess. He tamped tobacco into his pipe with his thumb as he stood near the door. He lit up as he watched the crew go through the serving line, rattling dishes, knives, and forks onto their trays.

"Steak and eggs this morning." He sighed wistfully to himself, smelling the aroma of the fresh-cooked food. He took one of the white porcelain mugs, stepped up to the coffee urn, and drew himself a cup. He walked to a vacant table and slipped into the built-in bench.

He took a long drag on his pipe, allowed a little in his lungs with a quick intake of breath, and blew it out. He washed it down with a mouthful of coffee. *I might live after all,* he thought, as the nicotine and caffeine gave his heart a kick start.

"Good morning, Josh," Chief Dietz said in a voice that was a little too loud, a little too cheerful for this time of morning. He patted Clark on the shoulder and slipped into the bench seat on the opposite side of the table. He slid a tray filled with ample portions of everything the mess cooks were serving onto the table.

"You'd better get some of that breakfast steak before it's all gone," Dietz said, shoveling eggs in his mouth, fork held in his fist like a trenching tool. Chief Dietz contrasted sharply with Clark. Small and wiry, he always seemed full of nervous, good-natured energy.

"Borkum Riff and black-and-bitter coffee are all I

need. I want to keep myself slim and trim in case we pull into Nice for a swim call."

"Swim call? This ain't no damn cruise ship. The old man will give the crew swim call when pigs have wings. Now if you could figure a way to convince the captain that his fitness report would look better if the crew had some fun, then we might get some liberty time." Dietz wrapped his fist around a knife and started on the steak and hash brown potatoes.

"Perhaps we can call it physical fitness training," Clark volunteered.

"Good morning, Senior Chief." An enlisted man walked up and stood at the side of the table.

"Well, good morning Smith," Clark said automatically checking Smith's blue chambray shirt and denim trousers for proper military appearance. "What brings the auxiliaryman of the watch down to the crew's mess?"

"The captain wants you to come to officers' call this morning, Senior Chief," said the young auxiliaryman. He shifted nervously back and forth from foot to foot as he stood at the edge of the chief's table.

"Oh, my, my, ain't we getting fancy," Dietz said, as he continued to shovel bits of egg and pieces of steak into his mouth. He had switched from a knife to a piece of toast to push food onto the fork in his other hand. "Go to officers' call, and next you'll want your own stateroom."

"Did he say what the problem was? Is there anything I should know about before I go up there?"

"Nothing that I know about, Senior Chief, but all the officers have been up since early this morning. The CO was up on the sub tender with the commodore before reveille."

"OK, thank you, Smith, I'll be right up." Clark finished his coffee in a gulp and tapped out the ash from his pipe into the empty mug. The bowl of the pipe made a solid thunk as it hit the edge of the heavy porcelain cup.

"See you later," he said as he eased out of the booth and headed forward.

Turning left into the passageway, he walked forward past the trash compacting room and the officers' quarters, and turned in to the officers' wardroom. All the officers were already there except the captain and his own division officer, Lieutenant Jones.

"Morning, Senior Chief," the XO said, "have a seat. The captain will be down in just a minute." The XO motioned him to one of the seats at the end of the long table with the junior officers.

"Yes, sir."

"Would you like some coffee?"

"No, thank you, sir," Clark said. If the meeting lasted more than an hour, he didn't want to be stuck trying to hold two quarts in a one-quart bladder. He took a seat at the foot of the table. The captain's seat at the head of the table was empty. The seating arrangement around the table was, by tradition, according to rank. The more senior the officer, the closer to the head of the table he sat. The junior officers joked that the rankest person on board was the captain.

The wardroom was as quiet as a wake. Worse. At a wake, there was usually some sniffling from the bereaved. Whispered comments. Young boys shifting around in their seats, waiting to get back home and play baseball. This was much worse. The officers were all too old to fidget, even the young lieutenant (JG), although he was still young enough to have acne.

The silence made Chief Clark feel even more awkward, since he was the only enlisted man in the room. He took his pipe out of his pocket and looked down the table to see if any of the other officers were smoking. The M

Division officer had a cigarette going, so Chief Clark pulled his pouch of tobacco out of his shirt pocket. Holding the pipe in the pouch, he pushed tobacco into the brown, wooden bowl, and carefully lit up. There was a time when almost everyone at any type of military meeting smoked, Clark thought wistfully. Now almost no one did. Congress was even considering putting women on subs. Maybe it was time to retire.

He looked around the room. The silence was unnerving. Even the communications officer, Lieutenant Dick Rogers, who was always so full of excited good humor that he chattered almost continuously, was subdued. Something was up. Where was Lieutenant Jones?

The captain entered the room and went to his place at the head of the table. The executive officer called attention on deck. Even before everyone had completely pushed back from the table, the captain motioned with his hand for everyone to remain seated.

"Keep your seats, gentlemen." The captain remained standing. "Some of you may have already heard, Lieutenant Jones was killed out in town last night." There wasn't any of the head twisting and murmured comment that usually accompanied this type of announcement, so it appeared that the officers, at least, had heard the news. Rumor, not subject to the usual laws of nature, did travel faster than the speed of light. Clark wondered how he had missed hearing it. He had been up at least twenty minutes.

"The circumstances are still under investigation, but it appears that there was a fight of some sort. The Navy Investigation Service will be conducting the investigation here on the ship, so let your men know at quarters this morning that individuals will be called in for routine questioning." The captain took a seat as he continued.

"Emphasize that this is just routine questioning to get details such as when Lieutenant Jones left the ship, who his regular companions out in town were, was he friends with any foreign national, when was the last time he was seen alive, etc."

The pudgy little captain had turned his chair at an angle to the long, green wardroom table and crossed his legs. He tapped out each point with his fingers as he spoke. His voice was barely above a loud whisper. Not what you would call a command voice, but more like a midlevel, civil service type.

"The investigation out in town will be conducted by the *Guardia Civil*. There doesn't seem to be any problem with the locals as far as redeployment of U.S. submarines in Rota, so we expect that the civilian police force will be cooperating fully and working closely with us on this matter. No protest about nuclear reactors or weapons on board or anything like that.

"I spoke with the commodore this morning, and he sees no reason to cancel liberty or change our operational procedures in any way. However, he did emphasize that personnel going on liberty should not go alone. This is always a good practice, but especially under the circumstances.

"XO," he said jabbing his index finger at the executive officer, "make sure that word is promulgated." The XO nodded and made an entry in the pocket steno pad he carried everywhere.

"Are there any questions?"

There was some hesitation. No one seemed willing to break the silence. After a few moments that seemed to drag on longer than they actually did, the M Division officer spoke up. He was the maverick in the wardroom. He even rode a motorcycle to work.

"What happened, Captain? How was he killed?"

"The top of Lieutenant Jones's head was crushed." The captain looked annoyed at the question. "He had a strong odor of alcohol on him, and it appears that there may have been a fight of some kind. The details are sketchy, but apparently he wasn't robbed." The captain was a puritan when it came to proper conduct.

"I've sent a message to the commodore formally requesting an immediate replacement since we are due to get under way soon. In the interim, Senior Chief Clark will be acting as A Division officer and will report directly to the engineer." The captain pointed at Clark as he spoke.

"Any problems with the test of the O_2 generator, Senior Chief?"

Clark took a measured drag on his pipe. "No, sir."

"Good. When you are ready to bring it up for a test run, get permission from the engineer

"That's all, gentlemen. Carry out the plan of the day."

8. VOLUNTEERS

Charleston

CELIA Jones watched her four-year-old son, Jason, manipulate his latest toy, transforming it from a truck into a helicopter and back again. He sat, legs spread, on the Persian carpet. He was as completely absorbed in his toy as his mother was in him. His father, Paul, had shown him how to work the first one before he left on cruise; the rest he had figured out himself. It must be a guy thing, because it was beyond her abilities.

He sneezed, and his whole body lifted off the ground with the force of it. Celia could see he was distracted from his work, as he rubbed the back of his sleeve across his nose, but only for a minute.

We will probably have to store the carpet if his allergies get any worse, she thought. *And he wants a dog. Or a cat. Or a baby sister.* Given the alternatives, choice A might not be so bad, even with his allergies. *What will he be doing in another twenty years,* she wondered, *taking apart and rebuilding automobile engines? In medical school learning to repair human bodies? Troubleshooting computers?* Surely it would be something mechanical, working with his hands. He went back to his task. Bend, flex, twist.

"Time for a nap, little guy," she said.

"I'm not tired," he said reasonably.

That's actually a good sign, she thought. If he were tired, it would be temper tantrum time, feet kicking, whining, and screaming. It was one of the oddities of parenthood that if the child wasn't tired, he could be reasoned with and talked into bed. If the child was tired, no amount of logic, or sometimes even bodily force, could get him into the sack.

"Well, you will be tired," she said. "By the time we get your pajamas on and sing a few songs, you will be asleep."

"Can I go to bed in my underpants?"

"I think that can be arranged," she said, smiling. A few minor concessions always helped the cause. The new Garfield shorts were his favorite. Good thing she had bought several, or she wouldn't be able to get him out of them to do the laundry.

"Do you want to take Panda Bear to bed or Dragon?" she said. Another easy strategy: whichever animal he chose, going to bed was conceded, and it was just a question of choosing which animal would keep him company. Child psychology was wonderful.

"Panda Bear," he said, hardly glancing up from the transformer. The red plastic helicopter was now fast becoming a truck. Celia still couldn't figure out how the toy worked. She had watched him many times, and she had tried, but she couldn't get the parts to move right.

"Can I have a story?" he said. Delay the inevitable.

"OK," she said with a sigh. "But a short one. What story would you like?"

"The flying ship."

"You mean *The Flying Dutchman*?" She rolled her eyes. It was longer than she wanted, but she had given him the choice.

"Yes, the one that sails forever."

"Very well. But we have read this one all week. Aren't you tired of it yet?" Her voice said she was.

He shook his head, straight blond hair standing out with centrifugal force. "I'm going to be a Navy like Dad."

"You mean a naval officer."

"Just like Dad," he said, agreeing.

She opened the book as he climbed into her lap, abandoning the Transformer on the battleground the living room floor had become. It was strewn with a multitude of other toy causalities.

Jason was getting to be tall enough that Celia had trouble seeing the book over the top of his head. She smelled his hair. Babies, even at four years old, still smelled sweet—provided you dipped them in the tub once a day. She ruffled his hair just to be touching him.

"A long, long time ago, there was a sailing ship with a cargo of gold in her hold." She paraphrased the story, flipping quickly through the pages. Only rarely did Jason catch her skipping paragraphs and pages. To Jason, it was new each time he heard it, but after the first several times, Celia was so bored it was painful.

"One day a fight broke out between the bad man, who wanted to keep all the gold for himself, and another man on the ship who was good. The bad man won. He killed the good man and threw him overboard. No one helped the good man.

"Why didn't other people help, Mom?"

"We are going to find out. Let's read a little bit more and see if we can find the answer." She gave him a squeeze.

"The crew became very suspicious of one another,

each one thinking that the other wanted to steal the gold, and each ashamed that no one had helped the good man in his fight. After a while, the ship was becalmed and didn't sail for weeks because of lack of wind. They ran out of food, and a plague broke out on board.

"A plague is where people get sick and die," she explained, tilting her head to the side to look at him. He nodded, running his finger over the picture of the ship.

"Finally, a wind picked up, and the ship sailed on. Eventually, it pulled into a port, and the crew asked for help. But in those days there weren't hospitals and doctors to look after the sick and make them better. So the people at the seaport wouldn't let the ship land because they were afraid of catching the plague."

Jason kept trying to turn the pages to look at the pictures. Celia gently restrained his hands.

"So the *Flying Dutchman* sailed on. Each port that the ship came to turned the ship away because the people were afraid of the plague. Finally everyone on board died, and the ship kept sailing on by itself.

"Some people say the *Flying Dutchman* is still sailing the seven seas. Sometimes on a foggy night sailors see it appear almost by magic out of the fog and sail across their bow. Sometimes it causes ships to go aground and sink."

"Why, Mom?" He swiveled his head halfway around to look at her.

"Well, some people think that the story was made up and not really true. Other people think it's an allegory. That means that it is a lesson using a made-up story to show people what happens if you don't do the right thing. The lesson is that the bad men were being punished for fighting over the gold by not being allowed to come into port. Maybe they are out there at sea still trying to come into port."

She was interrupted by a knock on the door. She

threaded her way carefully through the sea of toys. Jason followed in her wake.

"Mrs. Jones?" A Navy lieutenant stood at the door.

"Yes?" she said. She made the answer a question.

"I'm Philip Seat, a chaplain at the Navy base. May I come in for a few minutes and talk to you?"

A ball of hard, cold ice formed in the bottom of her stomach.

She barely noticed Jason holding tightly to her leg as she stood at the door, nodding her head yes. She led the chaplain into the living room, avoiding the cluttered toys by instinct. She sat on the sofa and motioned him to a chair, afraid to look at him.

Please, God, let Paul be OK, she thought. *Don't let it be Paul.* "May I get you some coffee?" she asked, more to change the subject than to be polite, or to delay the bad news. By now she was sure it was going to be bad news. She put her arm around Jason.

"No, thank you. There is no way to cushion bad news. I regret to inform you that your husband, Lieutenant Paul Jones, is dead. The Navy has assigned me full-time to assist you in any way possible."

Celia Jones hugged Jason tightly, her mind blank, not hearing the details as the chaplain continued. Jason started crying. With a fragment of detached thought, Celia knew he didn't understand what was happening, was reacting to her anguish. His pain brought her back, helped her focus.

"It's OK, Jason," she said, but she knew it would never be.

Groton

THE commanding officer of the Submarine School was a captain. As an O-6 he was equivalent to a colonel in the

Army or a CEO of a small corporation. Yet his office was on the plain side. Government-issue desk, chair, coffee table, and sofa all purchased through the lowest bidder. The desk was the usual gunmetal gray. Thomas had begun to suspect that the old six-hundred-ship Navy was now office furniture. He sat on a small sofa across from the captain. It was too soft to be comfortable sitting all the way back, but too low to sit forward on the edge.

"Lieutenant Thomas, I don't like to pull students out of class, but there has been a major change in your assignment, and I wanted to give you all the notice that I can," the captain said.

"Yes sir," answered Thomas.

The captain had been looking at his hands in front of him on the desk, or perhaps admiring the four gold stripes on the sleeves of his blues. He looked up. Thomas thought he seemed startled to have his speech or train of thought derailed. The captain cleared his throat and resumed his contemplation of his hands. Thomas thought he looked distracted, and the captain paused as if choosing his words.

"Yes," the captain said, getting back on track. "I see that you initially expressed a preference for a Charleston boat. Well, we are going to be able to meet your requirements.

"One of the officers, Lieutenant Paul Jones, on a submarine out of Rota, Spain, was killed in a fight or something in town during refit." The captain shook his head and looked like he had swallowed something unpleasant. "So we need someone to replace him before the *King* leaves on patrol. You've been selected."

Thomas hesitated. "Thank you, sir, and normally I would be very excited about being assigned to the *King*. In fact, the *Martin Luther King* would have been my first choice if she had been available at boat selection. I actually prefer a missile boat, and since the *King* is the newest missile boat in the fleet, with all the latest technology, that's the best I could have hoped for."

"Stop right there." The captain held his hand up. "The *King* is not a missile boat; it is a fast-attack submarine of the Centurian class, which has been extended in length to carry extra cruise missiles and vertical launchers. You will recall that some of the 688-class fast-attack submarines also carried cruise missiles and vertical launchers; therefore, this is nothing new. Even the Seawolf class carries cruise missiles, normally fired out of the torpedo tubes."

The captain was visibly agitated, but Thomas couldn't figure out why. Something must have hit one of his hot buttons.

"I realize that many of the enlisted men have been referring to the *King* as a missile boat, but as an officer, you have the responsibility for setting an example. The Strategic Arms Reduction Treaty, START, specifically limits the number of submarine missile launch platforms that each side is allowed." Portraits of famous Navy admirals on the wall looked sternly down on Thomas.

"The Russians are playing this up as usual," the captain continued. "They claim we've launched a new class of missile submarines. We are falling right into the trap if we do the same thing and call the *Martin Luther King* a missile submarine. The cruise missiles are tactical weapons, not strategic weapons, and have a short range." He tapped the desk with his finger for emphasis. "That is why the submarine has been redeployed to Rota, Spain, to be close enough to probable targets to launch these missiles if needed."

Thomas was surprised at the lecture. It sounded like he'd plugged into Navy 101, the Navy line on missile subs. Thomas closed his mouth, which he suddenly realized was hanging open. "I understand, sir. As I said, under different circumstances, I would have been happy to serve aboard the *King*. But my wife and I have already made all our arrangements for moving to the West Coast."

Thomas realized his voice had grown plaintive and consciously lowered it a half octave. No sense whining in front of this guy. That would be counterproductive. "Our household goods have been shipped to San Diego, and I had to do some talking to persuade her that living on the West Coast might be fun. Now we're actually sort of looking forward to going there."

"I understand that this may cause some disruption in your plans; however, it's not a request, Lieutenant." The captain leaned forward. "Your orders have been cut, and you are going to the *King*.

"The executive officer has arranged for medical to update your immunization card after class today, and then you are to report to the Personnel Support Detachment for your orders. You will complete the remainder of scheduled courses tomorrow and will fly out on Saturday. The *King* leaves on patrol on Sunday. Any questions?" The captain sat back in his chair. His attitude said there had better not be.

"Well, yes, sir." Thomas said. He didn't notice the warning signs. He sat forward on the edge of the sofa. "My household goods have been shipped and are somewhere between Idaho and San Diego. Also, my wife is visiting her family in Maryland."

"Yes, well, what is your question?"

"What should my wife do? What about my household goods?"

"Tell your wife to go to Charleston, and tell Household Effects to ship your goods to Charleston." The captain's voice was sarcastic. "You're not the first officer to have his orders changed between duty stations. And your wife will manage without you. They usually do."

"Aye, aye, sir."

The captain picked up a paper on his desk and started reading. This time, Thomas recognized the signal. He was dismissed. He picked up his hat.

"By your leave, sir?"

The captain nodded without looking up.

NEIL Thomas pushed open the gray metal door to the personnel office. Desks marched in rows from the door to the back wall of the medium-sized room. Each desk had a chair next to it for a client, not unlike your friendly neighborhood loan officer, he thought. Even a Please Take a Seat sign stuck on a waist-high wooden post in the small waiting area by the door. He obediently took a seat.

At least the chairs were semi-comfortable: standard gray-painted metal, Navy-issue with padding across the upper back and extra heavy-duty padding across the seat, sufficient to accommodate the battleship-sized part of the anatomy that many senior Navy chiefs and officers developed after years of hard work performed in a sitting position in the service of their country.

Thomas impatiently looked around the room, noting the tastefully painted walls. A nice two-tone pattern, mud brown from the hip down, and mundane yellow above. The earth tones, though bland, were a daring innovation from the standard battleship gray found worldwide in cookie-cutter Naval offices.

He looked at his watch. Seventeen hundred hours. Almost quitting time. Like bureaucrats everywhere, everyone was getting ready to secure—getting ready to bolt was more like it. Actually, many of them had started their wind-down after lunch, Neil thought with the disdain that seagoing sailors felt for their landlocked brothers. Still, these were Navy people, and even landlocked sailors were several cuts above a civilian. Too much shore duty could dull the best sailor.

There were only three desks occupied by enlisted men working with clients. One finished up as he watched. As the chief she had been working with left, the personnelman gathered up her paperwork and said to Thomas, "I'll be with you in a minute, sir." She motioned to the chair next to her desk and looked at his name tag. "Please have a seat."

Thomas returned the smile automatically as he changed chairs. *I get the plain Jane,* he thought, looking enviously at the attractive young female third class personnelman at the next desk. Hair so blond it was almost white. Eyes so blue you could forget your name.

He watched Plain Jane as she came back to her desk. No danger of this lady being a threat to the good order and discipline of this man's Navy. Her name tag read Hoggins. Not a great name for a lady, especially this one. On the plump side, with eyes a little bit too far apart, nose a little too big, skin too coarse, blond hair too thick. Nothing was too terribly bad; everything was just abundantly plain. She was just a very bland blond.

"Let me look over your paperwork for a minute, Lieutenant Thomas, and we'll get your travel set up. I see you're going to Spain, to the *Martin Luther King*." She flipped rapidly through his personnel folder. "Charleston is your home port. Will you be flying out of McGuire, or will you be going out of Charleston?"

"I haven't thought about it. I assumed that I would be going out of McGuire, since I have to meet the ship before she gets under way."

"All right, sir. I'll set it up for McGuire and get you on one of the Air Force MAC flights. Travel from New London to McGuire will be commercial at your own expense, subject to reimbursement." She was filling out forms as she talked.

"Will you need a travel advance?"

"No, I can put everything on a credit card, and I may catch a ride with a friend partway."

"Then if you'll just stop by tomorrow, sir, I'll have everything ready."

PETTY Officer Cynthia Hoggins watched Neil leave. She busied herself with minor, routine paperwork while the last of the personnel staff left. After locking the door, she made a photocopy of Lieutenant Thomas's paperwork. She double-checked the stack of orders written that day, although she had done it earlier. No other officers bound for Rota, Spain.

Why Max would want to know which officers were going to Spain, she didn't know. He said he had a friend in Charleston in the real estate business. Crews of submarines making patrols out of Rota, Spain, were stationed in Charleston and flew to Spain for crew change before patrol. Max said that he wanted the names of people moving to the area to help his friend get a lead on selling homes to the new people moving to Charleston. His story didn't sound quite right, but she wanted to believe him. She didn't really want to challenge him. Telling him he was lying was unthinkable.

Max had come into her life like a whirlwind. She had been out in town with a couple of girlfriends. She was always out with the girls. Max had approached them and danced with one or two of the other girls before centering his attentions on her. With his dark hair and handsome features, Max could have been with any of the women there that night, but he chose her. At first she had been embarrassed by his attentions, dancing with her, buying her drinks. She thought he must have been joking with her or teasing her. No one had ever paid that much attention to her. Actually, no one had paid any attention to her.

That night when he had asked if he could take her home, she had been afraid to say yes. But she was even more afraid to say no. Later, while driving home, he had suggested that they stop at his place. She wasn't surprised and also wasn't prepared to say no.

He led her to his bedroom, kissed her as he unbuttoned her blouse. She made a halfhearted attempt to push his hands away, but he saw through her false protest. She held her stomach in as he pushed skirt and panties down around her ankles. She felt self-conscious about her weight as she stepped out of the skirt. Would he think she was fat? He pushed her back upon his bed. After they had made love, he asked her about her work. She told him everything she could think of. He was interested in her, and she wanted to hold his attention. He asked questions, where orders were written to, especially overseas orders. What airport did personnel fly out of? She could deny him nothing.

He said he would like to see what a set of orders looked like to see what type of work she did. He said that, being a civilian, he had never seen that type of document and was curious. She said she didn't think that was allowed, but he made a joke of it. He said he would reward her handsomely for it and that she should bring a copy of some orders when they went out the next night. He dropped her off the next morning at the barracks with just enough time to change into her uniform and get to her workstation before muster.

She met him that night as arranged and, of course, had the copy of some orders with her. Max gave her a gold wristwatch after she gave him the copy of the orders. He laughed and said it was a bribe for the paperwork. That night they had dinner, drinks, and dancing. She kept hoping to see one of her girlfriends so they would know what a handsome guy she was out with.

That night back at Max's apartment, Max had taken pictures of them making love. Holding the small autofocus camera off to the side with one arm over their heads, he took picture after picture. She was embarrassed but didn't know how to tell him to stop. He was so self-confident in everything he did.

The next morning, driving back to the sub base, he said that a real estate friend of his might be able to use the information about officers going to Charleston, or officers who were going to Spain and were home-ported in Charleston. Would she make a copy of all the orders prepared in that category? She said she didn't think she could. He told her to call him when she could do that small favor for him. Later that afternoon, she had called him and told him she had made copies as he had asked.

And so it had gone for the past week. It didn't seem quite right, but maybe Max really was just helping a friend sell some real estate in Charleston. After all, someone has to sell Navy people a house when they were transferred. Also, she didn't like the way he kept subtly reminding her that he had those pictures of them tucked away for safekeeping.

She finished making photocopies and locked up the office. Max's insistence on getting physical descriptions of all the officer transferees was also difficult. That information was not in the officer's record. The medical file had it, but that didn't always cross her desk. At least she had interviewed Lieutenant Thomas herself. She typed out a half page on his height, weight, hair and eye color.

Moscow .

COLONEL Borzov unconsciously ran his hand across the close-cropped gray stubble on his head as he studied the file. He closed the file and pushed it to the side of the uneven desk. The gray-painted steel desk was as heavy as a small car. Borzov suspected that disgruntled workers made it at a tank factory on a Monday, angry that capitalism was taking so long to improve their lot. The desk was empty except for the single file.

The rest of the small office was spartan, the military equivalent of the bleak, barren, civilian bureaucrat's office after a budget cut. A lighter shade of gray paint showed the spot on the wall where Gorbachev's photograph had hung. The photographs of many others had hung there before him. Now the leaders changed so fast there wasn't time to print new pictures before the next leader came along. The single window behind Borzov didn't do much to dispel the gray gloom. The young psychiatrist sat on the forward edge of the chair, directly across the desk from the colonel.

"We are at a point in this operation where a candidate has to be selected," Borzov said. The office wasn't big enough for his voice to echo, but the barren, concrete walls gave it a hollow sound. "A tentative decision has been reached that Yuri Amelko should be our operative for this evolution." He looked up from the file at the doctor. The doctor's head bobbed up and down in agreement, even though he had not been asked a question.

"The first choice of the language instructors is Yuri Amelko. His command of the English language and his use of contemporary idioms is as good as any American. Of course, he has had an advantage in that he has actually lived in the United States," Borzov leaned back in his chair and spread one hand expansively. "This gives him the background material to draw on and a broader database to use in the event of any unforeseen situations, of which there will be many. In hand-to-hand combat, Gregor has also grudgingly picked Amelko as his first choice."

Borzov did not mention that he was also near the height, weight, and body type of the officer he would replace. In the spy business you told people only what you had to tell them, no more. The more people in on a secret, the greater the probability it would not remain a secret.

Borzov could see that the psychiatrist was unable to break eye contact and Borzov wasn't going to let him look away for a minute. Borzov didn't blink. It was amusing watching the man squirm. Being questioned by the AFB made everyone feel guilty, even if they couldn't think of anything they had done wrong.

"This brings us to your psychological profile of Amelko's suitability for covert operations. You recommend against him." Borzov leaned forward. "Why? I have read your reports, but I want to hear it from you."

The psychiatrist cleared his throat and looked at the desk, then at Colonel Borzov, looked away, then looked back at Borzov and looked away again in another direction. Borzov noticed that now that he was done talking, the psychiatrist couldn't seem to look at him. Before, he couldn't look away.

"Well, uh, he may perhaps be, uh, suited for some operations, but without, uh, the details of the operations, it was felt that he could not be recommended. In other words, there are certain situations in covert operations in which he could not be counted on to perform the task assigned." He shifted in his seat, could not get comfortable, shifted again.

"Be explicit," Colonel Borzov said. The man was making him irritated.

The psychiatrist seemed to find it hard to think with Borzov staring at him. Perhaps it was the uniform: brown, with blue collar tabs, standard AFB. The AFB could still lock someone up and forget about them, really forget and move on to something else, and no one would question it. *Glasnost* was fine, but this was the AFB.

"Well, I mean that if the candidate were ordered to terminate a member of the opposition, there is a strong possibility he would not comply with the order."

"You mean he would not kill someone if ordered to do it?" Borzov smiled at the physician's squeamish choice of words.

"Depending on the circumstances involved and the threat posed by the individual, that is correct." The psychiatrist's eyes darted around the bare, gray walls of the small office. He seemed unwilling to let Borzov capture his eyes again. Borzov saw his eyes run around the wall. Perhaps he was thinking a prison cell would smell like this. It was certainly cold and damp and musty enough.

"But he has received extremely high marks in hand-to-hand combat. In fact, he has even been characterized as aggressive. How do you explain that?"

"In certain situations, where actions of a defensive nature are required, the candidate would respond aggressively, but only in defensive situations. He is competitive and likes to win, but he questions everything. Yuri Amelko is a maverick." He lifted his hand as if instructing a student, thought better of it, and put it back down in his lap, where it clung to his other hand for support. "We, uh, felt that if ordered to terminate an individual in a premeditated manner, the candidate may refuse to comply. Perhaps further testing—"

"No," Borzov cut him off in a loud voice. "There will be no further testing. I will make the decision based on the information available. That's all."

Colonel Borzov sat back in his chair as the psychiatrist fled from the room. These psychiatrists were as weird as their patients. But if you talked to crazy people all day, every day, was it possible to remain completely normal?

He tapped his pencil on the desk. He decisively flipped open the file, made some notes, and closed it. Yuri would do.

YURI stood in front of the plain, unmarked metal door. He rapped sharply twice.

"Enter," came the muffled voice through the door.

Yuri opened the door, walked to the desk, and came to attention.

"Yuri Amelko, reporting as ordered, sir."

The desk faced the door squarely. Colonel Borzov sat behind the desk, hands laced together with his chin resting on his hands. *He looks like a cobra,* Yuri thought. Behind Borzov, a window looked out on the backs of other buildings. It was not very impressive for a colonel in the AFB. The bare room held filing cabinets, two chairs, and a single desk. Even monks had more than this.

Yuri remained standing at attention, his eyes fixed on the wall above Borzov's head. He was calm and confident. He would stand here all day if the colonel wanted. It was a nice break from the never-ending classes.

Borzov grunted and gestured toward the chair. "Sit." As Yuri took the indicated seat, Colonel Borzov pressed a button on the bottom of the desk, and the door eased shut.

Without preamble, Borzov said, "I ask you point-blank: if during the course of a mission you were ordered to kill someone, would you do it?"

Yuri hesitated. "If it were necessary to kill someone, I could do it."

"That's not what I asked you. If you were ordered to kill someone, would you do it?"

"That would depend on the circumstances," said Yuri. He looked thoughtful as he considered the question. He sat back on the hard, wooden chair, alert but not on edge. "I would have to know the situation and have more information."

"There will be times when there is no time for explanations. When there is only the order to kill, you must do it immediately. There must be no hesitation." Borzov paused. "I have selected you for this mission."

"I don't want to go," Yuri said immediately. He was surprised at his statement but realized it was true. This was the first time he had the opportunity to express his desire not to participate in the operation. Borzov's comments about killing for the state made the decision easier. What was done in a war was one thing; during peacetime, it was murder.

Borzov slammed the desk with his hand. "What you want is unimportant!" he shouted. Yuri's body jerked at the loud noise and bark of Borzov's voice.

Borzov stood and walked to the window. He looked out, his hands clasped behind his back. After a moment, he returned to the desk. Leaning on it with both arms, he looked intently at Yuri. "You are the most knowledgeable in American language and customs. You have learned the American submarine systems and the theoretical knowledge behind their operation better than the others. Even Gregor says that you are the best choice, at least in hand-to-hand combat. He doesn't like you, but he says you are the best. Therefore, you will go."

Yuri said nothing. Borzov continued. "When you return, you will be a hero—a secret hero, perhaps, but you will have a medal for your uniform, and your career will be assured. You can return to Navy life, if that's your wish."

"Will it be necessary to kill anyone on this mission?" Yuri said.

Borzov sat down, running a hand over his close-cropped gray hair, relaxing a little. "Hopefully not. However, there is always the unforeseen event. Something may occur that we cannot plan for and that you cannot anticipate. Therefore, you must be ready to act at once if it becomes necessary to protect your identity. Also you must realize that your life will be at risk. If you hope to return to see your family and friends again, you must protect yourself." Borzov held Yuri with his eyes.

Yuri nodded. The implied threat was there. To see his family and friends, to see Illya, he must return not only alive, but he must return. Colonel Borzov put a blue and white paper-wrapped package on his desk. It was a bar of American soap.

"You will take several of these with you, along with other disguised items. You will never be questioned about soap, even if we believe you were going to be searched, which we do not. These packages of soap appear just as if they had come from the factory," Borzov said as he removed the paper and the cardboard from the bar of soap. "The soap itself looks normal, down to the printing embossed on it. It smells like American soap. Even an X ray would show nothing unusual about it."

Borzov broke the bar in two pieces against the edge of the desk to reveal a plastic-wrapped packet inside the soap. Yuri recognized the faint smell of Ivory from his stay in the United States. Could he ask the colonel for permission to take the discarded soap home to Illya without looking foolish? He picked up a small piece and crumbled it between his thumb and fingers and smelled it. Soap was still a scarce commodity in Russia. Even though there was more soap, toilet paper, and other commodities in the stores, there were still long lines to buy it. The old *babushkas* often stood in line to buy it and then sold it on the street corners for a profit.

"There is a packet containing a chemical substance inside. When this chemical is mixed with an acid, a very potent anesthetizing agent is produced. This agent will render everyone on board the submarine unconscious in a matter of seconds. When you prepare the anesthetizing agent, you must be in a self-contained breathing apparatus so that you are not overcome. If you are rendered unconscious, the ship will sink, with you and everyone else aboard.

"The acid will be available on board ship. It is used to test the nuclear propulsion plant water system," Borzov continued. "That is fortunate, since acid would be much harder to get aboard without detection."

"What type of anesthetizing agent is this?" Yuri asked.

"That is unimportant." Borzov said, irritated. He waved his hand to dismiss the question. "You'll be given further directions on the amount of acid to use and the number of packets necessary to give the desired concentration of gas in the ship. All you must know is that this chemical, in the presence of acid, is an anesthetizing gas.

"There will be several radio transmitters hidden in your personal items. You will receive more instructions on this later, but they will be in your electric razor, after-shave bottle, camera, and other places. The transmitters will not be for two-way communication but only for signaling the location of the ship. These items may be detectable and will be in your baggage. You will check your bags to avoid the X-ray inspection.

"Each time you transmit a location, you will offset the actual location by twenty miles north, twenty miles west. This is very important. Do not put in the actual position of the submarine. Understood?"

Yuri nodded his head.

"You will speak to no one else of these instructions. For now, you are dismissed."

Yuri stood to attention, turned, and left.

9. SUBSTITUTION

New York

DROPLETS of water on the outer plastic pane of the airplane's double window magnified parts and pieces of the world outside. Yuri sat in the window seat on the left side of the plane watching the covered, phalliclike passenger loading tunnel telescope slowly into a mating position with the door. The other passengers crowded against each other in the aisle. They had jumped up from their seats like rabbits when the plane stopped. Now they were bottled up, pushing at each other with bags and briefcases.

Yuri shifted his attention to the front of the airplane. The airport was not nearly as interesting as the blond stewardess he had watched most of the flight, who was now preparing the door for arrival. Would Illya object to his watching? Probably, but women are pretty, so men will look at them. He was just doing his job. Women, on the other hand, want your total devotion. To look is to lust, at least as applied to men. Women certainly looked at other women, but that was to check the length of the nails, the cut of the hair, and for the visual evaluation of the competition.

He smiled as he watched the stewardess's long, shapely legs and imagined them continuing upward from her hemline all the way to her hips. He stood as the other passengers began to disembark. *Not like Russia,* he thought, still looking at the stewardess. *Anyone showing that much leg in Russia would wind up with frostbite of the knee.* He sighed. It was good to be back in America.

Yuri nodded as he passed the stewardess on his way out of the plane. Her eyes were the clear blue of a cloudless, winter sky. She held his gaze and smiled.

"Have a nice day," she said. He was sure the look held some secret message, offering more than a nice day, perhaps a nice night also.

He glanced behind him as he started up the ramp. Sure enough, she watched him, shivering in the moist cold that edged around the exit seal.

The stewardess, Betty Ward, kept Yuri's back in sight until the tunnel turned. With his dark hair and intense, hazel eyes, he looked larger than he actually was, she thought. The eyes fixed your attention and made everything else in the picture seem hazy.

A ripple of fear or excitement ran up the back of her neck. Perhaps she should have given him her phone number. There was danger in letting a stranger in your life, but sometimes you had to take a chance. She hugged herself against the cold.

YURI stood in line with the rest of the passengers waiting to pass through customs. His turn came, and he drew a middle-aged man.

"Passport, please," the agent said.

Yuri pushed his passport over the counter without

comment. The customs official looked at the picture on the passport and back at Yuri with a glare. Yuri guessed the customs official gave everyone else that same intimidating look, trying to make the smugglers sweat with fear. Yuri felt excited. It was a little like a game.

"What was the purpose of your trip to France, Mr. Smith?"

"Business," Yuri replied.

"How long were you in France?" The customs official tried to stare him down.

"Two weeks." Yuri maintained eye contact as he had been taught. He knew the information in the passport by heart.

"Do you have anything to declare?"

"No." Yuri had been well briefed on giving straightforward, simple answers. Don't volunteer information. Don't be chatty going through customs. Maintain eye contact. Borzov was an obnoxious human being, but he knew his spy craft. There had even been videotaped practice sessions with critiques afterward.

Yuri had no doubt that the passport would pass inspection. After all, it was a genuine passport, stolen in the last few days. He didn't want to know what had happened to its former owner.

The official grew tired of the game and waved him through. Yuri was careful not to sigh with relief as he walked away. If you looked confident, you got away with only questions. If you looked guilty or fit a profile, they took your luggage apart, and everything in it. Then they strip-searched you for fun.

Gregor waited at the edge of the crowd, near the exit from the customs area. He stood out from the multitude of fathers, mothers, brothers, and friends by more than the few feet that separated him from the masses. Gregor was larger than life. Standing next to Gregor, even tall men had to look up. But there was an aura about him.

Women passing him gave him a wide berth, held their children close, as if he might reach out and pluck them from their arms.

Yuri was careful to stop several feet short as he walked up to Gregor. There was little chance the mountain would fall on him today, but there was no need to tempt fate by standing closer to the precipice than necessary. Yuri also had no doubt that Gregor remembered the bruises he had given him.

Gregor turned and walked away without speaking. Yuri noted he was no longer limping from their karate match. That didn't mean the injury was forgotten.

Yuri followed. A white Ford Taurus waited at the edge of the loading area. Gregor got into the front seat and motioned for Yuri to get in the passenger side. Yuri relaxed; at least there was no one else in the backseat. There was still a fear, so pervasive in most Russians that it seemed inherited, about going for a ride with a carful of AFB thugs.

The seat was big enough that he wouldn't have to sit close to Gregor. Sitting next to Gregor made him tense. In the close confines of a car, fancy karate would not save him.

They stopped at a cheap hotel off the main roads in New Jersey. Cheap places were chosen because there would be fewer questions asked, but also because it was easier on the AFB budget. The entire military establishment in Russia was now on a budget. The military and AFB no longer had all the money they needed. It would never be a business because there would never be a profit, but now there was accountability.

Yuri pushed open the door to the small room. There were burned places on the close-cropped orange carpet. The concrete floor beneath showed through places where the carpet was ripped out. Faded, forest green spreads covered the two twin beds. Stale smoke permeated the drapes and furnishings. Yuri walked into the room. It had been rented by a local contact.

Yuri lifted a package from the bed. He stripped the plain, brown paper wrapping from the package, leaving Gregor to secure the door. Inside was a uniform for a United States Navy lieutenant junior grade (JG). Appropriate ribbons were mounted above the left pocket of the coat. The gold stripes on the arm were correct, one wide stripe with a second, narrow stripe above the first, to signify junior grade. Yuri took off his civilian clothes and put on the plain, white cotton shirt, black tie, and black wool trousers. He looked in the mirror, checking the soft shoulder boards on the white shirt. He slipped on the dark, navy blue wool coat. It felt comfortable. He had been wearing a similar uniform in training for months. The embossed eagles on the gold buttons looked back at him from the mirror.

Gregor removed another uniform from the package and changed into a navy blue jumper and bell-bottom trousers. He put a black rolled scarf over his head. A white canvas cap completed the uniform. Yuri smiled. The small cap looked obscene on Gregor's big head. He looked like Bluto from the Popeye cartoons, only more so.

"How did you get these uniforms, Gregor?"

"In the United States it's easy to impersonate a military person. Merely stop by a military uniform shop in any town that has an Army or Navy base, and buy the items off the shelf." Yuri was sorry he asked. Gregor liked showing off his knowledge almost as much as he liked hurting people. Now he would have to listen to Gregor brag.

"You can even order them cut to size, or they can be tailored at the store," Gregor continued. "Correct information is provided on where to put the medals on the uniform, and the rank insignia. A good operative will know these things."

"How do I look?" Yuri asked, straightening his tie as he looked in the mirror. To get Gregor to be quiet, he had to start talking. Sometimes even that didn't work.

"Your uniform is correct."

"You mean, 'Your uniform is correct, sir.' When you talk to an officer, you must say *sir*."

In the mirror Yuri could see Gregor was getting angry, but Yuri pretended not to notice. He adjusted his jacket.

Yuri and Gregor left the room and got back in the car. "How will we get on the Air Force base?" Yuri asked.

"That is also easy. You are a lieutenant (JG) naval officer. I'm a petty officer, first class, your driver."

"Surely it can't be that easy. We will have to show official papers, orders, identification?"

"If asked, you have official papers, but the question is almost never asked. On this car there is a sticker for the military base. The car was liberated from a military person on temporary deployment. It has a decal appropriate for getting on base. The guard waves everyone in with the decal without checking papers or ID cards. After we are finished with the car, it will be left in the same location it was taken from. No one will ever know it was used."

"It is unbelievable that American security is this lax."

"Believe it." Gregor smirked as he put the car in reverse. The American idiom rolled easily off his tongue, pushed along by his gravelly voice. "In the United States, if you look like you know what you are doing, almost anything is yours for the taking."

McGuire AFB

THE raindrops traced patterns of clarity on the dusty window world. The damp and somber day outside the bus matched the mood of the young naval officer watching the rural countryside roll past.

An extra rough bump, orchestrated and exaggerated by the worn-out shocks of the blue school bus, lifted the officer out of his seat and out of his reverie. *Do the armed forces buy old school buses, or do they order them pre-aged from the factory?* Thomas thought. It was a safe bet that the U.S. military establishment was in possession of the largest fleet of used school buses in the world. There was probably some connection between grown men playing soldier and still riding school buses, but he couldn't put his finger on it.

"Almost there, Lieutenant," the airman driving the bus said to the young lieutenant in his rearview mirror.

"Thank you." Thomas smiled.

It had been a long trip since deciding to go submarines. This was the next to the last leg of the journey, and he felt more than a little anxious. Submarine School, Nuclear Power School, and Prototype were all starting to blend into one, like a tunnel stretching away into the distance. A few vivid memories, like silver threads, stuck out here and there, making the fabric of his life beautiful.

He gazed unseeing out the window. Prototype training in Idaho was one of the best times, more so, in retrospect, of course, than while in progress. During training, working ten- or twelve-hour days, rotating to a new shift once a week, there was little time to enjoy anything. But the mind stores up vignettes that were often overlooked on a day-to-day basis that can be enjoyed later. Walking home from the bus stop after the ride back from the evening shift at the test site was a favorite. At two in the morning, with snow up to your knees, it was so quiet the hair on the back of your neck would stand up. The air was so clean and cold it burned your nose. And you owned the night. That memory got much replay. It would go platinum before the grooves wore out.

Thinking of Idaho, thinking of anything, for that matter, usually branched off on a trail that led to thoughts of Dee.

When he called to tell her that he had orders to Charleston, there had been silence on the line. Talk about burning up the telephone lines—this lady could do it without words. There had been no choice but to wait it out, give her a few minutes to think through it. Good thing she was visiting her family and not in New London, where he would have had to tell her face-to-face. There are some acts of bravery that even soldiers and sailors should not be required to do in peacetime, like telling Dee Thomas she had to change her plans.

She managed to outwait him. "Hello, still there?" he said.

"Yes, I'm still here. As a matter of fact, I might stay here. As a matter of fact, you can go to Charleston by yourself."

"You don't mean that, do you, Dee?"

"Try me. You go to Charleston, you're going by yourself."

"You don't understand. The Navy is sending me to Charleston. I didn't ask to go."

"Tell them you won't go." She said it matter-of-factly, as if it were obvious that the only way to handle the United States Navy was to be firm with them.

"Dee, you don't just tell the Navy you won't go. They give the orders. You might tell them you don't like the idea, and I did, but even that's not such a good idea."

The black plastic receiver hung in his hand like the inanimate object it was. Silent. Like the lady on the other end of the line. This lady had one of the best silences in the business.

"Well, if you have nothing further to say, I guess I'd better say good-bye."

Still silence. This had to be the most frustrating person

on the face of the earth. She wouldn't talk to you, but when you said good-bye, she wouldn't say good-bye, so if you hung up even after saying good-bye, you were hanging up on her. And you would never be forgiven.

"Dee, try to moderate your emotions. You are either full speed ahead, angry and in a rage, or so sad that you are crying, or so happy that you are euphoric. You have a right to be angry about it, but we have to talk about it. Be angry at the Navy, not at me.

"Look, Dee. You initially wanted to go to Charleston. So, we are going to Charleston. The only difference is that the Navy made the choice for us. How about some flexibility?"

There was a very pregnant pause.

Finally, "OK," as if ripped reluctantly from her body by Cesarean section.

"I said we're here, Lieutenant Thomas," the airman said, replacing the gray Connecticut daydream with the gray New Jersey day. "McGuire Terminal."

"Thanks. Daydreaming, I guess."

And thanks for the promotion, he thought. Lieutenant (JG) was just too much of a mouthful, so you got the verbal promotion rather than the extra syllables. The real-life promotion to lieutenant (JG) was new enough so that when someone called him Lieutenant, there was still a tendency to look around to see whom they were talking to.

The McGuire MAC terminal was superficially similar to most airline passenger terminals. It was a military version of what the armed services thought a civilian passenger terminal looked like. The high ceiling, the check-in counters, the endless lines. The crowd waiting for a flight was the big difference.

There was the usual assortment of military dependents. Anxious wives surrounded by obnoxious children. Retirees, old and gnarly, and their wives, were taking advantage of their free flying privilege. A group of midshipmen waited for transport to a summer training assignment. All leavened with a very large mixture of military personnel—Air Force, Army, and Navy—in the more somber hues of the rainbow. Some in navy blue, or sky blue, or forest greens, or tan, with gold stars or silver bars. No uniform contained red, lest it remind them of their ultimate purpose.

Thomas looked around. No skycaps. He dragged his government-issue bag off the bus. Not that he wouldn't rather carry his bag himself, but it was nice to have the option of having someone else do it for a dollar. Especially since the Navy required that you carry all your worldly possessions, or at least those you would take on a cruise, in your bag. Three months of clothes, shoes, and toiletries weighed a lot.

Check-in at the flight desk was standard operating procedure: hurry up and wait. Hurry up and get a place in line at the flight desk, then wait. Produce your orders and ID when your turn came, and then wait again—five hours, this time—for your overseas hop. And of course the hop was on a C-141, one step above a dinosaur and one mile per hour faster than Orville and Wilbur Wright. Sitting on a cargo net for an eight-hour flight on a C-141, with a box lunch, would probably qualify as cruel and unusual punishment, except they were all volunteers.

It would be nice if the Air Force would purchase several of the new 747s, but no such luck. Military passengers were cargo. If there was room. Actually, they were less than cargo. Cargo usually took precedence.

"Hurry up and wait." Thomas sighed and looked at his watch. Still hours to go before flight time. No time to see the wife before leaving, but plenty of time to wait around at the airport. Thomas settled his bags and himself on a wooden bench. He pulled a book from his B-4 bag. A man with a good book who likes to read is seldom bored. *The Bridges of Madison County*. Not his kind of book, but it was a present from Dee. He held his hand over the cover as he opened the paperback book to the dog-eared page that marked his place. Light reading.

After reading for a while, Thomas stood up, stretched, and looked around for the head. The area at the far end of the building was a good possibility, he thought, as he headed that way. Civilians called their toilets restrooms. The Army called them latrines. Thomas wondered what the Air Force term was.

A sailor with a balding head and a fringe of hair around his ears sat several benches away. He looked over his magazine as Thomas walked toward the men's room. Reaching into a travel bag on the bench beside him, he keyed a button on a small metal beeper.

At the far end of the building, a janitor pushed his mop in lazy circles. He stopped and touched the hearing aid stuck in his ear. A wire led to a receiver in his coat pocket. The three quick beeps that only he could hear set him in motion. He leaned his mop against the wall, walked to the door of the men's room, removed the Closed for Cleaning sign, and placed it inside the door.

Thomas noted the Air Force had settled for Men, proclaimed proudly by a simple sign on the door. A metal plate on the right-hand side was surrounded by an area where the wood finish had been worn off by thousands of hurried hands, too anxious to take proper aim at the push plate. Thomas swung the first door open and then the second. The restroom was deserted except for a pair of disembodied feet below the door of one of the stalls.

Thomas took his position at the first urinal on the left, farthest from the door and in the corner where the stalls began and the urinals ended. Graffiti seemed to be universal. One would have thought that ceramic tiles would discourage the usual inane comments on the bathroom walls, but the dedicated writers had merely written smaller, with ink pens, on the grouting between the tan ceramic tiles. "You hold the future in your hands," someone had written. Another had added, "Small future." Yet another had added on one of the vertical seams, "Why are you laughing, the joke's in your hand." Of course, there was the usual assortment of names and phone numbers.

The door to the men's room opened, and Thomas glanced at the large sailor who entered. The man turned, pushed the door shut behind him, even though the mechanism automatically pulled it closed. He walked down the row of urinals to the stalls. Thomas couldn't be sure, he didn't want to stare, but it seemed like the man had knocked on the occupied stall before coming back.

Thomas felt a rush of adrenaline as the large man stepped up behind him. All the other positions were open. Gregor's hand slipped around Thomas's mouth just before the knife entered his back. The blade passed easily through the dark blue wool of the service dress blue uniform coat. The thin nylon lining of the coat was even easier. The white cotton shirt and the undershirt were nothing.

The knife entered the epidermis just above the third dorsal vertebra, left anterior. There was a brief resistance as the knife penetrated the skin, like punching a hole in leather, then less resistance as it passed into the hollow body cavity. The knife hit the vertebra a glancing blow, dislodging a portion of the transverse process. Deflected slightly, the blade slipped between the third and fourth rib and punctured the left ventricle. Continuing forward and angling slightly to the left and down, it stopped just short of the front of the rib cage. The blow was not instantly fatal, but it was enough.

As the hand slipped around his mouth, Thomas hesitated, filled with fear, undecided as to whether to zip up or whether to defend himself exposed. Carefully weighing all the alternatives, knowing he was already dead but not believing it, the world turned black, with his eyes still open. His last thought, fleeting and incongruous, was that Dee would be pissed.

Yuri stood behind Gregor, watching. He was filled with an infinite emptiness, tinged with a touch of nausea. He felt like saying he was sorry as he watched the body slump in Gregor's arms, but he didn't know who he should say it to. This business of being a spy was not nearly so romantic as he had hoped, and his hopes in that department had not been high. Careful, abstract planning could not prepare one for the reality of a dead human being on a bathroom floor.

"Move, you fool," Gregor said as he backed into Yuri. He dragged the dead body toward an open stall.

"Hold the door open." Gregor sat the body on the toilet and searched through Thomas's pockets. He removed the rings from his fingers.

"Quickly, open the duffel bag."

"Why did you stab him?" Yuri said. "You were to choke him. Now there is blood everywhere."

"Not everywhere." His voice was matter-of-fact. "Just a little if we leave the knife in. The rest we will clean up.

"Here." Gregor took the items he had gathered and stuffed them into Yuri's hand, taking the duffel bag from Yuri. Yuri stood motionless, staring at Thomas sitting on the toilet.

"Never seen a dead man before, have you?" He grabbed Yuri by the neck with one hand and roughly pulled him forward, pushing his face against Thomas's face. Yuri could smell the copper scent of blood.

"Take a good look. It won't be your last." Yuri struggled and finally, with a laugh, Gregor released him. "A knife is faster. I am the field agent. I will make the decisions when changes are necessary."

"You weren't worried about the speed of the kill."

Anger was in his voice. "You enjoy this. You just wanted to try something new, didn't you?"

"Hold this," Gregor said. "What makes you think it's new?" He opened the duffel bag and pushed it into Yuri's hands. "You break their neck, choke them, stab them. Its all been done before." Gregor pulled Thomas's knees up against his chest and wrapped him in the fetal position with heavy tape. He slipped a heavy-duty plastic trash bag over the head of Thomas's now triple-folded body and slid it down around his body like a sausage skin. He tied it securely beneath his feet. Then he put the plastic bag, with Thomas in it, into the duffel bag.

"A tidy little package," Gregor said, smiling. He straightened the small, white hat on his head and hoisted the canvas bag.

A few minutes later, a large sailor, bald except for a fringe of hair around his ears, walked out of the men's room with a military duffel bag slung over his shoulder. A young lieutenant (JG) followed. A third man wearing the khaki trousers and khaki shirt of the janitorial service, removed the Closed for Cleaning sign and nodded to the large sailor. The lieutenant (JG) returned to the bench where he had left his bag. He sat and started leafing through the folder, which contained his orders, his medical records, and his personal history. His past and his future.

Rota, Spain

"USS *Holland*, petty officer of the watch speaking, sir. This is a nonsecure line."

"This is Lieutenant Thomas," Yuri said, smiling into the phone as he pronounced his new name. The only way to distance himself from his namesake was not to think of him. That was Gregor. He was only an observer of the murder.

"Has the *King* sailed yet?" Yuri asked.

Hesitation. "We aren't allowed to give out that information, sir."

"I'm calling from the airport. I have orders to report to the *King*. I need to know if there is anything there to report to."

"Hold, please."

The petty officer first class standing the quarterdeck watch on the submarine tender punched the Hold button and turned to the officer of the deck. "You better take this one, sir. Wants to know if the *King* has sailed."

The OOD looked up, put his pen in the logbook, and picked up the phone. He stabbed the blinking light at the base of the phone with his finger. "Officer of the deck speaking, sir."

"This is Lieutenant Thomas. I have orders to the *King* and want to know if she has left for patrol yet."

"Lieutenant Thomas, we've been expecting you, sir. The *King* is not in port now, but we have arranged a transfer. If you will check into the BOQ, I'll have Squadron Operations contact you to make arrangements. We should be able to put you on board when we pick up the commodore tomorrow. I'll send a car over to the terminal for you."

Yuri's smile got wider as he hung up the phone and picked up the bags. It was good to make a plan and see it work. Perhaps he would be home with Illya for the summer after all.

Offshore, Rota, Spain

THE fog was so thick he could see no more than two or three hundred yards ahead of the tugboat. The sun was up somewhere, but everything in this part of the ocean still had the look and feel of predawn, even though it was midmorning. The sea itself was as calm and flat as the surface of a lake, as if it were still asleep. Only the drone of the tug's engine and the screech of seagulls broke the silence.

The lieutenant (JG) stood on the quarterdeck of the tug. He wore a faded green foul weather jacket, on loan from a member of the crew, with the collar pulled up around his ears. The wheelhouse partially shielded him from the relative wind as the tug churned its way through the water at a respectable fifteen knots, rocking slightly back and forth. The tug sought its target through the fog with invisible electromagnetic radar waves.

A submarine slowly materialized out of the haze, broadside to the tug and dead in the water. Jet-black in color. Even the numbers on the sail were painted out. It appeared surreal against the foggy background. A ghost ship, an apparition. It seemed to be closer than it was, and only as the tug continued on did its true size become apparent. It was a black behemoth, a seamount in the middle of the ocean.

As the tug approached and slowed, a whirlpool developed near the stern of the submarine, just aft of where the rudder rose from the water. It was impossible not to be impressed at the massive power of the submarine as he watched those tons of water fall into the hole in the ocean created by the propeller as the ship gathered way.

As the submarine's speed increased, it started a slow turn to starboard. The tug altered course to port, slowed, and drew abreast of the submarine on its port side. They were on a parallel course, close aboard. The tug lowered a brow that stretched from the deck of the tug to a hatch located at the aft end of the missile deck of the submarine. The lieutenant (JG) grabbed his B-4 bag in one hand and scrambled across.

A disembodied head watched him from the hatch. As the officer boarded the sub, a body followed the head out of the hatch and onto the deck.

"Let me help you with that, sir," said the sailor, taking the bag from the JG's hand.

"Welcome aboard, Lieutenant Thomas," said the sailor, saluting. Yuri smiled and returned the salute.

Charleston

DEE Thomas pulled into the cul-de-sac. *What a beautiful location,* she thought, looking at the brick houses surrounded by the pines and Spanish oaks that lined the little half circle. An enclave of serenity, just two blocks off the main drag. It was like entering a hidden world, tucked away in a time warp in metropolitan Charleston.

Number 429 was a two-story house with light, multi-colored bricks. A red Toyota was parked in front just as Sarah had said it would be. Dee turned into the driveway. She pulled the rearview mirror toward her and pushed at an imaginary stray piece of hair. Damn, long hair was a bother. Worse, it was hot, even tied back into a bun. But Neil, her husband, liked it long.

She looked at her watch. Almost fifteen minutes late. She was getting better with time management. Good thing Neil was not around, he was such a stickler about being on time.

She got out of the car, went up to the door, and knocked. The dark red door shouldn't have gone well with the brick, but it did. The effect was bright and cheerful. The door opened, replaced by a lady with a smile just as bright as the door.

"Hi, you must be Dee. I'm Sarah Clark," she said and extended her hand. Please come in."

Sarah closed the door behind them. "Did you have any trouble finding the place?"

"No, not at all, the directions were very good."

Dee studied Sarah out of the corner of her eye as she

took her hand. She was beautiful, that was the only word for it. No, exquisite was better. Dark skin, moderately tall, long, black hair with a few silver strands through it, not frosted, but more like silver woven in. Her face was hard to fit into any category. The dark eyes meant she was probably Mexican, Indian, or African American, or maybe even Asian, but there was no epicanthic fold at the corner of the eyes. *Do all Asians have an epicanthic fold?* The clothes she had on set her off beautifully. Who would have thought that a peacock blue blouse with a chocolate brown vest and skirt would go with such dark skin? But it did. Dee felt a twinge of jealousy.

"Would you like some tea, Dee?"

"That would be nice."

"Good. Just sit down, make yourself at home, and I'll be right back. I put the kettle on when you called, so it shouldn't take but just a minute."

Dee sat as she was told and looked around the living room. "You have a beautiful place here, Sarah," she called out to the kitchen.

The deep red tones of the outside trim had been carried through to the thick Oriental carpet that covered most of the living room floor. The dark wood floor showing around the edges of the room made it a little dark but set the tone nicely for the rest of the living room.

"Thank you, Dee," said Sarah, bringing in a serving tray with tea and cups. "I keep adding to it as I go along. Fortunately, we've never had enough money to buy so much furniture that it's cluttered. I've never been able to decide if I wanted a modern or an antique look, so it is sort of a combination of both. The only thing I was sure of was that I didn't want French Provincial." She laughed.

"Well, you've done a nice job."

Sarah sat on the sofa beside Dee and poured two cups of tea. "One lump or two, Dee?"

"No sugar, thank you. I'll take mine straight up. I'm watching my weight."

"Aren't we all?" Sarah said. "Have you ever met a woman who wasn't watching her weight? You heard about the woman who was rescued from a desert island? She had nothing but raw fish and coconuts for three years, and very little of that. They asked her how she felt. She said, 'Overweight, but other than that, not so bad.'"

"You said you had already found a job when you called. That's pretty good for just being in town a couple of days."

"Finding a job wasn't the hard part," Dee said. "Nurses are virtually interchangeable parts. You can go from one part of the country to another, and the job will be essentially the same. There is always a vacancy, especially in a Navy town. Wives quit on a regular basis and follow their husbands when they are transferred."

Dee blew on her tea as she held it to her lips with both hands. "With so many nurses coming in at entry-level salary and leaving after two years, the pay is so low that many nurses don't even work in their field. They are out doing other jobs, such as waitress or barmaid or whatever, and getting more money for it.

"The difficult part is finding a place to live. Coming into a city cold like this, not knowing a single person, not knowing which areas of the city are the good areas and which are the bad areas, makes it difficult. I don't even know where Neil will have to go on a daily basis when the ship gets back. Knowing where the other families live would also be helpful."

"Well, I'm glad you came over, Dee." Sarah put her cup down. "That's just what the wives' club is for, to help out when the husbands are at sea. At least you have a job.

"Some of the young wives, eighteen, nineteen years old, come to town with their husband, and never had a job. They got married right out of high school, and have never been out of Hometown, U.S.A., until their husband received orders. And then here they are, a strange town, no family or friends, and their husband is out to sea. Those are the ladies who go to pieces. So finding you a place to live will be easy compared to what you could be facing."

"Thank you, Sarah." Dee sipped her tea. "I called the XO's wife—that's the only number that Neil was able to give me—and she said you might be able to help."

"Be glad to. She doesn't enjoy the social aspects of the Navy, but she knows I love it. First of all, where are you staying now?"

"The Holiday Inn just over the Ashley River, the big one that looks like a huge cylinder right at the end of the bridge," Dee put her cup down. They both sat forward on the edge of the sofa, at an angle to each other. "It's a nice place, but it's expensive. So that's another factor that makes my search for a place to live more urgent."

"Well, you're moving in with me until we can find you a place to live," Sarah said, taking Dee's hand. "And we are going to start house hunting right away."

"Thank you," Dee said, almost out of breath. It felt odd to have another woman hold her hand. Odd, but pleasant. Sarah was self-confident and so beautiful.

Sarah smiled and gave her hand a squeeze and released it. She stood and walked to the secretary in the corner and took out a map of the city.

"First, we'll look at the layout of the city and talk about the advantages and disadvantages of certain areas. Then we'll see what's available in the newspaper." Finding the map, she sat on the sofa near Dee and spread the map on the coffee table.

"If you've got the time, maybe if you're not too busy, you could go look at some of these homes and apartments with me," Dee said, pushing the tea service to the side. "I would really feel uncomfortable looking at homes with some of these agents by myself."

"Certainly. With the ship at sea, I've got plenty of time. In fact, I've got much more time than I'd like to have," Sarah said with a smile.

10. ON BOARD

USS Martin Luther King

THE open door was latched against the bulkhead. Yuri reached inside the room and knocked. The walls were covered in a low-cost, fireproof plastic that was colored to look like wood. It was the government version of a wood-paneled office.

"Good evening, Commander," Yuri said as a Navy commander looked up from a pile of paperwork on his desk. "The messenger of the watch said you wanted to see me."

The commander was short and portly, a middle-aged man, not in the least like Yuri's—or Hollywood's—idea of a ship's commanding officer. "Commanding officers of naval vessels are referred to as 'Captain,' regardless of rank," he said. He rose and gestured toward a fold-down chair attached to the bulkhead. "They didn't teach you everything at the Academy, I see.

"Come in, Neil. Have a seat." He closed the door to the cabin. "Well, what do you think of us so far?" The captain stood with his hands on the small of his back.

Yuri could see he was proud of his command. "Very impressive, Captain." Yuri took a seat at the small fold-out table. "I'm still learning to find my way from the engine room to my stateroom, but what I've seen so far, I like."

The small cubicle was bigger than a walk-in closet, but not by much. There was an outline of a fold-down bed in the wall. A fold-down sink was located below a mirror, which hid the built-in medicine cabinet. Not an inch of space was wasted. *Just like Russian submarines,* Yuri thought, *but with nicer amenities.*

"Good. Treat this ship like your home, because that's what it will be for the next three months. It helps if you like it."

The captain puffed as he sat down across the table from Yuri. Months of enforced idleness and plenty of good food had taken its toll. Yuri guessed that the commanding officer would not finish first in the annual physical fitness test.

"By the time you're done with your submarine qualification program, you'll know just about every nut, bolt, and pipe in the ship. You'll get to know your way through the ship backward and forward, top to bottom, so well that you could find your way in complete darkness. In a submarine, if the watertight door goes shut and the compartment is flooding, you may be the only one in that space. Saving the ship may depend on your knowledge."

Yuri nodded his head, holding up his end of the monologue.

"As you know, we're one man short on this run," the captain wheezed. He raised a finger to emphasize one man. "We had one officer transferred shortly before flyway and another officer met with an accident during refit. Hence, the hurry to get you over here before the start of patrol.

"I want you to start on your qualifications for diving officer first, because we need watch officers forward more than we need them in engineering right now. Also, we have an Operational Reactor Safeguard Examination at the end of patrol. If we qualify you as an engineering officer of the watch, the ORSE Board will test you as part of the exam, and that's one more chance to fail, and I don't intend to have my ship fail." He looked at Yuri.

Yuri nodded his head. He had no intention of failing any test.

"After you qualify as diving officer and officer of the deck, then we can start you on your qualifications as engineering officer of the watch."

The captain huffed as he talked, his plump stomach cinched in by his web belt. His bushy gray eyebrows wagged up and down to the random cadence of a distant drummer. Yuri stopped himself as he felt his eyebrows going up and down in unconscious imitation. Yuri nodded his head again. It was clear the captain was going to do all the talking.

"Lieutenant Rogers is the most newly qualified officer on board," the captain continued. "He should be able to give you the greatest amount of help. However, all the officers will be pushing you along, because the sooner you are qualified, the sooner they will be able to go into three section watches. Right now they are in port and starboard watch sections. They stand watch for six hours, then have six hours off before their next watch.

"This may all be a little long-winded," the captain said.

Yuri started to nod his head but caught himself just in time.

"But the essence of it all is that we want you qualified as soon as possible. Do you have any questions?"

"Yes, sir. About how long should this qualification take?"

Yuri sat with his hands on the table, fingers laced. He still felt nervous about being aboard a U.S. warship. Nervous and excited, even exhilarated. It was the most exciting thing he had ever done. There was a sense of unreality about it, much like a play but more like a game.

"I expect by the end of the patrol you'll be qualified driving officer and possibly officer of the deck. During off crew and next patrol, you should finish officer of the deck. Next patrol you'll work on engineering officer of the watch qualification."

The captain stood. "That will be all for now, Neil." He put his hands on the small of his back. It probably helped him brace up his stomach, Yuri thought. He looked like he might topple forward if it was unsupported.

"And see the chief of the boat and have him issue you some coveralls. We don't have the laundry facilities to wash those khakis as often as necessary."

"**MASTER** Chief Johnson, I'm Lieutenant Thomas," Yuri said, offering his hand to the chief. Yuri noted the two silver stars at the top of the anchors attached to the chief's collar of his one-piece blue coveralls; two stars for master chief, one for senior chief, and a plain unadorned anchor for chief. The amount of information he had been forced to swallow would choke a horse, but Yuri felt grateful. He knew more about the U.S. Navy than most Americans.

The chief stepped out of the booth and reached for Yuri's hand.

"How do you do, sir? You must be the new A Division officer." His smile seemed genuine, Yuri thought. Then again, any new face must be a welcome event in a small crew like this. It broke up the day-to-day routine.

"The captain said that you might have some coveralls that would fit me."

"Well, I don't know," the master chief said with a hint of a Southern drawl. He scratched his head. "We issued just about everything during refit. All we've got left is a couple of size large.

"Thank you, but I could go swimming in a large size."
Yuri stopped. He wasn't sure about the idiom he had
used. Too late now to call it back. "I guess I could just
continue to wear khakis."

"Actually, you can't, at least not on patrol. These
poopie suits are made of a special lint-free fabric. Normal clothing produces lint when it's washed. That can
foul up the electronic equipment, collect in the air ducts,
and cause fires. Also it looks like hell, since we don't
have the facilities or the manpower to press uniforms."
He turned to the chief sitting across the table.

"Chief Dietz, do you have any poopie suits that might
fit the lieutenant? You're about his size."

"Matter of fact, I do, COB. Come with me, Lieutenant." Dietz put his coffee mug down and bounced out
of the booth. "We'll fix you right up. Got them right
across the passageway here in the goat locker.

"On second thought," Dietz said, stopping so quickly
that Yuri bumped into him. He turned to face Yuri, put his
hand in front of Yuri's chest to hold him in place. "You
wait right here. Those old chiefs see a sweet young thing
like you, you might never get out of there." Chief Dietz
smiled as he continued across the passageway to the
chief's quarters.

Dietz disappeared into the chief's bunk room across
the hall. The master chief smiled, noticing Yuri's startled
look. "I realize this is your first submarine, sir, so I'll give
you a word of advice. The enlisted men, chief petty officers included, will be gross. Vulgar if you will. They
don't mean any disrespect by it. It's more like a game,
even though they're the only ones amused by it. The best
way to handle it is to ignore it. If you blush or get angry,
you've made their day."

"Thanks Master Chief, I'll do my best." Yuri tried a
smile.

"Not to change the subject, Master Chief, but what do

you mean by poopie suits? I thought you were going to issue some coveralls to me."

"Same thing, sir. Why don't we sit down while we wait," Johnson said, motioning to the seat Dietz had just vacated. He waited until Yuri sat down, then took his seat.

"Poopie suit is just a nickname the crew has for the coveralls. You'll understand why after your first patrol. You pack the coveralls in your suitcase, go home, and stick them in your closet. Then three months later you take them out for your next patrol. That's when you'll know why they call the coveralls poopie suits. In fact, then you'll understand why the old diesel boat sailors used to call the submarines sewer pipes."

The master chief put his cigarette out in the metal ashtray. "You get used to anything cooped up inside a submarine for three months. You sort of get used to what a submarine smells like and don't even really smell it anymore. It's not the worst smell in the world, but it makes Charleston seem like roses."

Yuri tilted his head to the side. "I don't follow you, Chief."

The master chief waved his free hand to clear the smoke. The other hand was anchored firmly to his coffee mug. In his short time aboard, Yuri had heard the rumor that coffee mugs were grafted onto the index finger of chiefs when they were promoted. They were a chief's security blanket. Yuri was starting to believe it. He had never seen a chief without one.

"It's like this, sir. Say the submarine is down a couple of hundred feet, and you flush the toilet. Where is that stuff going to go? The pressure outside the ship is greater than the pressure inside the ship, so it can't go overboard. So it goes into a holding tank. Well, eventually the tank fills up, so then what do you do with the tank full of sewage? You pressurize it to a pressure greater than the pressure outside the submarine, open a hull valve connected to the tank, and allow the pressurized contents to run overboard until the tank is empty.

"Well, now you've got a tank full of high-pressure air. Now you can't flush the toilets into the tank because the pressure in the tank is higher than the pressure inside the ship. So what do you do? You vent air in the tank back into the submarine. The only problem is that the air in the tank now smells like what used to be in the tank." The master chief smiled. "We vent the air through a charcoal filter, and that takes part of the smell out, but not all of it.

"So, after doing this for all patrol, the air inside the entire submarine has a peculiar odor. You smell that day in and day out, week in and week out, and month in and month out, and pretty soon you don't smell it anymore. It's still there, but you build up a tolerance for it. But that odor is in your hair, in your clothes, and everybody back home notices it. Hence, poopie suit." The master chief smiled over his cigarette.

Yuri laughed, too.

"Master Chief, are you politely telling me I will smell like shit after patrol?"

"Yes, sir," the master chief said. "By the way, Lieutenant, I heard that you're an Academy man. There's a man on board named Davis who wants to talk to you about the Naval Academy. He's in A Division. His brother went there and was probably a classmate of yours."

"That's interesting," Yuri said. It was more than interesting, it was frightening. Suddenly the room felt warm. Yuri felt sweat break out on his lip.

"ON board a submarine you are considered a lowlife until you have qualified in submarines," Lieutenant Rogers pontificated.

Yuri caught up with Rogers in the engine room. The

guy was always on the move. Yuri had checked three other places and was forwarded from watch stander to watch stander before running him to ground. At each location the report was the same: "He was just here."

"Even the enlisted men who are qualified are going to feel superior to you," Rogers continued. "They will let you know it at every opportunity. Until you're qualified, you're a no load." He emphasized "no load," striking forward with his head. "That's a person who uses up breathable air, consumes food, and serves no visible, useful function. So get qualified!" He looked like he could fly, the way he flopped up and down.

"Yes, Lieutenant." Yuri nodded his head meekly, remembering his many submarine cruises on board Russian ships.

"Hey," Rogers said, grabbing Yuri's arm. "My name's Dick. You can call me Ray, and you can call me Jay, but you doesn't have to call me Lieutenant. The captain is the only one that gets called by his rank around here." He stopped to think. "Maybe the master chief, also, and XO, but officer to officer, first name only," he added.

"That's the official part of qualification requirements," Rogers continued, laughing. He let go of Yuri's arm and rubbed the salt-and-pepper mustache on his lip. "My job, and the job of everyone else on board, is to get you qualified as soon as possible. It is a little bit like a fraternity; there is some hazing, but we all want you to be qualified as soon as possible. My ass may depend on what you do in an emergency. I want to make sure the number of times we surface is greater than or equal to the number of times we dive."

He winked, but Yuri got it without his help. Rogers pushed his straight black hair off his forehead. His constant motion, shifting back and forth from foot to foot, made Yuri nervous. He must have been hell in high school, squirming in his chair, questioning everything, talking to the other students. He was the kind of student teachers love to have in another teacher's class.

"If you have any questions while you are studying different systems, ask anyone. Ask the most knowledgeable person. You can even ask the person you want to give you a checkout and then go back later for your checkout." Rogers walked in small circles while he talked. His glasses crept down his nose. He pushed them back in place with his thumb.

"Since you are the A Division officer, you should start with the A Division systems. That way you will be learning your division responsibilities as well as getting a checkoff on those systems."

Rogers leaned back against the engine room bulkhead, finally sitting still for a minute. Yuri checked his watch. He half sat on a large, stainless steel locker, hands stuffed into the oversized pockets of his blue coveralls.

"Here's how it works." Rogers's hand jumped out of his pocket of its own volition, fingers together, pointing at Yuri. Yuri looked at his watch hopefully, staring at it for about forty-five seconds. "You get your qualification card for diving officer of the watch from the diving officer, the engineering officer of the watch qualification card from the engineer log room yeoman, and an officer of the deck qualification card from the senior watch officer. The captain has said that you are going to start off with the diving officer of the watch qualification card. That's mainly auxiliary systems anyway, so you are in luck."

Yuri rested his head on the gray rubber insulation lining the inside on the hull. His head was buzzing with all the information that Rogers was putting out. Rogers had one patrol head start, and Yuri could see he thought he was an expert on everything. With a piping diagram stuffed in one pocket and a flashlight in the other, he looked like a large leprechaun. Yuri decided he liked him.

"There are about a thousand signatures on the card,"

Rogers continued. "To get signed off, you have to read different publications, physically go and locate all the parts in the system, mechanical and electrical, then hunt down the person to sign it off, and get a verbal checkoff from him. When you complete the diving officer of the watch qualification card, you have a written exam that is graded and then an oral examination by the captain, or by an examining board, if he chooses. It's a lot of work, and you're not going to have much free time during the patrol. Don't even think about seeing a movie or getting much rack time."

Yuri listened intently, letting the engine room blower ruffle his hair. The ninety-degrees-plus temperature in the engine room felt good; hot, but a dry heat. His body had adjusted to it comfortably. The best way to learn is to listen. As long as Rogers was willing to talk, Yuri was willing to do his part. You can't give yourself away just listening.

"What I'm going to do now is to introduce you to Senior Chief Clark," Rogers said. "He's probably in the machinery room. That's his domain. Most of the A Division's equipment is there. Senior Chief Clark can get you started," Rogers said. He hopped up and started forward. He gave a *follow me* gesture over his shoulder.

"Now, one of the first things you need to learn is right here at the watertight door." Rogers pointed to an oval-shaped opening in the thick metal bulkhead dividing the compartments. "This is a new system for automatically closing watertight doors in the event of an emergency." Rogers placed his hand on a high-pressure air flask mounted next to the opening. "We're the first ship in the fleet to have this new watertight door, and I doubt it was covered in your Sub School course. That's because it's secret. If you tell someone about it, you have to kill them first."

Rogers paused. "Feel free to laugh if you like." Yuri

smiled. Rogers was funny, but he talked so fast he was hard to follow.

"In older subs," Rogers said, "since day one, watertight doors have been big slabs of metal, weighing six hundred or seven hundred pounds, balanced on hinges so that they could be swung shut in the event of flooding. They were dogged down with a large hand wheel to prevent flooding in one compartment from flooding the entire ship. Those doors were all manually operated, and if something happened quickly, you might not get to the door and be able to close it. If you got to the door, the water flowing through the hatch might prevent you from closing it against back pressure. So what is the solution?"

"I don't know," said Yuri.

"An automatic door!" Rogers yelled, waving his arms and rolling his eyes. "That's what I have been talking about. The door is set up so that it can be closed automatically, either from control, or on loss of air pressure in the high-pressure air header. That way if we have an emergency that causes loss of high-pressure air, the watertight door shuts. It's a fail-safe system. If we have flooding or any other emergency, the doors throughout the ship can be shut from control.

"These doors aren't hinged but ride along tracks like a sliding glass door," Rogers said, bending down and pointing to guide rails in the solid metal doorframe. "Except these babies are just as big and as heavy as the old ones."

Rogers straightened up and turned back to Yuri. "Now, the important lesson here is, don't get caught in a watertight door when it is closing. You are going to learn how the door operates in more detail than you ever wanted to know, before you get your checkout on the system. But for right now, all you need to know is, when the Klaxon goes off— it's like the diving signal but continuous—stand clear of the door. When the officer of the deck operates the doors, he is required to sound the alarm beforehand. When the door operates automatically, the alarm sounds while the door is closing. So be on your toes, or you're liable to lose your toes, or some more important body part, in the watertight door." Rogers tilted his head down to look at Yuri over his glasses. "We don't want your wife suing the Navy for loss of consortium, do we?

"Can you imagine what OSHA would have to say about this door?" Rogers asked. He got no reaction from Yuri. "Occupational Safety and Health Administration. They would want a hundred-page operating manual and eighty-eight safety interlocks. The door would never close."

Rogers didn't wait for a reply. He ducked his head and stepped through the watertight door into the auxiliary machinery room. He waved his head for Yuri to follow him. Yuri warily watched the slab of metal, slidably mounted on the bulkhead. He raised his foot to clear the elevated sill of the oval as he ducked his head in what was becoming a familiar two-step.

Rogers stopped just inside the door beside a blue, coverall-clad Navy chief who was head down in his paperwork.

"Senior Chief, I'd like you to meet the new A Division officer, Lieutenant Thomas," Rogers said. Turning to Yuri, he explained, "Senior Chief Clark is the A Division chief."

Clark shifted his attention from the paperwork on the stand-up metal desk to Yuri. "How do you do, sir?" he said, extending his hand.

"I'll let Senior Chief Clark show you around A Division spaces," Rogers said. "He is more familiar with them than I am, and I've got the next watch. See you later. And get qualified!" He poked Yuri in the chest with his finger, eyebrows raised for emphasis.

Rogers gave Yuri a wave and a smile as he disappeared forward, not waiting for a reply. Yuri watched Rogers disappear into the missile compartment, already at warp factor four and accelerating. Yuri turned to Clark.

"Senior Chief, this is my first submarine tour, so don't worry about telling me things that might seem obvious. It's all going to be new to me." Yuri was pleased with how the pieces were falling into place. The qualification program would allow him to learn everything he needed to know about the ship without appearing suspicious.

Yuri saw Chief Clark check him up and down while Yuri talked. Nothing overt, but taking a measure of the man who had been appointed his boss.

"OK, sir," Clark said. "First of all, let's go over the spaces that A Division is responsible for.

"We're standing in the auxiliary machinery room, middle level." He waved his hand at the equipment that surrounded them on all sides. "As with most everything else in the Navy, we're not content to speak English when we can use acronyms, so we usually call the auxiliary machinery room, AMR or AMR 1. There is no AMR 2 on this boat, but some sailors can't learn new tricks.

"The machinery room is actually part of the missile compartment, which is one of the three watertight compartments on this class submarine. The other two are the operations compartment and the engine room. The layout is a lot different than the old George Washington–class missile boats, but then we have learned a good bit since then. Fewer compartments but stronger bulkheads. Still, I wouldn't give two cents for any of these internal bulkheads if the pressure hull fails.

"AMR is where most of the Auxiliary Division's equipment is located, including the oxygen generators, the CO_2 scrubbers, and some other machinery. As is the case with most submarine equipment, we have two of everything. If something breaks, we have a backup, and sometimes we even have a backup for the backup."

Clark took out his pipe while he talked. He dipped the

bowl into the tobacco pouch and started loading the tobacco in with his thumb. Yuri had never smoked, but he
watched enough people who did to know that the simple,
mechanical preparations were often as satisfying as the
hit the nicotine would bring. The paraphernalia was like
worry beads.

"Most of the items that A Division is responsible for
are related to atmosphere control. We're responsible for
the high-pressure air banks, which are used to blow the
ballast tanks. The same air banks can also be used to supply breathing air to the ship if needed. We're also responsible for the air-conditioning system that maintains the
internal temperature constant.

"Another area we're responsible for is what you might
call the plumbing system. We own the sanitary tanks and
the piping connected to them. That includes the sink
drains, the shower drains, the toilet drains, and miscella-
neous drains. Of course, the pressurized air system is also
connected to the sanitary system and is used for blowing
the sanitary tanks overboard when they are full. The
charcoal filters that remove odors from the air used to
blow sanitaries when vented back to the ship also belong
to us."

Clark placed the pipe in the corner of his mouth and
fired it up with a match. One eye winked shut as the blue
smoke curled up around his head.

"Why don't we start with the aft end of the ship and
work forward?" Clark said, pointing over his shoulder
with the stem of his pipe. "I'm not responsible for the
space in the engine room; however, we are responsible for
the air-conditioning equipment, which is located there."
Clark had a slow, easy manner, which Yuri liked. A nice
contrast to Rogers, who looked like he was constantly
ready to jump out of his skin.

"It's too bad Davis isn't on duty," Clark said. "He had
the mid-watch. He's been looking forward to meeting

you. He thinks you might know his brother from the Naval Academy." Clark started aft.

"I don't recall anyone named Davis at the Academy, but it was a big place," Yuri said. He felt a twitch under his left eye. It passed unnoticed as Clark headed toward the engine room. He resisted the urge to put his hand up to calm the twitching muscle. This Davis must have told everyone on the ship he wanted to meet Neil Thomas.

GATES sprawled on the machinery one workbench, his eyes half-closed. A Naugahyde cushion was propped at an angle between the storage locker and the workbench to support him in a half-reclined position. One leg dangled just off the metal deck.

Wilson climbed halfway down the ladder from the upper level, ducked his head down, and looked around. Seeing Gates, he continued down the ladder. Wilson looked around the space. He looked undecided whether to wake Gates or come back later. There were no clues about which course of action he should take in the immediate vicinity. He bent over to look more closely at Gates's face to see if his eyes were closed.

"Arrg!" Gates roared at the top of his voice, and then laughed as Wilson jumped back several feet. There were no cameras to record the standing jump, but it surely would have been a record.

"Don't you know better than to wake a sleeping man, Wilson?" Gates put his feet on the floor and sat all the way up. "If you must wake him, you stand back as far as you can, then tap him on the foot in case he comes up swinging. Better yet, tap him on the foot with a broom handle."

"I didn't know you were sleeping, sir."

"Don't call me sir," Gates said emphatically, shaking his head. "I'm a first class petty officer. Commissioned officers are sirs, and who said I was sleeping? I'm on watch. You don't sleep on watch. I was just checking my eyelids for pinhole leaks."

"You said be careful how you wake someone up."

"I just asked if you know how to wake up a sleeping man. I didn't say I was sleeping."

Gates stood on his toes, stretched, and flatulated loudly. Wilson's nose wrinkled in disgust, but he said nothing. Gates's smile broadened.

"What do you need?" Gates sat down again.

"I need a machinery one checkout for my submarine quals."

"Well, I don't know, I'm on watch. I've got to watch these dials on this oxygen generator." He gestured to the machine adjacent to the workbench. "That's a task with a high degree of responsibility. I can't be engaged in any idle chatter.

"Then again, there doesn't seem to be a lot of oxygen consumption right now. The movie tonight is a western rather than a skin flick, so not much heavy breathing is going on. I reckon we can risk a checkout as long as you don't do any heavy breathing. You are not planning on doing any heavy breathing, are you, Wilson?"

"What do you mean by that?" Wilson's ruddy face flushed a darker red and his eyes narrowed.

"I don't mean anything by that," said Gates, irritation in his voice. "I was just joking with you. But if you do get into some heavy breathing, that's the end of the game. We'll have to send you to the showers until you get a hand on yourself," he said, laughing loudly, his mood changing back.

Wilson's pudgy face wasn't even wrinkled by the hint of a smile as he watched Gates through narrowed eyes. Wilson wasn't sure what the joke was, but he probably assumed he was the butt of it. Gates's laughter tapered off rather quickly.

"That's quite a sense of humor you got there, bud. When you come to someone for a checkoff, you have to pretend their jokes are funny and laugh a little whether you like them or not. Where are you from?"

"Alabama."

"Well, expand on that a little bit," Gates said in a booming voice, waving his hands toward his chest in a rolling motion. "What part of Alabama—Birmingham, Tuskegee, Chattanooga? This part of the interview is called 'getting to know your shipmates.' With one hundred and two men on board, by the end of the patrol you'll know each of us by name and face, whether you want to or not."

"I'm from Birmingham, and Chattanooga isn't even in Alabama. If you don't mind my saying so, I don't think this a proper part of the checkout."

"Well, I'll be damned. I do mind your saying so, and you are one smart-ass little prick. Give me your card."

Gates grabbed the qualification card from Wilson and initialed it next to the section marked AMR 1. "I also think you are going to have one hard time getting the sign-off for machinery one. You see, once I initial your card, that means that you have to come back to me for the signature. No one else is going to sign that blank, even if they are qualified, now that I have my initial on it. And in case you have not noticed, you have pissed me off, 'if you don't mind my saying so.'" Gates mimicked Wilson's high-pitched voice.

"Now here is your first checkoff question: Why is the *Martin Luther King* painted black?" Wilson's jaw muscles worked, but he didn't say anything.

"I guess that means that you don't know, bubba. You go find out and come back when you have an answer. Also, we are going to test your knot-tying skills. Bring back a couple feet of water line when you come back. Now get the hell out of here."

Wilson started up the ladder, suddenly in a hurry to be gone. He stepped back off the ladder when he saw that Honeybear was on his way down. Honeybear turned to Wilson after he climbed down.

"Hey, Bill, how's it going?" Honeybear said with a drawl and a shy smile.

Wilson looked back at Gates, turned, and went up the ladder without answering.

"What's the problem with Bill?" Honeybear looked up the ladder. "Didn't the checkoff go well? I pumped him up for it pretty good, so he should have known all the answers."

"We never got that far. The guy is just plain stupid. We barely got past the 'Hi, how are you?' stage." Gates threw his hands in the air.

"I don't know if I agree with that," Honeybear said. "He may not be a genius, but he's not stupid. He is just a little bit unfriendly."

"Well, he's going to be social with me if he wants a signature." Gates shook his head and blew air out of pursed lips, like a boiler releasing low-pressure steam. "I started him off with 'Why is the *King* black?'

"Hey, enough of that. Are you ready to do this watch relief?" Gates's mood was improving again. "I'm just about ready for Miller time."

"I guess so. What is the answer to the 'Why is the *King* black' question?"

"Because it is harder to see from airplanes. If the *Martin Luther King* or any other submarine was white, you could see it from an airplane even if it was submerged. That's the real answer, but the answer for him is going to be, 'Because black is beautiful.' Now, I don't want you to tell him. I want to hear that Southern turkey say 'black is beautiful.' I bet he can't get it out." Gates laughed.

"Besides, what other color would you paint the USS *Martin Luther King*?"

* * *

YURI tried the stainless steel doorknob. Locked. It would be locked, of course. This was where they stored the low-level radioactive waste material generated by routine sampling of the reactor plant primary coolant. Unfortunately, this was also where they stored the chemicals for analyzing primary and secondary water samples. This was where they stored the acids.

Pressing against the door with one hand, he grasped the doorknob in the other and rattled the stainless steel door in frustration. An adjacent door opened, and Mark Gates looked out.

"Oh, hi, Lieutenant Thomas. I thought you were Norvak. There's no one in there right now. We don't have any samples due for awhile. You wanted to talk to one of the ELTs?"

"Not really. I just wanted to look around and familiarize myself with the layout of the sampling laboratory to get up to speed for a checkout. Maybe read over a couple of the chemistry procedures. I guess I can come back later." Yuri looked longingly at the door. If wishing it open would work, he would be in by now.

"That's OK. I can let you in. I've got an extra key over here somewhere. Norvak is always losing his key and keeps an extra in the log room so he doesn't have to go forward and wake someone else up to get in. Come on in, and I'll see if I can find it."

Yuri stepped into the little stainless steel office behind Gates. As Gates dug through drawers filled with log sheets, a picture taped on one of the metal cabinets caught Yuri's attention. A mountain goat looked out over a bright blue sea from a high, rocky elevation. The perspective made Yuri feel like he was there, gazing from great heights on a limitless horizon.

"Beautiful, isn't it?" said Gates, standing beside Yuri, looking at the picture.

"Yes it is. What is it?"

"I don't know. I pulled it out of a magazine. It's a painting by Wyeth. I think it's from the top of a Greek island or something, but it just caught my attention, and I liked it."

"This is beautiful, too," said Yuri tapping the bulkhead below a photograph taped beside the picture.

The color photograph was of a woman with dark hair drawn into long ponytails on either side of her face, Indian-fashion. The white skin was a sharp contrast to the dark hair. She had her face crinkled up in a little-girl smile that went with the denim shirt with the cut-off sleeves, blue jeans, and hiking boots. The overall effect was strikingly beautiful, more an imp than a woman.

"Isn't it, though? That's my prize."

"Your wife?" Yuri bent closer to look at the woman-girl. The black hair reminded him of Illya, and he felt the familiar tingle in his belly.

"Yes, sir, she is," Gates said with obvious pride. He stopped his search to admire the picture with Yuri. "That's Sweet Jane."

"Why Sweet Jane?" Yuri turned his head to look at him.

"I don't know. The crew just started calling her Sweet Jane, and it sort of stuck. She's always been the life of the party, almost one of the guys, except she's a lot better than just one of the guys." He started searching in the drawer again. "I suppose Good Time Charlie would have done just as well, except her name is Jane, and Sweet Jane it is.

"I don't mean she's bawdy," he added quickly. "It's just that one of the guys squeezes her buns, she'll turn right around and squeeze his back. Course with me there, that type of thing doesn't happen much. It's just more in the nature of holding her own. If a guy tells a salty story and she's around, she'll come right back with one that will make a sailor blush."

"She sounds like a lot of fun. I'd like to meet her

sometime." She did look like the kind of person Yuri would like to know, but it would never happen. He would be back with Illya, and Gates would be in a secluded Russian prison along with the rest of the crew.

"Well, you will. We have an off-crew party for the entire ship back in Charleston. That is, if Congress doesn't shut down the naval base before we get back. Just about everybody on board comes. When we first get back, we have R & R, and everybody goes home or takes vacation. After several weeks of that, you're ready to see some of your old buddies again, and that's when we have our party. We sometimes have two parties, if the recreation fund can stand it. So, I'll be there, and you can bet Sweet Jane is going to be there, so you can get to meet her."

"So, did you find the key?"

Yuri knew the hard part of patrol was being separated from your other half, maybe better half. The sense of something, some part, missing was always there. Usually it was submerged, buried by the everyday business of operating the ship, but sometimes it surfaced unbidden. But talking about it made it worse.

"Oh, yes, sir. Here it is," Gates handed the key to Yuri. "Just be sure to lock up when you are finished and bring the key back. If I'm not here, just put it in the drawer. But make sure the door is locked behind you. You leave the ELT lab open, and the engineer is liable to make you write up an incident report. That door's supposed to be locked if nobody is in there."

"Thanks." Yuri stepped out and closed the door behind him.

Gates continued to look at the picture a while longer. After a few minutes, he touched the picture gently with his hand. Gates stepped out of the log room and walked to the ELT lab. He knocked on the door. "I'm going forward for some chow, sir. Lock up when you're done."

"Right. Thanks," Yuri said, his voice muffled by the door.

Yuri quickly opened cabinets and lockers, coming at last to one filled with brown glass bottles. Hydrochloric Acid, Reagent. Yuri took several bottles from the rear of the cabinet and put them into his bag. He stuffed rags between the bottles to keep them from bumping and breaking. He wiped sweat from his forehead. The fun of the spy game was fading fast.

Charleston

SARAH Clark walked into the large, dim interior of the church and looked around. The building had that old familiar musty smell, from an air-conditioning system that only comes to life once a week on Sundays. The church had a capacity crowd, and it took her a few minutes to locate Dee Thomas near the front of the church. She walked up the red-carpeted aisle and took a seat beside her on the old oak bench. The red, bench-length cushions were small comfort.

"Glad to see you could make it, Dee," Sarah said in a whisper, tilting her head close to Dee. "Sorry it was such short notice, but you weren't on any of the call-down lists, the officers' wives call-down list, or the enlisted list, so you were called last. Also, the whole thing was on rather short notice."

"That's OK, Sarah. I understand. I do feel a little awkward being here though. You're the only person I know, and this is the funeral for the old A Division officer, the man who Neil is replacing."

The air conditioner hummed, barely audible in the high-ceilinged room. There was an early heat wave in Charleston, and it was warm outside, a warning of the warmer weather to come. Inside it was cold. Like a meat locker. Like the grave.

"Well, this will be a good opportunity for you to meet some of the wives." Sarah tried to keep her voice cheerful, but it was hard to be. "Most of the wives from the Gold crew wardroom will be here and some of the wives from the wardroom for the Blue crew. I'll try to introduce you to some of them later."

"There aren't very many men here." Dee said looking around. "Why is that?"

"The submarine is at sea with the Gold crew aboard. These are all wives of the Gold crew, so of course, they'd be here by themselves. There may be a few of the Blue crew people here, but not many. The crew split after construction. It wasn't that long ago, but many of the Bluies that went through new construction have been transferred. A few of the Blue crew officers may come, but they're on R&R.

"See the lady in the front row? That's Mrs. Jones." Sarah said, nodding toward the lady on the front row, in front of the casket. "Her husband was the A Division officer, the one who was killed."

"Who's the officer sitting next to her?" Dee said, leaning her head closer to Sarah.

"I don't recognize him. He's probably the casualty assistant's control officer or something like that. The acronym is CACO.

"When there's a death, the Navy makes an officer available to provide full-time liaison with the deceased's next of kin. He takes charge of everything, from getting the military insurance payment, to getting the balance of pay and allotments, even to arranging the funeral if that's what the widow wants. He's the first one on the scene and the one to break the news to the family and answer any of their questions and be available full-time if need be. He's probably from the Blue crew, but he could be someone who has been assigned by the naval base. The Blue crew probably also provides the pallbearers, since the Gold crew personnel are out at sea."

"Who's that?" A woman waved casually to Sarah as she passed. The woman had dark hair, wore a black open-necked dress, and sat several rows farther forward.

"That's Jane Gates. Her husband, Mark Gates, is a first class petty officer in A Division. Lieutenant Jones was his division officer. Most of the crew calls her Sweet Jane."

"Why Sweet Jane?"

"I don't know how it got started, although she is always the life of the party. Usually it is the guys who get nicknames rather than the girls. Like Honeybear, another one of the A Division men who's big and very sweet. I suppose that's how he got his name, Honeybear, big as a bear and very sweet. But with Jane, I don't think she got her nickname because she was so nice, or maybe that is why she got it." Sarah stopped, embarrassed. She was starting to gossip.

At the front of the church, Celia Jones held Jason's hand in a tight grip. Despite the strain of the funeral, she was careful not to squeeze it too hard and hurt him. She tried to swallow, but nothing would go past the lump in her throat. Even the Valium was not enough to dissolve it.

Jason looked up at his mother. He knew something was wrong but was not quite sure of the problem. Dad was dead, but people die. Mom was very sad and kept squeezing his hand. She needed to hold hands, and he could do that. He leaned his head against her arm.

Conversation died out as the minister started the service.

11. SUSPICION AND DECISIONS

Moscow

THE command center was dark, enclosed in a perpetual twilight. Those who played the war game lurked in shadows and spoke in whispers. Men with ghoulish faces, inverted shadows extending upward from their chins and eyebrows, tended tabletop cathode-ray screens and LCD panels. They monitored their machines, abject as any acolyte that tended idols. Dimly seen specters hovered behind Plexiglas status boards, tabulating the movement of ships and planes half a world away. Playing the war game. The global situation maps along the walls disappeared into darkness as they approached the invisible ceiling.

Colonel Borzov stood near the door, waiting as his eyes adjusted to the artificial night. Perpetual night. After several minutes, he identified the watch section duty officer in front of the large sectional map of the Mediterranean. The watch officer was reviewing a message board. Coming up behind him, Borzov ordered, "Report the status of the American submarine."

The startled officer turned and came briskly to attention and saluted. "Good evening, Colonel Borzov," he said.

Borzov ignored the salute. "You have established the position of the American submarine?' "

The watch officer snapped his hand down. "The detectors on our geosynchronous satellite indicated that the submarine has transited the area north of Crete within the last several hours. They have changed course to the south."

The watch officer walked to the status board and used a laser pointer to indicate a square area, fifty nautical miles per side. "They are in this quadrant." He glanced at Borzov.

"As you know, Colonel, the satellite detectors only give an indication of where the submarine was." Borzov could tell the officer had shifted into his briefing mode, a more formal delivery reserved for senior officers. Borzov wasn't much for small talk, but he was hungry for information, so that was fine with him.

"This is based on changes in surface temperature and other surface effects, and doesn't give the current submarine location. The last radio message from your source, hours ago, indicated the *King* would continue due east at three knots."

"Have there been any sonar contacts? What is the position of our ships, the *Kresta* and *Kinda*?" Borzov concentrated on the board. Magnetic models of ships clung precariously to the metal map, marking the positions of the ships they represented. If one were sunk, the marker would be removed. The battle with real ships wasn't won as easily.

"The *Kresta* is here, Colonel," the watch officer said, pointing with the laser. He illuminated a magnetic ship model clinging to the wall map just below the Dardanelles, the narrow channel of water that led from the Aegean Sea to the Black Sea.

Borzov knew Russia's desire to control this water highway to the Mediterranean had been a driving force in its foreign policy for centuries. For Russia, the Black Sea was a warm-water port; for the Ukraine, it was their only port. In hostile hands, the Russian Black Sea fleet could be bottled up.

"*Kinda* is here," the officer said, indicating another ship model just north of Alexandria, Egypt.

"As ordered, both have remained out of the area. However, specially equipped merchant ships have transited the area but have not made detection. It is believed that the American ship is patrolling at two to three knots and will remain almost undetectable on passive sonar."

"And the magnetic detection?" Borzov asked.

"An aircraft carrying magnetic detection equipment received indication of a submarine here." He pointed to a position ahead and south of the puck that marked the *King*'s position. "Since this was not along the track predicted by the last message, and since the American ship does not usually come shallow at this particular time, it was felt that this was probably not a valid contact. As was noted on your orders, no search pattern was established, just the one overflight."

"You have done well." Borzov looked at the young lieutenant for the first time and smiled. "You will continue to insure that all forces remain well clear of the area occupied by the *King*."

BORZOV pulled the collar of his greatcoat up around his ears as he waited. Today didn't feel much like spring, no matter what the calendar said. The beast of a Russian winter had not had all its teeth pulled and was still ready to grab you by the neck and shake you roughly if you were not careful.

He looked impatiently at the crowd in the square. He

turned and walked toward the end of the block. Better to keep moving than to stand conspicuously in one place. The old, frozen and refrozen snow crunched beneath his boots.

Caution was all very well, but his contact was waiting until the end of the appointed time slot to establish contact and was trying his patience. Worse, he didn't know what his new contact looked like and wouldn't recognize him if he bumped into him. Borzov knew his contact was hanging back, checking Borzov for a tail. Paranoia was an important part of spying; still, the waiting wasn't easy.

Borzov stopped and rocked on the balls of his feet as he watched the crowd rush by. *Babushkas* on their way to a bargain, their string bags clutched at the ready in case some item should become available at a shop they passed. That much had not changed with the end of Communism. Everything was still in short supply.

At least the grandmothers had a purpose, or so it seemed as they rushed off to somewhere, or perhaps nowhere. The number of men of working age slowly walking about showed they had nowhere to go. Worse, they had nothing to do. Troops from disbanded units in Eastern Europe. Workers laid off from factories that were no longer competitive. Borzov shook his head. Russia's first taste of capitalism was a bitter recession.

His breath blew out in a frosty puff as someone bumped him from behind.

"Excuse me," said a young, pretty woman, as Borzov turned to face her. "I must have slipped," she said.

Borzov nodded and started to turn away.

"Russia is colder than the Ukraine," she said.

Borzov quickly turned back to face her. She was medium height and very blond. Her hair spilled out from the sable hat pulled over her ears. The bulky coat couldn't completely conceal her figure. "A cigarette may warm you," he said, giving the answer to the recognition signal.

"But not as much as a breeze from the Black Sea," she responded, completing the code.

"But you're a woman," he protested.

"Thank you for noticing." She smiled.

She stood toe to toe with him; she didn't seem intimidated by Borzov and looked like she could be aggressive. Though Borzov liked that in a woman, he preferred them more shy and timid.

"Perhaps we should walk." She tossed her head and turned. She strolled slowly up the street and seemed confident he would follow.

"Of course we should walk," he said, catching up with her. "We would attract attention standing in the middle of the square talking. I wasn't expecting a woman."

"That is obvious. Perhaps no one else will be expecting a woman if you are being watched. Even an AFB colonel can see a woman without making anyone suspicious." She stopped talking, waited for a couple to pass them.

"What information do you have?" she continued.

"The American submarine has changed course to the south. It is approaching the optimum position for an intercept by our forces. We must act now or lose the opportunity."

Borzov looked casually around. "The *King* is heading into an area clear of Russian and U.S. ships." He stumbled on a broken slab of concrete as he surveyed the street behind him.

She laughed as she took his arm to steady him. "Perhaps you are a good analyst, we will see, but you are not an operative. Here," she turned him toward a shop window. "This is how you check for a tail. You stop in front of a shop and look for someone behind you that stops to look in another shop. You repeat this several times. No one can turn their head one hundred and eighty degrees without falling down."

He looked at their reflection in the glass, her holding his arm. It had been a long time since a woman held his arm.

He sighed. "Have the *Udalog* turn north at top speed on an intercept course. The American submarine will be at these coordinates on Wednesday." Borzov gave her the latitude and longitude. She repeated them. Even her voice sounded good, full of confidence.

"Code and send the release message to Gregor," she said. "Wednesday will be the day you will surface the submarine. Our crew will be ready to come aboard, and the Ukraine will have a new ship."

USS Martin Luther King

YURI held the toggle down as he drew a cup of coffee from the large urn in the crew's mess. Conceived in a stainless steel pot, the coffee was sterile, if not tasty. He put the heavy porcelain cup to his lips. Making a face, he swallowed the bitter brew. Not as good as tea, but it kept you awake. It was a still day, somewhere. The mess was mostly empty. Everyone was on watch or working.

"Lieutenant Thomas? Hi, I'm Fitz Davis."

Cornered. On a small steel ship, sooner or later you saw everyone. Some sooner than you wanted.

The tall, thin second class petty officer led with his head as he looked around Yuri's shoulder. He saw he had Yuri's full attention and stuck his hand forward, smiling.

"How do you do?" Yuri grasped Davis's hand. He checked the name tag sewn on the right chest of Davis's coveralls. Like a party, everyone on board wore name tags. It was the military way, everyone neatly labeled and categorized by collar devices into ranks and ratings.

"I understand you are a recent Naval Academy grad, sir. I wonder if you knew my brother."

"The Naval Academy is a pretty big place. There are

four or five thousand people there." Yuri spoke slowly, choosing his words carefully. He took another sip of the coffee, careful not to burn his tongue. "Hard to know them all."

"Yeah, but if you graduated a couple of years ago, he was a classmate of yours, and there are only eight hundred or nine hundred left by June week," Davis said, waving his hands in exasperation. He glanced at the large gold Naval Academy ring on Yuri's hand. Yuri was glad the ring he took from Thomas fit. It was a little loose, but it wouldn't fall off. He even memorized the words on the crest. *Ex Scientia Tridens*: through knowledge, sea power. Borzov wasn't pleasant, but he knew his spy craft and had taught Yuri well.

"That's still a pretty large number." Yuri smiled. "Each class started out over a thousand strong."

"But still, you probably heard of him. Brad Davis, he played football." The frustration stood out in his voice. Like a terrier with a slipper, he couldn't, wouldn't let go.

"No, can't say that I have. Sorry," Yuri turned away.

"But you had to have heard of him," Davis said, putting his hand on Yuri's arm. "He was first string halfback for his last two years," Davis said, raising his voice. The mess cook in the galley looked up, then went back to working, breaking out the frozen meat for dinner. "There was even some talk he might get the Heisman Trophy."

Yuri turned back toward Davis. He looked down at Davis's hand on his arm and looked back up at Davis. Davis quickly removed his hand. Yuri held him fast with a hard, direct stare and drew the silence out. Davis squirmed, blinked, and finally looked away.

"Maybe I did hear his name," Yuri said, his voice hard and flat. "But I had to spend a lot of time at my studies. I struggled with academics. I didn't have time to go to the football games. We were there to study, not to follow football statistics."

Davis opened his mouth as if to say something, worked it several times, then shut it, deciding against speaking. He turned on his heel and left. Didn't stamp his foot, but Yuri felt he would like to.

Yuri watched Davis's back as he disappeared around the corner and headed aft. He had been briefed on the Naval Academy, but he hadn't been there. There was no way to plan for everything. Davis reminded him of a petulant teenager. *There goes trouble,* he thought; trite, but true. Yuri hoped the order to surface the ship would come soon.

CLARK leaned on the metal desktop, scanning the pile of legal-sized sheets filled with numbers in front of him. The Navy's penchant for paperwork was legend. There was a plethora of gauges throughout the plant. Every pipe, bend in a pipe, valve, machine, and motor had gauges. Many had more than one. They all had to be recorded at least hourly, twenty-four hours per day. Then all logs from all watch standers had to be reviewed. Clark wondered if it was to give everyone something to do on the long, lonely hours of patrol.

Davis climbed down the ladder from the upper level. "Hi, Senior Chief, what's up?"

"Just reviewing equipment logs," Joshua said, continuing to read.

"Looks boring." Davis shuffled his feet. "It's bad enough to take readings on all the equipment on your watch station every hour for six hours. I just can't imagine reading through the logs for all the A Division watch stations. How long does it take to do that?"

"Not too long, actually." Clark said. He looked up from the papers, trying to decide if Davis planned on staying. He hoped he wouldn't.

"Everyone has their own style of doing it." Clark took out his pipe and tamped some tobacco into it. Davis wasn't going away soon, he decided. This wasn't like the "What are you doing, Josh?" type of questions he would get from his younger brother. It was more like the "We've got to talk, Josh," that his wife would ask, not knowing how to get started.

"What I like to do," Clark said, "is check the midnight readings fast. Then I scan across the row to see if I can find any trends. If the numbers are getting larger or smaller, then I look in the remarks to see if there's a reason for the change. Then I check related readings to see if we've got equipment problems, even though all the readings may be in spec. If any of the readings are out of specifications, of course, the watch stander circles the reading in red, which makes it jump right out at you." Clark set the tobacco on fire and took several puffs to get it going.

"If I do my review every day, I can knock the whole thing off in fifteen minutes. That way, when the engineer or the division officer holds a spot check, I'm one step ahead of them."

"Well, have you got time to talk, Senior Chief?"

Clark smiled. Davis was finally ready to get down to whatever was bothering him. "Shoot. I'm going to scan the last of these sheets while you are talking, if you don't mind. What's the problem?"

"It's our new division officer, Lieutenant Thomas. There is something not right about him." Chief Clark looked up from his log sheets but didn't say anything. Davis had his complete attention now.

"He is supposed to be a Naval Academy graduate," Davis continued. "But he has never heard of my brother, and he was there at the same time my brother was there."

"Well, that's not so strange." Clark smiled and relaxed. "I wouldn't have heard of your brother, either, if you weren't on board to keep us constantly updated. I don't think your brother has his own personal public relations man aboard the rest of the ships in the fleet." Clark went back to reviewing the logs as he was talking. He put his pipe between his teeth.

"It's not quite so simple as that, Senior Chief," Davis said, his voice urgent. "You don't understand how the Naval Academy works, how sports-oriented it is."

Clark thought about telling Davis that he did know. The two years Joshua had spent at the Academy before dropping out to marry Sarah were the best training he ever had. Still, he had chosen not to publicize the fact.

"In your first year," Davis said, "you're almost always at attention. You sit at attention at the meal table. You jog at attention in the passageway, you do just about everything at attention except sleeping.

"But, when the football team wins a game, you get to carry on and relax for a while. You're real people again for a while, even the plebes. So the members of the football team are heroes. They're all heroes, and you have a vested interest in how they do in the weekly college football game."

They both stopped to listen as the electric hum from the oxygen generator changed pitch. On a submarine, everyone's life depended on how well the oxygen generator functioned, how well the CO_2 scrubbers ran, the efficiency of the distiller, which made fresh water out of seawater. Satisfied that there was nothing abnormal, Clark again turned toward Davis.

"If that wasn't enough of an incentive by itself," Davis said, "the upperclassmen ask you the names of the starting players and their statistics. If you don't know the answer, you better be able to knock off ninety push-ups. If the football team is working so hard to get you to carry on, you damn well better know who they are. Not only that, for the home games, the whole brigade of midshipmen, from plebe to first class, forms up as a unit and marches over to the stadium and sits together. So there is a lot of built-in enthusiasm; it's a herd instinct. It carries through the four years you are there, mostly about football, but also for the other Naval Academy sports. I visited often to see my brother, and you just get a feel for the place. The enthusiasm is contagious."

"But, isn't it possible that Lieutenant Thomas could have been there without knowing your brother?" Joshua puffed his pipe, the log sheets forgotten. Davis was a fanatic about the Naval Academy, but what he was saying made sense.

"Sure, Senior Chief, anything is possible." Davis said, his voice filled with sarcasm. He stuffed his hands into his pockets. "It is possible that I just might make admiral tomorrow, but it is very unlikely. My brother was being considered for the Heisman while he was there, and that's equivalent to being canonized at the Naval Academy. They retire the football jersey and number for those guys who win the Heisman Trophy. They set up a little shrine with the guy's jersey and his football helmet encased. They probably have his jock bronzed. You *know* who's up for a Heisman at the Academy."

"What did Lieutenant Thomas say? Did he say why he didn't know your brother?" Clark studied Davis carefully.

Davis looked away. "He said he studied a lot." Davis's voice had subsided to a monotone, barely audible over the pervasive hum of machinery. "Nobody studies that much at the Naval Academy. Hey," his face lit up with a new thought. "He said he struggled with academics. But I thought you had to make good grades to get into Nuclear Power School."

"Let me think this over, Davis. Thanks." Clark went back to reviewing the logs. Davis recognized his dismissal.

* * *

"THANK you for reviewing the high-pressure air system with me, Senior Chief." Yuri folded a multicolored diagram back into the three-by-eight-inch book, the trainee's handy reference guide. All ship's systems were colorcoded by function, all except the reactor plant. He stuffed it into the large back pocket of his blue coveralls.

"Happy to do it, Mr. Thomas. After all, it is my system. Your system, too. It's obvious you studied the system; all I really did was help you find the individual components. You know more than enough for a checkout in this area. Anything else I can help you with, sir?"

"There is one other thing, Senior Chief. The subject of 'the black box' keeps coming up in relation to the speed of the ship. I can't find anything written about it in the Ship's Information Book."

They talked in loud voices, controlled shouting, like a conversation in a noisy restaurant. The sound from the pumps and motors that kept the ship alive bounced back from the metal wall and echoed in Yuri's ears. The hum of heavy machinery added a subliminal note that was felt in the bones. The smell of hot lubricating oil was a heavy, almost sensual smell.

"That's because it isn't there." Clark said. "It's a very hush-hush item, and no one knows very much about it. We can go back and take a look at it if you want," Clark tilted his head toward the aft end of the ship.

"I'd like to do that. It seems that subject should be related to the diving officer's qualifications, since it has to do with the speed capabilities of the ship. There's not even a signature block for it."

They walked aft past the switching gear in the upper-level engine room as they talked. They stopped just aft of the number one and number two ship's service turbine generators.

"Well, this is it." Clark patted a heavy metal shroud at the forward end of the number three turbine generator.

The eighty-degree temperature was just on the bare edge of comfortable. The air-conditioning couldn't cope with the heat, but it dried the air. It was a little like the desert air, except for the ubiquitous smell of the oil, which was almost pleasant. Yuri felt a fascination for the machine that went beyond the job that Borzov had assigned him.

"I never even noticed that before," Yuri said, raising his voice. He tilted his head close to Clark's ear. From a distance, they looked to be whispering. The noise of the equipment that packed the engine room set up a resonance in Yuri's body, made him feel like an extension of the ship.

"I thought that was part of the turbine generator."

"No, if you look close, this extra two feet of casing has been added on at the end of the generator. If you look at the steam system diagrams, you can see that there is a third turbine." Clark picked up a systems booklet from the workbench. He pointed to the proper place on a brightly colored page on the steam system.

"Now look at the electrical diagrams." Clark flipped to a different page. It was a piping diagram for electricity.

"You'll see that the third turbine generator doesn't feed any of the electrical buses. Off in one corner, though, there is a breaker indicated for the number three generator." Clark traced the diagram with fingers well worn with years of work, a hint of grease in the creases in the skin that would never go away. "That's because the number three turbine generator only feeds this one component, which almost everyone calls the black box.

"Look at this." Clark pointed to the seam between the black metal shroud and the navy gray, cast iron of the generator. "There are no bolts holding this part of the case. So how do you get it apart?"

Yuri shrugged his shoulders.

"You don't," Clark said, answering his own question.

"There's a preset timing mechanism that's set before patrol so that the box can't be opened during patrol. At the end of the patrol period, when the preset time has expired, and with the proper key, the box can be unlocked. If the mechanism fails during patrol, we have to do without it until we get back. No one, but no one, not even the captain, gets to take a peek."

"Well, that does sound mysterious." Yuri crouched down and ran his hand around the metal seam. "Who does the repair work on it? The tender personnel?"

"No, civilian tech reps are the only ones who touch that mechanism. Maybe it will change in the future, but for right now, no one knows."

"Interesting. Any idea how it works, Chief?" Yuri stood and brushed his hands off.

"Good question, but I don't know the answer. There's a lot of speculation. My guess is that it has something to do with changing the boundary layer of the water on the ship's surface. You have probably seen the charts that show the correlation between the ship's speed and power. The curve is exponential. At the high end of the curve, you require a large increase in power for a small increase in speed. The faster the ship goes, the greater incremental power requirement for each incremental speed increase."

"How fast does the ship go, Chief?" Yuri watched Clark closely. This was why Russia wanted this ship: its speed. Yuri was amazed that so much information was available for the asking. In Russia, even today, you weren't allowed to ask these questions. On board a submarine it was even better; you were expected to ask questions as part of the qualification program.

"Balls to the wall, we get right about fifty knots," Joshua said enthusiastically. "That's phenomenal when you think how big this ship is. Even with a fast-attack, which is smaller, you're talking thirty, maybe forty knots, top speed. Now, they have a smaller reactor, but even this new two-hundred-megawatt core we have just couldn't push this ship through the water that fast. So that leads us back to the boundary layer.

"There has been talk of changing the boundary layer for a long time to make a ship slip through the water easier." Clark lifted the flap on the breast pocket of his coveralls and pulled his pipe out as he warmed to the subject. Yuri noticed he used it like worry beads, something to keep his hands occupied.

"For example," Clark continued, "if you coated the ship with grease, like the English Channel swimmers, it would move through the water much faster. But coating a submarine with grease would be impractical. The grease would wear off just from the action of the water, or the barnacles would eat it. So the change in the boundary layer wouldn't last long. You could use a chemical, a petroleum-based chemical or polymer, and pump it out through the hull of the ship up near the bow to continuously reduce the friction of the ship moving through the water. But then you are adding extra pipes and pump and that adds extra weight. And you've got some material that has a limited supply, is probably expensive, and may even float to the surface and make the sub more detectable. So what's the answer?" Clark pointed at Yuri with the stem of his pipe, stuck out from his fist like an extra finger.

Yuri smiled. He knew no answer was required of him. Clark would tell him.

"Now, here is my theory." Clark leaned against the turbine and patted the black box possessively. "I really don't want to know what goes on inside the black box, so it is just a guess. What got me started thinking about it was the oxygen generators. We run electricity through the cells of the oxygen generators, and we break down the water into hydrogen and oxygen. Little bubbles of hydrogen collect at the anode and cathode. You collect the oxygen for the crew to breathe, and you pump hydrogen overboard.

"We've got this extra turbine generator feeding the black box. That's a lot of power to do something. My guess is that we are putting the power into the hull of the ship to cause electrolysis of the water. In other words, we are making little hydrogen and oxygen bubbles on the surface of the ship to change the flow path of the water. It makes the submarine more slippery."

Clark smiled shyly, his bronze skin flushing faintly. "I could be completely off base. We could be doing something like changing the magnetic signature of the ship to reduce the possibility of detection. I guess if the Navy wanted me to know, they would have told me."

"You've done some serious thinking on this, Senior Chief, haven't you?" Yuri leaned against the turbine casing, his hands in his pockets.

"I guess I have, sir, but it's got my curiosity up." He shook his head. "It's pretty much the same with everyone else on the ship. Usually when you go to sea on a submarine, there are no secrets about anything, except possibly what goes on in the radio shack. You need a secret clearance to even stick your head inside the radio room because of all the encoding equipment. To have a black box on board that makes your ship go faster than anything else afloat or submerged when its turned on, just makes me curious."

"I guess all I have to really know is that it works, Senior Chief." Yuri pushed off from the turbine. "Thank you again for the information on the high-pressure air system and the black box. I guess I'll head forward and study some more." Yuri turned to start forward.

"I'll walk back with you, sir. I'm headed to the goat locker." They started forward together, walked several paces in silence. "How's Navy doing in football this year, sir?"

The question dropped on Yuri like a bombshell. His heart skipped a beat. Davis had shared his suspicions with Senior Chief Clark, his doubts about the new division officer. The knowledge was like a revelation, instantaneous. It was one of those things that you know for certain without having actually seen the event or overheard the conversation. Whether it was an extra semi-quiver in the chief's voice when he asked the question, Yuri couldn't have said with certainty. Clark's question came too close on the heels of his conversation with Davis to have been coincidental. The proximity was probative. Until now, the senior chief had not expressed an interest in sports. How did Navy do in football? The world wants to know.

"I didn't know you were interested in sports, Senior Chief," Yuri said, looking over at him as they continued forward. It was an effort to keep his voice calm. When possible, avoid the question rather than answer it.

"Oh, I'm not, really," Clark said, keeping his eyes straight ahead. Yuri suspected that they were both playing a game with words, one in which neither was entirely sure the other was playing, or if so, playing in earnest. "It's hard to follow a sport on a regular basis being out at sea as much as a submarine sailor is. It's just always nice to keep track of our own Navy team."

"We had an OK year, I guess."

"Did we beat Army this year?" Clark persisted.

"You know, I just can't remember. I probably heard, but I was at Prototype, in shiftwork at the time, and it must have slipped my mind."

"Yeah, Prototype can do that to you." Clark gave Yuri a quick glance.

Yuri knew it was a good answer. He was starting to feel confident, perhaps a little smug. He would get away with this yet.

"Not being a nuke, I never had to go through that, fortunately." Clark said.

They had passed through the missile compartment and were now standing in the operations compartment just aft of the control room.

"Well, I guess I'll head on down to the chief's quarters. If you have anything else I can help you with, just let me know."

"Thank you, Senior Chief."

Yuri watched the chief climb down the ladder. So Davis hadn't believed him. Not only that, he had talked to Senior Chief Clark about it. The question now was, would Clark say something and to whom? It was best to remain above suspicion. Once under scrutiny, all actions were suspect. *Am I being paranoid? That might not be so bad.* Borzov had stated during a lecture that the best spies are paranoid. Look for shadows in the shade.

Charleston

THUNK! *Thunk! Thunk! Thunk!*

Dad was chopping wood again. Getting ready for winter. Mom always said he liked swinging that ax more for the exercise than for the savings on the heating bill. Dee watched him from the hillside, bright sunshine giving picture-perfect clarity to the scene. Soon his red flannel shirt would be soaked with sweat.

Thunk! Thunk! Thunk! Thunk! The hollow sound of the ax on wood was pleasant.

Dad was chopping in an odd pattern today. Usually he took slow, methodical swings, more like listening to a metronome than like someone knocking on a door.

DAMN, *it is the door,* Dee thought. She surfaced slowly through several layers of sleep. The evening shift at the hospital plus a pizza with the girls after work didn't make for early mornings. Here it was, some ungodly early hour, and some itinerant, who couldn't read the No Solicitation signs at the apartment complex entrance, was pounding on her door. She lifted her head and squinted at the clock in the half-light that seeped around the venetian blinds and curtains. Nine o'clock, and someone was at the door. She pulled the pillow up over her head and rolled over on her stomach.

Knock, knock, knock.

It was probably just some salesman, she thought, trying to shut out the sound. He or she would go away if ignored long enough.

Knock, knock, knock.

Like some Chinese water torture, waiting for the next knock was almost as bad as the knocking. No way to ignore that.

"Just like Pavlov's dog," she said. Dee jumped out of bed. She angrily threw the pillow on the floor and slipped into her robe and slippers. She cinched the bathrobe belt tight with a vengeance. With no soliciting allowed at the apartments, it had to be either a friend or one of those Air Force pilots borrowing a cup of sugar. If it was one of those Air Force Romeos pestering her again, they'd be sorry this time. This was one wolf at the door who would think that he'd stepped in a bear trap.

She paused for a moment before the hall mirror to push at her hair, and gave it up. *If someone doesn't like how my hair looks, he shouldn't be waking me at nine a.m.* As she opened the door, she was already warming up to what she was going to tell that airplane jockey. She swung the door open and gasped. She took an instinctive step backward, clutching the robe tightly at the neck.

The largest man she had ever seen was standing in the doorway. His fat, bald head almost touched the top of the doorframe. The little tufts of gray hair above his ears looked like an obscene caricature of a troll doll, the ugly little rubber toys that were popular years ago.

As Dee stepped backwards, he started to enter. She recovered quickly and pushed him with her outstretched fingers. She swung the door half closed with her other hand.

"Wait a minute, where do you think you are going?" She held the door in position with her foot, as she re-closed the top of her robe, which had fallen open.

He stopped just inside the threshold. "Oh, excuse me," he said, his voice deep and heavy. "We had a report that your telephone is out of order. I just wanted to check it out."

"That's strange, it was working last night. Who reported it out of order? I didn't report it." She looked him over carefully, from his black, lace-up boots to his matching forest green trousers and shirt. The green ball cap didn't quite cover his baldness. It had been so long since she had seen a telephone repairman, she couldn't remember what their uniforms looked like.

"I do not know," his voice rumbled with a trace of some accent she couldn't place. He sounded respectful. "I had orders to check it out when I called in. Probably somebody tried to telephone you, couldn't reach you, and reported it out of order."

"Well, you just wait right there," Dee said firmly. "Let me check the phone."

Dee, starting for the phone in the kitchen, hesitated and looked back. Should she close the door and make him wait outside? She shook her head and continued to the kitchen. There was such a fine line between caution and rudeness. One good way to make sure who this joker was would be to call the phone company and ask if a problem with the telephone had been reported. This guy looked just strange enough to make her feel uneasy.

She picked up the telephone, put it to her ear. No dial tone. She punched a few buttons on the touch pad. Dead.

Well, at least there was something wrong with the phone. She felt a little better already.

She turned and walked back into the living room. "The phone is dead. It's—" She stopped in midsentence when she noticed that he had stepped inside the door and closed it behind him.

"It's out here in the kitchen," she pointed back at the way she had come. Her hand was at her neck again. She followed him into the kitchen.

"What did you say your name was?"

"I didn't, but it is Gregor." He set his toolbox on the Formica kitchen counter and stared openly at her.

"Well, there is the phone," she said, irritation overcoming fear. She pointed at the wall-mounted telephone near Gregor's shoulder. "It's dead."

"I know," said Gregor, continuing to stare. She felt embarrassed as he looked from her face to the thin blue cotton robe that covered her small breasts, to her rounded hips, and back to her face.

"You . . . you know," Dee stammered, starting to feel a little lightheaded. His eyes, crawling over her body, made her feel violated. She felt nauseous. And afraid.

"Yes, I cut the wire." A grin spread over his face and made him look more ugly, if that was possible.

Dee felt her heart give a tremendous thump like a kettledrum, shaking her ribs with its intensity. It paused for a moment and then took off at a fast gallop. Her stomach felt like a rock, exactly as if someone had punched her in the belly. Her knees were weak and tried to fold up underneath her. She remembered she had not been to the bathroom since she woke up and suddenly didn't know if she could hold it.

"What do you want?" She thought she already knew. Rape and robbery, and sometimes murder, were things you read in the paper every day. But they happened to other people, not to you. *Not in my own home. I won't cry in front of this oaf,* she thought. She tried to swallow, but her throat was as dry as her eyes.

Gregor let the silence draw out between them. The tick of the wall clock above the refrigerator was suddenly audible.

"I want you to send a message for me," he finally said. "That's all. I want you to read a message for me over the phone, and that will be the end of it. This is a job I have been paid to do, not a criminal act, so you can stop worrying about that."

"What do you mean, read a message? What are you talking about?" She tried to keep her voice from breaking. Her left arm was wrapped protectively across her stomach.

"What I am talking about is sending a message to the ship the USS *Martin Luther King*. The people I work for have to get a message to a man on board that ship. The family grams from members of the family ashore to husbands on board the ship are the only means of doing that. So you're going to assist me by sending one to your husband."

"But why can't you send a message directly?" Her voice refused to stay on pitch and cycled up and down on its own, like a violinist searching for a note. "Why send the message to my husband? And how do you know my husband is in the Navy and on board the *King*?" Her eyes wandered around the kitchen, looking for a weapon or a means of escape while she was speaking.

"I will ask the questions. I will give the orders." Gregor grabbed her face with his hand and twisted it toward him. "And do not look around when I speak to you. If I have to slap you to get your attention, I will be happy to do so."

Dee felt her bottom lip start to quiver and bit the inside of her lip to keep it steady. She noticed the way his mouth twisted down at the corners as he smiled. He held her face harder than he had to just to make her face him.

"Good, I have your attention." He released her. "Here is the message you will read." He handed her a slip of paper. "You will read it to me before you say it on the telephone, to make sure you have it right. Your voice must be calm. It must be routine."

"But we can't use the telephone for family grams. We have to take them to the office. Besides, the telephone is not working."

"Stupid woman, of course the telephone is not working, I cut the wires." She quivered at the anger in his voice. "You will telephone your friend, the Clark woman, and tell her you are sick. Ask her to take the message in for you. Tell her that it must go today."

Gregor opened the toolbox he was carrying, removed a standard cellular telephone. "What great devices you Americans have invented."

Dee looked at the cellular phone. The box he had put her in was getting smaller. She looked at the message and read it aloud, "Grandmother eighty-four on Wednesday. Her only disappointment was you could not be there."

"Good. You are a good girl. We'll have this over in no time, and I'll be on my way."

Could she believe him? Would he really let her go?

"And why are you calling," Gregor said, "rather than taking the message in?"

"I'm sick and couldn't go down there myself."

"Excellent, and when should the message be turned in?"

"Today," she said. If she did exactly as he said, maybe it would be all right.

"Good girl. Now I will dial the number. You will talk, and I will listen on the speaker. But remember this." He bent down to bring his face close to her and lowered his voice to a whisper. She could smell the rotting remains of his last meal on his breath, something with pastrami in it. "If you say the wrong thing, it will be a long time before they come. Plenty of time for me to leave and still make you wish you hadn't called for help. Do you understand?"

Dee nodded her head. She couldn't talk with him this close. Couldn't even breathe.

"Good, we call now." Gregor said matter-of-factly. He dialed the number and handed the receiver to Dee. The rings came over the small speaker built into the phone. After the fourth ring, Dee began to be afraid that no one would answer and she would have to spend more time with this man.

"Hello?"

"Hello, Sarah," said Dee, too anxiously, her voice rising at the end.

"Dee, is that you, are you all right?" Gregor frowned at her and grabbed her upper arm and nodded his head.

"Yes, I'm all right," she said, nodding at Gregor. Her voice steadied. "Just sick. Caught the flu or something. Look, Sarah, I need a favor. I had wanted to send a family gram to Neil today, and I'm just too sick to stop by the off-crew office. Would you mind terribly if I read a message to you and had you take it in for me?"

"Certainly. That's fine, Dee. I have some shopping out at the base. I would be glad to do it. Is there anything I can get for you? Is there anything I can do to help?"

"No, thank you. I should be fine. If you would just take the message, I'd appreciate it."

"Sure. What is the message?"

Dee read the message, her hand shaking and her voice almost steady.

"Eighty-four, well, that lady has reached a fine old age." Sarah's voice echoed from the speaker, disembodied by the electronic circuitry.

"Well, Neil is close to his grandmother and always looks forward to news of his family if I have any, so if you could get that in today, I would appreciate it."

Gregor whispered, "Hang up."

"Good-bye, Sarah, talk to you later," she said sadly. A frequently used, casual phrase that suddenly had significance. She mouthed *I hope*, as Gregor depressed the receiver.

"You did well. You are a brave lady."

"You'll leave now?" she asked plaintively. She hated the way she sounded, like a little girl.

"Of course, but I can't just let you run around loose. You would call up and stop the message from being sent. So I'm going to have to tie you up before I leave to make sure the message has had time to be sent."

"Please don't tie me up," she said. Tears welled up in her eyes.

"Put your hands behind you." Gregor grasped one arm and roughly pulled her around before she could think about complying. Taking the other arm, he taped both wrists together. "And, of course, I have to put a gag in your mouth," he said, roughly turning her to face him again.

"No," said Dee and started to struggle, too late. Gregor forced her back against the edge of the white, metal-bound Formica countertop. He held her in place with his body, his hips heavy against her, while he took a handkerchief from his pocket. He stuffed it in her mouth and wrapped tape around her head to hold the gag in place. She gagged on the piece of cloth as a vagrant thought fluttered through her mind: *Is the hanky clean?*

"Of course, while I have to leave, I have no pressing appointments," Gregor said, smirking. He did that a lot. Twisted smile on florid face. He held her body firmly between his body and the countertop. She twisted and arched her back to keep away from him as he brought his face close to her. He grabbed her bathrobe in both hands, holding her pinned with his hips. He ripped the robe open, running his eyes over her body. Dee struggled more violently and screamed, but all that came out was a sound like a groan, a moan, indistinguishable between pleasure and pain.

"Ah, I see you sleep in the nude," he said, running a hand over her exposed breasts. He roughly pinched one nipple. She squeezed both eyes shut tightly, moisture leaking out at the edges of the eyes, gagging again on the handkerchief.

"And you need not worry about committing adultery," said Gregor leaning over her, trying to look into her face as she arched backward over the counter. "I killed your husband."

Dee's scream was rage, not fear, but her gag muffled the sound. She brought her knees up sharply, using the counter top behind her back as a pivot point. Anger had freed her from her weak-kneed paralysis.

Gregor's breath was expelled sharply, and he slumped to a half-crouched position. Even in his pain, he maintained his hold on Dee. His face was only inches from the top of her head. She arched forward, her forehead striking Gregor on the side of his head, near his temple, crashing her forehead against the soft part of his skull, pure instinct rather than plan. He tried to turn away and to hold her firmly, but he couldn't have it both ways. His hand slid from her to the floor. Through white dots swimming around the edge of her vision, she saw him sag to his knees.

Surprised, she stared at this bull of a man, momentarily crouched before her. Then, definitely by plan, she brought her knee up sharply to his Adam's apple. During nursing school, she had seen a man brought in with a crushed larynx. This man, Gregor, would suffocate in a matter of minutes.

Gregor grabbed his throat, his eyes wide with disbelief, his face rapidly turning red. With his other hand, he grabbed Dee and half pulled himself up and half pulled her down. He fell heavily on top of her, and her last conscious thought was how bad his breath smelled.

12. IN MOTION

USS Martin Luther King

YURI sat alone in his small stateroom, hunched over the small, fold-down desk. The light from the tiny, fluorescent bulb above the hinged desktop lit a multicolored diagram spread out in front of him. The three built-in bunks and the fold-out sink that constituted the rest of the small stateroom cast cold shadows on the walls of the dark, dollhouse-like room.

He studied intently the diagram of the ship's ventilation system as if preparing for a final exam. He traced the red-coded supply line leading to each compartment with his fingertips, as if reading Braille. He referred frequently to the detailed description in the printed information behind the fold-out flow diagrams. His fingers followed the green-coded return air back to the fan room. His studies were interrupted by a knock on the door.

"Yes?"

"Lieutenant Thomas?" An enlisted man in blue coveralls leaned into the doorway. The yellow light from the passageway lit him from behind.

"Yes, what is it?" Yuri answered. He was anxious to get back to the diagram.

"You just got a family gram. I was going off duty in radio and thought I would bring it down." He handed Yuri a one-inch-by-eight-inch slip of yellow paper. "Pretty tame compared to most of the stuff we get."

"I thought family messages were supposed to be private," Yuri said.

"They are." The enlisted man chewed his gum with his mouth open. He looked as though he might have been old enough to have graduated from high school. "But somebody has to take them off the decoding machine. Of course we don't read them, but we have to see who they are addressed to," the messenger said with a broad smile. He didn't seem intimidated by Yuri's scowl.

"You should see some of them that come in though, especially from the wives of these newlywed, young enlisted men on their first patrol." He said this from the lofty precipice of, at the most, twenty years old. "Enough to make your heart stop." He placed his hand over his heart and closed his eyes for emphasis.

"I'm sure," Yuri said, turning back to his desk.

"There was one where the wife said she had oiled the bed springs and—"

"I would rather not hear about it," Yuri said, cutting him off. He stood and put his hand on the door. "Thank you for the message."

"Nothing to it," said the enlisted man. He smiled and touched his two fingers to his forehead in an imitation of a Boy Scout salute as the door closed in his face.

Yuri still had trouble with the casual attitude some of the enlisted men displayed toward the officers. They took the camaraderie found in a small unit and carried it to the edge of disrespect. It would not have been tolerated in the Soviet Navy.

Yuri looked behind the curtains on the bunks to double-check they were empty, to make sure his roommates were not taking a nap. In a submarine, night and day were arbitrary numbers on the chronometer. You slept when you were tired, when you weren't on duty, whenever you could. He was alone. He lowered the fold-out desk closest to the door and put the second chair between the desk and the door so the door could not easily be opened.

He read through the message. Good, the wait was finally over. Wednesday was the day. He could still hear his spy school instructor telling him, more than once, that the best code was the simplest. The time was from 8:00 p.m. on Wednesday night until 4:00 a.m. Thursday morning. By prearrangement, the operation was to take place at night. Grandmother meant to surface the ship. All that remained was to send a final position marker prior to Wednesday.

He opened the locker above the desk and took out his shaving kit. Taking a dark green plastic bottle of aftershave out of the shaving kit, he opened the top, folded down the metal sink from the wall at the far end of the cubicle, and poured the aftershave into the sink. The sweet aroma of cologne was overpowering in the small room. He wrinkled his nose as he twisted the spring-loaded water faucet handle to the open position and washed the aftershave down the drain. It would take a few minutes, but the ventilation system would soon blow the stink away.

Taking a penknife from his pocket, he sliced off the top of the plastic bottle. The metal waste receptacle mounted on the bulkhead rang with a heavy, hollow sound as he tossed the top in. He shook a two-inch-long metal cylinder out of the aftershave bottle and disposed of the remainder of the bottle.

He dried the silver-colored, stainless steel cylinder on

the towel and folded the sink back into position. Sitting down at the desk, he examined the cylinder under the small desk light, looking for defects.

Good, cylinder intact, pressure sensing orifice open. Using his ballpoint pen, Yuri pressed a detent on the side of the cylinder. He folded back the top and looked inside. In the larger end, a lightweight folded balloon filled the space. The CO_2 cylinder that would expand the balloon at the proper depth was somewhere beneath. Yuri looked at the opposite end, which contained a digital input device. Housed in the cylinder, behind the digital interface, was a miniature radio transmitter. He would have to enter information on the ship's course and speed. The red digital readout was all zeros.

All that was left now was a final position check, projected course and speed, and the time and the date. Yuri carefully reclosed the cylinder and put it in his desk safe. He closed the safe door and rotated the combination dial to relock it. When the officer in charge of classified material for the submarine had assigned the safe to Yuri, he had emphasized the importance of keeping track of classified documents. When you signed out a secret document, you made damn sure you didn't lose it. If it wasn't in your hand, it was in your safe. Yuri found it ironic that he, or at least "Lieutenant Thomas," wasn't allowed to read most of the secret material on the ship. Soon he would have it all, and the ship to boot.

He opened the door of his cubicle and went out into the middle-level passageway. He climbed the ladder to control. Entering the darkened control room, Yuri casually looked around. The officer of the deck was discussing some pending evolution with the chief of the watch, near the ballast control panel. Yuri walked over to the plotting table. The quartermaster of the watch was marking the ship's current position, using data from the inertial navigation system. He looked up as Yuri approached.

"Good evening, Mr. Thomas. How's everything with you?" He sounded glad to see him. Anything to break the monotony of the watch.

"Oh, pretty good." Yuri leaned against the heavy metal table, his hands in his pockets. "I just got tired of studying the ship's ventilation system and thought I would come up and see how everything was going. Anything interesting happening?"

"No, sir, just the same leisurely, slow, steady three knots. Punching holes in the ocean. Going nowhere at a snail's pace. This baby can run fast if she wants, but to remain undetected, it's all ahead slow."

Yuri put his finger at the point of the last fix and looked at the coordinates. Longitude thirty degrees, fifty-two minutes, twenty-three seconds east; latitude thirty degrees, forty-six minutes, twenty-one seconds north.

The quartermaster watched Yuri as he traced the ship's projected course on the gray and blue nautical map. Small blue numbers on the chart marked the depth of the water.

"You have a course of one hundred and fifty-five degrees true, speed four knots laid out," Yuri said. "Is that the course for the rest of the night?"

"Yes, sir. Straight out of the captain's night orders, and we always try to do what the captain says," the quartermaster said.

"What's the course for the next twenty-four hours?"

"We will be on this course for the next two days," the quartermaster said. "We're en route to a new patrol area and won't make any course changes except to clear baffles. I don't know who would be trailing us. The Russians spend most of their time in port these days, and they are the only one with subs sophisticated enough to get away with hanging on our tail. But still, every couple of hours, we reverse course and look behind us. Then it's right back on course."

"Good. Thanks," Yuri interrupted. The quartermaster was obviously ready to ramble on to whomever would listen. The position of the ship was supposed to be on a need-to-know basis, but officers got away with a lot. Besides, whom would he tell? The ship was submerged at sea. Yuri tapped the map with his finger, looked again at the last position fix, and went back to his stateroom.

Back in his stateroom, he retrieved the cylinder from his safe. He popped open the metal cylinder and entered the position coordinates. Just like setting a digital watch, he thought. He set the course, speed, date, and time. Now all that remained was to get the cylinder in the water. Tonight was as good a time as any. This marker was bigger than the others and would require some special procedures.

Charleston

DEE opened her eyes. She saw Sarah looking down at her. Dust motes danced in the early morning sunlight. With the sun from the window just behind Sarah's head, shining through her hair, she looked just like a princess in a fairy tale. Dee smiled at the thought. Like a Moorish princess with copper-colored skin and black hair, with strands of silver woven in here and there.

"Hi, Sarah," she said, feeling mellow. At the head of the bed, out of her line of sight, a bottle dripped drugs into a tube leading to her arm.

"Hello, Dee."

Dee pressed her lips together. "Thirsty."

"Of course," Sarah said, pouring water into a glass from a carafe on the bedside table.

Dee frowned as she accepted the water. "What are you doing here, Sarah?" She looked around. This wasn't her room. White, windup bed surrounded by pastel green walls. "Where am I?" She winced as she tried to sit up and put weight on her left arm. She looked down at the white plaster cast. "What happened?" She spoke through the great lethargy that engulfed her. Waking up with a broken arm seemed perfectly natural, part of a dream that had carried over to the morning.

"Here, lie back down, Dee," Sarah said and eased her head back to the pillow. "Don't you remember?"

"Oh, God." Memories flooded back with the force of a migraine. Dee squeezed her eyes tightly shut. She remembered Gregor's face, inches from her own, her robe ripped open, him falling on top of her, the sharp crack of bone breaking.

"It's all right," Sarah said. She took her hand and sat on the edge of the bed.

"No, it's not all right," Dee said, trying to sit up. Her voice was now as urgent as she could make it, muffled as it was by whatever pain medication they had given her. "He said Neil was dead. He said he killed Neil."

"Slow down." Sarah gentled her with her voice. "You are not making sense. Here, let me put a pillow behind you." Sarah helped Dee lean forward as she put a second pillow behind her.

"The burglar said that he killed Neil?" Sarah asked. "But that's impossible. Neil is at sea aboard the *King*. How could a burglar kill him?"

"He wasn't a burglar, Sarah. I don't know what he was, but he wasn't a burglar. What happened to him? How did I get to the hospital?"

"You sounded distraught when you called me about the family gram, so I stopped by to see you, but no one answered the door.

"I tried to call you later, about 4:00 p.m., at the hospital. I knew you were on the evening shift, but they said you didn't come in and they hadn't heard from you. That really had me worried. That didn't sound like you, so I called again and got no answer. I went back over to the apartments, and there was still no answer. Your car was out in the parking lot. I knew something was really wrong, so I had the manager let me in."

Dee shifted in the bed and grimaced with the pain. Everything hurt as her body woke up, even her face. She touched her head and felt a bandage. Her face felt puffy. She hoped it wouldn't be that ugly. Sarah took Dee's hand.

"We found you in the kitchen," Sarah said. "With that enormous man on top of you. You were unconscious, and your hands were bound. Your arm must have been broken in the fall. We called the police and an ambulance. You have been unconscious since. I guess he forced his way into the apartment after I talked to you this morning."

"No, no, Sarah," Dee said, her voice agitated. "He was in the apartment when I talked to you. He made me send that message."

"He made you send that message? He wanted you to send a family gram to the ship? I don't understand."

"I don't understand either, Sarah. Has he said why he made me send the message?"

"He's dead, Dee. His windpipe was crushed; they don't know how that happened, and he had smashed his head against the counter when he fell."

"I killed him," Dee wailed.

"You didn't kill him." Sarah took Dee's shoulders as she started to cry. Dee's shoulders shook with the force of it.

"I did, I did, Sarah. I hit him with my head in the soft spot at the temple, and then kneed him in the Adam's apple. I'm a nurse. I knew what I was doing. I wanted to kill him. I was trying to kill him." Dee's voice cycled higher in pitch. Her sobs were becoming choking gasps.

Alarmed, Sarah pressed the call button at the end of the cord looped over the head of the bed.

"It's all right." Sarah's voice was soothing. Dee had heard her use the same voice when her daughter, Nicole, fell down. "Let me call the nurse in here and see if they can give you something to calm you down. I promised that I would call them as soon as you woke up, and I haven't." Sarah sat at the edge of the bed with her arms firmly around Dee. She rocked her slowly back and forth. Dee's head rested on Sarah's shoulder, tears running down her face.

The nurse stepped into the room, prompt and efficient. "If you'll wait outside Mrs. Clark, I'll take care of this." Hysteria was not usually life-threatening, no matter how distressing to friends and family. "There is a waiting room at the end of the hall."

Sarah reluctantly left the room and walked down the hall, deep in thought. She looked at the pay phone mounted on the wall for a few minutes before she took a pocket phone directory out of her purse. She ran her thumb down the index to *B* for the Blue crew commanding officer. Joshua always gave her hell for her filing system, but she could find anything. Locating the number, she picked up the phone and dialed.

She resisted the urge to pace as the phone rang three long times. She contented herself with holding her arm across her stomach, which was starting to churn with stress. The hospital air, which had seemed comfortable before, now seemed hot and thick, like it was congealing around her. Finally a man's voice answered.

"Hello, Captain Tolson? This is Sarah Clark. I'm the wife of Chief Joshua Clark on the Gold crew. Sorry to bother you at home, but we have a problem that you need to know about."

Sarah felt relief. Giving the problem to someone else wasn't as good as solving it, but it helped.

USS Martin Luther King

YURI climbed down the ladder from the crew's mess to the crew's lounge. The ladder was not quite steep enough to make him turn around and back down, but he had to keep both hands on the rail. The more adventuresome of the crew lifted both feet and slid down the rails on their hands, which was frowned on by the captain, because it was likely to result in injury. The danger, of course, made it more appealing to the crew.

Yuri casually walked through the small crew's lounge and looked around. Good, for Yuri's purposes, it was completely deserted. "Lounge" was a generous description for the tiny room. It had bench seats and lockers stuffed with magazines and books. The books were new each patrol and were chosen by the recreation officer, a collateral duty assigned to one of the junior officers. Yuri had heard the crew complain this patrol that the recreation officer was a staunch Southern Baptist. All the selections were suitable for Sunday school, but not many were read by the crew.

He stepped to the outboard side of the lounge and lifted an oval, metal deck plate set into the beige tiles. Stepping into the opening, he lowered the deck plate over his head. Taking a Navy-issue flashlight out of his pocket, he crawled forward along the inclined outer hull of the ship. The two-foot-high space between the bottom of the lower-level deck and the hull slanted upward on his left as he moved forward on hands and knees. The uninsulated hull sweated beads of condensation from the cold water outside the ship. Even in summer, the water hundreds of feet below the surface was in the forty degree range.

He reached a large-diameter, stainless steel pipe extending from the submarine hull upward through the deck. Success; exactly where the book said it would be.

He reached into his pocket, took out a folded piece of paper. Block letters across the front identified the page as part of the Ship's Information Book. "Trash Disposal Unit Diagram" was written at the bottom of the page.

After a quick glance at the diagram, Yuri moved to the inboard side of the pipe. A square, boxlike block of metal was labeled TDU Actuator. Moving his hand between the actuator and the section of the pipe, which widened out where it passed through the hull, he located the limit switch, which was held in a depressed position by a raised portion of the valve stem.

Taking a metal clip from his coveralls, he slipped the flat portion between the detent pin and the raised portion of the valve stem and clamped the back part of the clip to the base of the limit switch. Looking again at the page from the Ship's Information Book, Yuri double-checked for any other valve position indicators leading from the TDU hull valve to the control room display panels. Good, that should give a closed indication on the ballast control panel, whether or not the valve was open.

The deck plates creaked above his head. Yuri held his breath. As the footsteps moved forward, Yuri pressed a stud on the side of his watch, illuminating the digital readout: 02:03. Auxiliaryman forward was starting his rounds in the lower level. Right on schedule.

Yuri remained motionless on the moist, sloping hull, letting the cold metal drain the nervous heat from his body. The sounds on the deck above him disappeared. The auxiliaryman forward had completed his hourly checks of the crew's head. Yuri retraced his steps, crawling on hands and knees through the darkened space, lit here and there by light leaking through loose-fitting joints in the deck plates.

He paused beneath the hinged deck plate through which he had entered. Not hearing anything, he raised the deck plate a few inches and glanced around. All clear. He lifted the deck plate and pulled himself out.

"Hey, Mr. Thomas, what's up?"

Yuri spun around, looking behind the hatch he was holding. He crouched with the flashlight, clublike, in his hand. His heart thundered in his chest.

Gates was standing behind the hatch, holding the hinged cover of a combination bench-footlocker open with one hand and going through it with the other.

"Didn't mean to startle you," Gates said in his gruff, overly loud, hail-fellow-well-met voice. "What are you doing in the bilge this time of night?"

Yuri resisted the urge to ask him to speak more quietly. "Oh, working on quals, tracing out some systems. How about you?"

"Just looking for some skin mags, *Playboy*, *Hustler*, or something. The closest thing to the real thing we'll see for a while." Gates smacked his lips. "But it looks like they are all gone," he said, flipping through the periodicals one more time. "Either that or the rec officer got them. I wish the president would get his ass in gear and put some women on board submarines, like he promised."

"By the way," Gates said, closing the locker. "There ain't nothing worth tracing in this part of the bilge other than the trash disposal unit hull valve, and it looks just like the picture in the Ship's Information Book."

Gates turned his head back toward Yuri as he started to walk forward to the ladder to the crew's mess. "But I reckon if you are going to get hands-on experience, the only way to do it is to put your hands on it, right sir?" He laughed as he disappeared through the hatch toward crew's berthing.

"Damn, damn, damn," said Yuri softly as he sat on the bench. He took deep breaths as he waited for his heart to slow down. He wiped his forehead with the back of his arm and glanced at his watch: 02:10. No more time to spare.

He pushed himself off the bench and climbed the ladder to the middle level. He stuck his head into the crew's mess; no one there. A quick look in the galley showed that it, too, was deserted. He stepped into the trash compacting room located behind the galley. Also empty. He closed the door to the galley behind him. He gave his eyes a few minutes to adjust to the dim light. He leaned against the cool metal bulkhead. The bag of food scraps against the opposite wall was ripe but not yet unbearable.

He removed another clip from his coverall pocket and snapped it into place over the valve position indicator button for the TDU inner door. Clamping the detent button in the valve-closed position, he pulled the page from the Ship's Information Book from his pocket. He double-checked the diagram against the hydraulic lines to the valves and the associated electric sensing switches. He ran his hand over each of them one by one.

Tucking the diagram back in his pocket, he began positioning valves on the hydraulic lines leading to the actuating mechanism for the TDU. He heard footsteps in the galley and stepped behind the door connecting the compacting room to the galley. He pulled up the right leg of the coveralls and quickly removed a ball-peen hammer, which was taped to his leg with black electrical tape. The all-purpose weapon. He leaned against the bulkhead and held the hammer in both hands. He breathed deeply, again trying to calm himself.

This is not working out right, he thought. The footsteps, barely audible above the heartbeat hammering in his ears, stopped at the door to the trash compacting room. The door opened. Behind the door, Yuri raised the hammer. The auxiliaryman forward shined his light around the dimly lit trash compacting room without completely entering the room.

The door closed. Yuri breathed.

Yuri slowly lowered his hand. The auxiliaryman forward had inspected the trash compacting room out of sequence. He usually did that before the crew's head. Yuri had walked through the auxiliary's route as part of his qualifications. At least now there should be plenty of time to put the position signaling device in the TDU so that it would be flushed out with the morning trash. Too bad it was not small enough to fit into the toilet in the head.

Yuri's legs quivered with the release of tension as he stepped across the room. He tripped over one of the large, one-gallon, empty tin cans left in the trash room ready for compacting the next morning. The racket sounded deafening in the small, metal-walled room as several of the cans cascaded over one another.

Outside the room the footsteps stopped, turned, came back, and stopped at the door. Yuri hurried to his spot behind the door, his teeth clenched with anger directed at himself. Opening the door, the auxiliaryman shined his light around the room. The beam settled on the one-gallon tin cans that had fallen in the corner. He stepped into the room.

Yuri pushed the door shut with his left shoulder as he swung the hammer in his right hand, the full weight of his fear behind it. The auxiliaryman started to turn as he saw the motion out of the corner of his eye and was caught on the right temple by the blow and dropped instantly. Yuri saw that it was Davis. He checked for a pulse. Davis was dead.

Yuri's stomach hurt, his stomach muscles were knotted so tightly with tension. He sensed everything more clearly than he ever had before; the smell of the garbage from mid-rations, the remembered sound and feel of bone crunching as the hammer hit Davis's head, the moaning, deep-throated groan Davis made as the life went out of him.

Yuri turned to his task with a vengeance. Working swiftly, he completed positioning the hydraulic valves to open the inner door. He yanked the hand crank up and down. He then opened the vent valve for the TDU and the sea water inlet valve and began flooding the TDU. When the large, open, TDU cylinder was about half full, he shut the sea valve.

A new complication—Davis would have to be disposed of. He had had no intention of killing Davis, but the deed was done. Unreasoning anger filled him, although he was unsure of the source of his anger or its object. Putting both hands around Davis's chest, he dragged him to the open end of the cylinder.

Turning Davis toward the hip-high barrel of the TDU, he pushed his head into the open end of the cylinder. He readjusted his grip and lifted Davis's waist above the barrel to force the body in. Sweat popped out all over him as he realized the body wouldn't fit into the TDU. He strained harder as he pushed downward on the body, twisting the shoulders backward and forward.

He stopped, tried to think. Would the shoulders be smaller with the arms over the head or with the arms at the waist? He couldn't think. The cooks would be coming on watch soon to start baking bread for the morning meal.

He ripped Davis's shirt off. The skinny, hairless chest and shoulders should fit easily into the TDU, but they didn't. He reached into a bag of garbage. Grabbing some of the cold, greasy meat scraps, he rubbed them on Davis's shoulders. He pulled the body's arms in front of the stomach, crossing the arms one in front of the other. Fear and anger gave him strength. He braced one of the body's shoulders against one side of the barrel and elevated the other side. Yuri pushed downward and inward, the muscles going rigid all over his body with the effort. Something in Davis's body gave with a sharp snap, like a chicken bone cracking, and the body slid slowly downward into the TDU.

Yuri picked up the flashlight and looked into the TDU

barrel. Davis's feet were sticking up just above water level, about four feet below the open end of the barrel. Davis wasn't sinking; he was floating. Sweat stood out on Yuri's forehead. It was all going to hell. *He can't float. He has to sink out of the barrel.* Yuri started to laugh but stopped himself when he heard the edge of hysteria in the sound.

Yuri grabbed several circular weights stacked on holders. He looked quickly around the trash compactor room for something to wrap the weights in. Finding nothing, he removed the top of his coveralls, took off his undershirt, and wrapped the weights in his undershirt and dropped them into the TDU.

Anxiously, he again looked into the barrel, shining the flashlight on the weights. They slowly sank out of sight in the murky tube of water. He took a bag of the compacted trash and dropped it into the TDU.

Quickly he pulled the top of his coveralls on and fastened the Velcro tabs. Yuri repositioned the hydraulic valves and started to hand pump the inner door shut. *Damn, almost forgot.* He pulled the small cylindrical metal position marker out of his pocket and tossed it into the TDU. He dropped another bag of wet garbage on top of it.

He completed pumping the inner door shut. Checking that the vent and seawater inlet valves were shut, he removed the clip from the position indicator on the inner door to the TDU.

There was no way to pressurize the TDU to flush its contents without alerting the control room. If the drain pump had been running for another purpose, he could have chanced flushing the contents to sea, but no such luck. He would just have to leave the TDU partially filled and hope the morning mess cook would just think the evening shift was lazy.

Yuri took the clipboard that Davis had carried and

filled in the readings for the next several hours. He wiped his forehead and walked to control. He looked around. No one was looking. He hung the clipboard on a hook just outside the control room with a note attached. "Emergency head call. I stand relieved." It was not proper watch stander relief, but the oncoming man would probably cover for Davis, thinking he was sick. With some luck, Davis wouldn't be missed for twenty-four hours. By then, it would be too late.

Yuri felt suddenly cold as the air conditioner chilled his sweat-soaked body. His arms started shaking from the adrenaline overload as he climbed down the ladder to his stateroom.

Borzov had stressed proper planning during training, but also had stated that Yuri should be ready to go in a new direction. He would certainly get an excellent grade for it, provided he lived to be debriefed.

13. CINCLANT

COMMANDER Brad Tolson tried not to look nervous, but he was. You could see it in the small gestures, the way he would pick at an imaginary piece of fluff on his spotless blues. The way he twisted his neck and pulled at his collar, as if it was too small. The way his hands couldn't keep still, like they had a life of their own.

At the same time, he was embarrassed about being nervous. As a full commander, with fifteen years in the Navy, considered a senior officer, he was too old—correct that, too mature—to be this nervous. After all, he was captain of his own ship with 102 men reporting to him, and here he was just as jumpy as if he were a schoolboy called into the principal's office. He breathed in deeply and exhaled slowly and completely to slow his body's pace.

CINCLANTFLEET compound was enough to do that to anyone, he thought, looking around the crowded briefing room. It had started with his first view of the stark, concrete, bomb shelter–type building. It wouldn't stand a direct hit by a nuclear weapon—not much would—but not much else would blow it down. And there was not a window in the place. There would be no daydreaming or sunshine for these folks.

And the Marine guards at the entrance could make you sweat just looking at you. The way they checked and double-checked your identification against clearance lists, making sure your photograph matched your face. After you signed in, they probably checked your signature against computer records. They didn't require a strip search, but Tolson didn't want to bring that to their attention. All the precautions made him feel more like he was trying to get out of Fort Knox with a mouthful of gold coins, than trying getting into a building to see an admiral. They scrutinized you so thoroughly, it was hard not to look down to see whether your fly was open.

Once he was inside, there were enough captains running around to man a battleship. The four-stripers here usually made coffee, not because they did it any better, they were just the low men on the totem pole in their office. It wouldn't be a surprise to see an officer for God here, perhaps with six stars to indicate his relative rank.

He turned his attention from phantom fluff to the off-going watch officer, a lieutenant commander. The officer was preparing for the morning briefing in front of the floor-to-ceiling map of the Atlantic Ocean. The positions of the major U.S. surface combatants and many of the Russian ships were marked by miniature ship models attached to the vertical map.

The Russians still kept more of their ships in port, compared to the Soviets during the Cold War days, but they were sending more ships out again, as their economy got better. Some of the U.S. economic aid was to put fuel oil in Russian destroyers, which neither side advertised.

The Russians didn't want their aid cut off, and the U.S. Navy needed the Russians out there to justify keeping the U.S. Navy as large as it was.

The small talk died as a captain stepped into the room. The yellow and black braid on his shoulder identified him as the chief of staff. "Attention on deck," the chief of staff called. He held the door open for the admiral.

Commander Tolson came to attention with the other officers in the briefing room. The admiral went straight to the long table at the front of the room, closely followed by his entourage. Like a medieval king, Tolson thought. Actually, as commander-in-chief, Atlantic, or CIN-CLANT, he commanded more men under arms than most medieval kings ever had, and certainly more firepower. There was also enough gold on the stripes on his arm to forge a crown.

"Good morning, Admiral," the watch officer said. He commenced his briefing as the admiral and the officers in the gallery and around the table took their seats. The briefing officer was the off-going watch officer. You would never know he had been up all night on watch, but then everyone looked his or her best for the admiral.

The status report was brisk and routine, location of major U.S. combatants, location of Russian combatants, one or two possible submarine contacts, and the status of the localization search on the contacts. There was a short update on the growing tension between Russia and the Ukraine. The admiral interrupted periodically with questions. One or two of the staff officers asked a question, but it was the admiral's meeting.

It was hard to believe he was actually here getting ready to brief the admiral, Tolson thought. It was just two days ago that he received the call, on a Sunday evening, from Sarah Clark. A visit Monday morning with Dee Thomas had convinced him something was very wrong.

He had checked with the local police and verified the information. A meeting with the squadron commander in the afternoon wasn't much help. The commander was reluctant to make a decision on such unsubstantiated facts. Yet, he didn't want to kill the story and be on the spot if there was anything to it. So he had passed the buck and sent Commander Tolson up the chain to CINCLANT. The chief of staff had put him on for the morning brief.

"If there are no further questions, Admiral, Commander Tolson will brief you on a special situation."

"Good morning, Admiral," Tolson said, standing up. Twenty pairs of eyes swung around to check him out. "I'm Commander Tolson, commanding officer of the Blue crew of the USS *Martin Luther King*.

"On Friday, the wife of one of the Gold crew officers was attacked in her apartment. She was found later that evening by another Gold crew wife and the manager of the apartment complex. The assailant was still in the apartment, dead."

The large, high-ceilinged briefing room was quiet as hell. Was hell quiet? *I'd rather be in hell*, he thought, *or at least at sea, than briefing the admiral.* He resisted the temptation to shift back and forth on his feet and concentrated on keeping the pace of his words moderate, and not letting them speed up and tumble over each other.

"Mrs. Thomas, the Gold crew wife, was taken to the hospital and regained consciousness on Sunday. I was notified Sunday evening of the situation and talked to Mrs. Thomas on Monday morning. The assailant had no identification papers, and the police have been unable to establish his identity." Tolson watched the admiral, waiting for some reaction. The admiral stared back, unblinking, giving Tolson his complete attention. It looked like a *so what?* look, or a *get to the point* look.

Tolson cleared his throat. "The unusual aspect of the situation is that the assailant forced Mrs. Thomas to send a family gram message to her husband on board the *King*."

"Was the message sent?" the admiral interrupted, holding his hand up, index finger raised. The admiral talked in a quiet voice, but it carried clearly in the quiet room. Everyone focused their attention on him. If he raised a finger, everyone became silent. Maybe even if he raised an eyebrow.

"Yes, sir, the message went out with normal traffic on Friday. I checked on Monday. We didn't really know there was a problem until Monday, and by then, the message had gone."

"Very well, continue."

Tolson breathed a small sigh of relief. It must have been the right answer, or at least it wasn't the wrong answer. "Mrs. Thomas reports that the man told her that her husband had been killed. We received standard communication that Lieutenant Thomas had reported aboard the *King* prior to departure for patrol.

"The facts are strange enough to indicate something is wrong. Any of them taken by themselves could probably be dismissed, but the combination of the assailant having no identity," Tolson ticked them off on his fingers, "forcing Mrs. Thomas to send a message, and stating that her husband was killed, while he appears to have reported aboard, would indicate to me that there is a problem."

"What do you think we should do about this problem, Commander?"

"Admiral, I think we should surface the submarine and verify whether the officer on board is in fact Lieutenant Thomas." Would the admiral think he was crazy? The whole thing sounded weird, but he had no other explanation.

"That's a rather drastic solution, but you are on the right track. If you surface the *King*, then her location will be known to the world. The primary object of boats on patrol is to remain undetected.

"The first thing we need to do is to find out if Lieutenant Thomas is who he is supposed to be. Send a message to the ship for the commanding officer's eyes only. Get a complete description of Thomas from his service record and send that: height, weight, hair color, eye color, and birth marks, everything we can think of as being useful in identifying him."

Tolson felt a rising tide of panic. How would he remember all of this? He relaxed as he saw the flag secretary taking notes.

"Can we check a man's blood-type on board the *King*?" the admiral said, turning to the chief of staff.

"I don't know, sir," the chief of staff said, making a note.

"Find out. If we can do a blood-type analysis, send that information also." The admiral turned his attention back to Tolson.

"When the CO has made an identification, or even if he's unable to make an identification, he's to break radio silence and report the results back as soon as possible.

"In the interim, you're to remain available here in the Norfolk area, Commander Tolson, until we get this problem resolved. See my chief of staff for office space and anything else you need."

"Yes, sir."

"And, how is Mrs. Thomas?"

Tolson was impressed. In the middle of running one of the biggest military organizations in the world, he took time to be concerned for the welfare of his troops and family. "She appears to be fine, sir. She has a mild concussion and a broken arm. She is being kept under observation for another couple of days."

"Good." He turned to his chief of staff.

"Send a message to the joint chiefs outlining the problem and my recommended course of action. Does anyone else have any comments?" The admiral looked around the table.

Silence reigned. The admiral looked like he really wanted suggestions, but he had covered most of the points himself.

"In the event there is sabotage on the ship," the admiral asked, "what units do we have in the eastern Mediterranean area?"

The chief of staff answered, "There's the carrier battle group just north of Sicily."

"Draw up a message for CINCEUR outlining the problem. Recommend that he have the battle group steam east to the patrol area for the *King*. Avoid close approach to any Russian units in the vicinity."

He looked around the room again. When no one said anything, he rose and said, "Thank you, gentlemen," and left as abruptly as he had entered, ploughing like a ship of state through the officers standing at attention. His entourage was pulled along in his wake, like flotsam and jetsam, by the force of his passage.

Tolson felt like he had been caught on the edge of a whirlwind, spun around several times, and spat back out. Finally, he had met the man who could and would make decisions. It's what you would expect from someone in that position in the Navy, but after the meeting with the commodore the previous day, it was a pleasant surprise.

Russian Federation Ship Rostov

CAPTAIN First Rank Stavros wearily shifted his bottom on the thinly padded captain's chair. It would be easy to get bed sores sitting around like this too long, he thought, yet he was too exhausted, too tired, to get up. For the first several hours, he had paced back and forth on the periscope stand. But he no longer had the energy. His energy account was overdrawn.

He ran a hand through his long black hair and over the stubble on his chin as he surveyed the control room of his ship, observing the watch standers from his seat. Even in the dim red light he could see that they were all as weary as he was. Too long at battle stations, even rotating people through for brief relief, dulled the mind as well as the body. Being rigged for quiet running certainly didn't help.

He shifted his attention to the executive officer, as he came through the hatch from the sonar room.

"Captain, we have just completed another full sonar search, and still no sign of the American submarine."

"That's not completely unexpected, is it?" It was an effort just to talk. "This new American submarine should be at least as quiet as the American Trident class, and those are so quiet that you can't hear them until they run into you, and perhaps not even then."

The political officer had come over to listen to the conversation. "True, Captain, but Moscow has provided the predicted course and speed of the American submarine. It should pass this spot at approximately this time." He still looked fresh, like he had just stepped out of a bandbox. That was reason enough to dislike him. Stavros scratched his stomach. It had been forty-eight hours since he had bathed. Or was it seventy-two hours?

"What do you recommend?" said the captain, looking at his executive officer, ignoring the political officer. With the demise of the Communist party, the political officer was a useless appendage, but somehow they still seemed to hang on. They were called by a different name, but their job was still to check up on everyone.

"The orders are to remain on station," interjected the political officer. "Therefore, our duty is to remain on station." His tone left no doubt as to what he would do.

Stavros moved the back of his hand in the direction of the political officer as if brushing away an insect. The man couldn't keep quiet. Stavros kept his eyes on the executive officer. "We will do our duty, of course, but how to best carry out our orders is what we are discussing, Citizen." Stavros said "Citizen" like it was a curse.

"Your recommendation, Executive Officer?" Stavros liked to use every opportunity to test his XO's judgment and ability to make decisions. He would someday command his own ship and training him for that day was the captain's responsibility.

"We should remain on station, Captain, and reverse course to expose another aspect of the sonar array to the target. We have been traveling approximately perpendicular to the course of the submarine at very low speed, and we are somewhat off their track to the north. They may be past us."

"Very good, Executive Officer. A good recommendation." Stavros felt subordinates responded well to positive reinforcement.

"Here is what we will do." Stavros regained some of his old enthusiasm. "We'll come about to close the track of the American submarine and zigzag back and forth across it at slow speed to allow her to overtake us if she has been delayed." He demonstrated with his hands. "We give up some of our quietness to do this, since drifting at depth is our most quiet condition. But this will increase the time it will take for them to pass us. It will give us more chances for detection. Also, we will come shallow to assure that the American doesn't pass us above the layer depth. If they are above the layer or near periscope depth while we are below it, they could very well pass almost directly above us without being detected.

"Officer of the Deck," the captain said to the young officer standing discreetly at the far side of the periscope stand in order not to eavesdrop on the conversation. "Order all ahead slow. Come left to three hundred and fifty degrees, make your depth forty meters."

"All ahead slow, come left to three hundred and fifty, make my depth forty meters, aye," the officer of the deck repeated.

As the officer of the deck passed these orders to the engine room and the diving officer, the large submarine came slowly to life. The throttles were opened in the engine room, more steam was drawn off the boilers, taking more heat from the primary system. The colder water returning to the reactor increased the neutron flux and the power of the reactor. The submarine, shuddered slightly as it gathered speed, like a large beast quivering with anticipation at the beginning of a chase.

Charleston

Dear Josh,
I know you won't get this letter until the ship gets back into port, but I wanted to have it waiting for you at the tender. I know you sometimes volunteer for duty the first night in port so the younger men can go ashore. Since you can't go over to the telephones to call, this will be your welcome home note.

Of all your many patrols, this has been the craziest. First, the A Division officer gets killed in Rota before patrol, and then there was a burglary and assault at Dee Thomas's house. Dee is the wife of the new A Division officer, Neil Thomas. Having the old A Division officer killed was bad enough. It really upset all the wives. I think all of us were thinking that it could have just as easily been our husband who was shipped home in a box. And it isn't even wartime.

I hope you are getting along well with the new A Division officer, Lieutenant Thomas. His wife, Dee, is really nice, and we get along very well. She's fairly cute, medium height, straight blond hair. She's also a nurse. She works at the local hospital, so that keeps her pretty busy. They don't have children yet, but that's probably just as well with her husband out at sea and her working. She has no relatives nearby to help look after children. If you can get over your phobia about fraternization with officers, maybe we can have them over for dinner.

Despite her busy schedule, she's made an effort to get to know the other wives in A Division. She went to the funeral for Lieutenant Jones with me. I think it was harder on her than she would like to admit. The wife of the new A Division officer going to the funeral of the old A Division officer. It was really hard on Mrs. Jones. She was worrying not only about herself but about her son, who has lost his dad. Having to look after her son may have actually been a blessing, since it kept her from dwelling on her own loss. It was heartbreaking to see the son trying to comfort his mother at the funeral.

The big news, of course, is that there was a burglary at the Thomas house. Dee wound up killing a man. He had her tied up, but she was able to hit him with her head, and he died. The interesting part is that he forced her to send a family gram beforehand to the ship and told her her husband was dead. I didn't think much of it, but I passed the information along to the Blue crew CO. He was probably playing mind games with her, but it is strange.

The problem is that now Dee is really distraught. She's not sure if her husband is alive or

dead. Of course all of us worry about our husbands while you're on patrol. We don't hear from
you during that three-month period, and anything
can happen. We are really not quite sure if you are
alive or dead. I know it's not like the early days,
when someone died on patrol, you put the body in
the freezer and continued with the mission. But we
still worry. In Dee's case, it is even worse, since this
is her husband's first patrol, and the burglar told
her he had killed her husband. Of course, that's
impossible. The ship's at sea. How could he kill
someone at sea when he's ashore?

Now for some happy stories. Baby turned one
year old, and we had a party for her with some children from the day-care center. They watch her when
I'm busy shopping or at meetings. I made a big cake
for all the children, and a small cake just for Nicole.
When I put it in front of her, she didn't know for
sure what was going on but was excited that something was happening. She sat there looking at us
with her fork in one fist, not quite sure what was expected, and then she went facedown into the cake. It
couldn't have been better if we planned it that way.
It was the cutest thing that she could have done. I
have some pictures that preserved the Kodak moment for posterity. Copies are enclosed.

Even though you missed the birthday, at least
you will be home for our anniversary. I sometimes
don't know which is worse: having a regular
schedule with two crews, when you are in for three
months and out for three months, knowing in advance that you are going to miss Christmas and
Thanksgiving, or being attached to a fast-attack
with one crew being gone nine months of the year
on an irregular basis. Here you are not even home

*yet, and I'm already thinking about you being gone
for Christmas on the next patrol.*

Well, I guess that is all for now. See you soon.

Love,

Sarah

14. CARRIER BATTLE GROUP

Strait of Messina

THE floating city moved at a stately pace through the narrow channel. Water foamed in an arc at the bow of the ship, like a bone caught in the mouth of a beast, a standing wave that surfers would love. In other oceans, dolphins would have frolicked off the bow, popping out of the water like champagne corks.

From his seat on the bridge of the aircraft carrier, USS *Nimitz*, some one hundred feet above the water, Rear Admiral Isaac Armstrong surveyed his domain. Ahead of him, the cruiser, USS *San Jacinto*, matched his speed. He knew that if he walked to the edge of the bridge and looked behind him, he would see another cruiser, the USS *Ticonderoga*, in a similar position. Not a standard battle group formation, he thought, but then it was not usual to sail a carrier battle group through the Strait of Messina.

He looked at the rocky slopes thrusting out of the water on either side. Would Charybdis let his armada sail past without swallowing a ship? Would Scylla pluck a few sailors from the deck with her six hungry heads, if they strayed too near the Italian shore? *What would Odysseus think of my gray, metal-hulled armada? What would he think of the giant ship?*

With more than six thousand men aboard, the *Nimitz* really was a city. With ninety aircraft, it had more planes embarked than many small countries had in their entire air forces. Such a machine of war would have been more difficult for that ancient Greek to imagine than a six-headed monster like Scylla.

A seaman who handed him a cup of coffee was so nervous that his hands were shaking. Armstrong carefully took the cup from him, hoping that the young sailor wouldn't spill the hot liquid on them both.

"Thank you," Armstrong said, giving his best friendly grandfather smile. "That will be all."

The seaman took a step backward, turned, and left. Armstrong shook his head as he watched him go. It still occasionally surprised him, the awe that an admiral's uniform inspired in young enlisted and even young officers. The two stars on the collar of his khaki uniform made all the difference. Put on a flannel shirt and dungarees, and he would merely be another gray-haired, middle-aged man. Maybe not; he liked to think he had a commanding presence, and an aura of authority. But the uniform certainly helped.

He turned his attention back to the bridge. The orders had said to proceed with utmost speed to a submarine operating area in the eastern Mediterranean. *But I'll be damned if I'm going to speed through the Strait of Messina.* Even at twenty-five knots, such a passage was dangerous. He could feel the raw power in the huge ship from the vibrations as the two huge nuclear reactors propelled her through the water. At twenty-five knots, the stopping distance was almost half a mile. While the width of the channel was a mile, at this speed the turning radius was a substantial portion of that, and if you ran your ship aground, or your entire battle group, it was your ass.

Then there was the wind and current. He looked out the bridge window. The wind was twenty knots from the port quarter and just whitecapping the waves. With the large surface area of the ship acting like a sail, wind could be a significant factor. And the current through the strait was tricky.

It didn't matter if the orders said to get there in a hurry. He was the one who was responsible. That was the price of the uniform and the stars. He was paid to make decisions, but if he guessed wrong, he would be hung out to dry.

Plenty of time to crank on the extra knots when the battle group turned west after rounding the toe of the boot on Italy. Then the speed was limited only by the speed of the escorts. The frigates and possibly some of the destroyers would have to be left behind, but he couldn't afford to leave all of the escorts. He would have to keep the speed of the battle group under thirty knots so his cruisers and some of the faster destroyers could keep up. The nuclear aircraft carrier was the queen in this chess game, and it was too valuable to leave unprotected, even during peacetime. The cruisers were antiaircraft protection, and the frigates and destroyers were antisubmarine protection, although there was some overlap.

There were Russian units on exercise in the eastern Mediterranean, but it was unlikely they would do anything. Everyone was friendly now that the Soviet Union had dissolved. Right. There was always the possibility of attack, and he didn't want to be the first admiral to lose a nuclear-powered aircraft carrier. The politicians had been wrong before.

Armstrong watched the CO of the ship pacing back

and forth. Of course, the aircraft carrier herself was the CO's responsibility. He wouldn't say anything to interfere with how the CO ran the ship, but Armstrong enjoyed being on the bridge. Watching the computer-generated satellite plots gave him a broad overview, but there was no substitute for seeing the ocean.

I know it makes him nervous, me being up here on the bridge, Armstrong thought. *But there is no reason to go down to flag plot just yet. There will be plenty of time spent in flag plot later, if the message traffic was right.* Many believed, Armstrong included, that the high point of a naval officer's career was as commanding officer of a ship. Nothing else was as fulfilling, even promotion to admiral.

USS Martin Luther King

YURI stood in the rear of the crew's mess, resting his coffee cup on the serving counter in back of the last row of seats. The flickering light showed the crew's mess was only about half full. Crew members watched in a desultory fashion the film *Flashdance* for perhaps the tenth time this patrol. The ennui was palpable. The random flashes of light from the movie danced over bodies loose with lack of sleep and boredom.

Yuri stared at the screen, but his mind was elsewhere. The auxiliaryman forward watch was on one and five, which meant standing one six-hour watch and then twenty-four hours off. Davis's absence probably wouldn't be noticed until 0600, when he failed to report for his watch relief. Initially someone would probably cover him and take his watch, but eventually a search of the ship would be made, and no trace of him would be discovered. Then there would be an unbelievable uproar. Then

Davis's remarks would be reexamined; questions about Yuri would be renewed.

He should have left Davis at the bottom of a ladder, making it look like he tripped and fell and met an accidental death. Even if foul play was suspected, at least the body would be found and there would be an element of doubt. It had just happened too fast, and he hadn't considered alternatives. He shook his head. Then again, hauling the body around the ship to find a suitable place for an "accident" would have left too much chance for discovery.

He sipped his coffee as he watched the male lead throw the female lead through a series of steps that would make a gymnast proud. The question now was whether to commence the operation early and hope that a rendezvous could be made or wait and try to complete the operation with the entire crew stirred up. Perhaps it would be best to wait. If the rendezvous could not be made early, the whole mission was a failure. There was a good chance of still catching the ship by surprise, despite the confusion when Davis was discovered missing. Yuri wouldn't be connected with that, at least not immediately.

"Hey, Neil, sneaking a peak at the movie?" Lieutenant Rogers slapped him on the shoulder, slopping the coffee over the edge of Yuri's cup. "You know trainees are not allowed to watch the movie until they complete their qualifications." Rogers squeezed his shoulder before releasing it to draw himself a cup of coffee.

"I was just getting a cup of coffee," Yuri said. He turned to go.

"Hey, wait," Rogers said, his voice loud and boisterous. He grabbed Yuri by the arm. "I was just joking. I don't care if you watch a little bit of the crew's movie. You can't study all the time."

"The captain might care."

"Sure, but he's busy in conference with the XO right

now. They've been buzzing around since the captain received a CO's "eyes only" message. In fact, that's why
I'm off watch for a few minutes." Rogers looked at his
wristwatch.

"Say, that's right," Yuri said looking at him. "You had
the evening watch in engineering didn't you?"

"Yup, but the CO says to check the radio equipment
and be ready to fire it up in the morning. So I'm starting
checkout procedures on the high-speed transmitter before
I take the watch. This will be the first time I've been
aboard when we've used this equipment at sea. I can't believe the CO's going to break radio silence during patrol,
but it looks like that's just what we are going to do.

"I see they're showing *Flashdance* again," Rogers
said, pointing at the screen with his coffee cup and shifting his attention back to the movie. "There's not even
much skin in it. Why in hell watch something without de-
bauchery in it? What's the Navy coming to? Well, get
qualified as soon as you can. I could use the extra sleep. I
better get the checkout started and get back on watch."
He took his coffee and was gone.

Yuri was apprehensive. For a missile boat to transmit
radio signals on patrol was more than out of the ordinary.
It was unheard of. One of their primary objectives was to
remain undetected. In the event of war, if the enemy took
out all your land-based missiles, you would still have the
submarine missiles, since no one knew where they were.
You certainly couldn't be undetectable while transmit-
ting, no matter how brief the message.

Of course, the message transmission might have nothing to do with him at all. Lieutenant Rogers, the operations officer, knew nothing about the reason for
transmission, and secrets were hard to keep on a submarine. What kind of operation would be kept secret from
the operations officer?

The chief corpsman came into the back of the crew's

mess and filled his coffee mug. He stepped up beside
Yuri, tugging at his beard. Submarines on patrol were the
last place in the U.S. Navy where you could legally grow
a beard. After Secretary of the Navy John F. Lehman discovered he couldn't grow a beard in the mid '80s, he
made everyone else shave them.

"Good evening, sir," the corpsman said in a serious
voice. Yuri had noticed that he was always serious, like
life was too much to be taken lightly.

"Good evening, Doc. How are you today?" Yuri
looked at the chief. A Vietnam veteran, going bald and
overweight, but always respectful.

"Fine, thank you, sir," the doc answered. "And you?"

"All right, I guess. What has you up this time of
night?" Yuri made a face as he swallowed the last of the
now-cold coffee. "I didn't know you liked these movies."

"I've seen this one once. Once is enough. I just wanted
a cup of coffee before I went up to sick bay. The captain
has just given me a little project to do. He wants me to set
up to run a blood test in the morning. We've got the capability, of course, but I haven't done one of those in years,
and I need to study up on the procedure.

"Why he wants one done is what puzzles me. No one
aboard is sick. I'd be the first to know." He took a sip of
the scalding coffee. "Then sometimes you just do what
you are told. See you later, sir."

The hair on the back of Yuri's neck prickled. Now, that
was too much to be a coincidence, Yuri thought. A message received for the CO's eyes only, the communications
officer preparing to transmit a message in the morning,
and the corpsman preparing to do some blood-typing
work. At this point you'd have to be stupid not to believe
something was wrong. They suspected him and were going to check his blood type. That had to be it. The possibility, no the probability, was just too strong to ignore.
Could all this be the result of suspicions by Davis? It

didn't matter; the best spies are paranoid—at least Gregor said so—and while he was many unpleasant things, it turned out he was good at spy craft.

Yuri could feel the adrenaline coursing through his body. Tonight would have to be the night. If there was no rendezvous when the submarine surfaced, the mission would have to fail. By this time tomorrow he would surely have been discovered. Davis, blood type, problems ashore. Something had gone awry.

You set up contingency plans to cover all possible divergent turns the course of events might take, but there was always the possibility of some unforeseen circumstance that had not been planned for. This was one. Yuri set down his coffee cup on the metal countertop and walked forward to his stateroom. The dark, tile-lined halls of officer country were dim in deference to what the chronometer had designated as "night." Even submariners slept sometimes.

In his stateroom, he unlocked his briefcase. One of his two roommates was sprawled in his bunk, asleep. His ragged snore was counterpoint to the steady hiss of the ventilation system. Yuri removed the last three ball-shaped pieces of soap from his briefcase and stuffed them into his pockets. Five others had been released periodically to mark the ship's position.

Yuri walked to the officers' head across the hall and locked himself in one of the stainless steel stalls. He took out his penknife and carefully cut the soap in a circle around the circumference. He removed the soap from the outer surface of the metal sphere contained inside. He placed the metal sphere and the pieces of soap in the toilet. He repeated the procedure with the second and third sphere. The radio messenger buoys would inflate upon reaching a predetermined depth, once flushed overboard. Unlike the larger, more complicated mechanism he ejected through the TDU, these were small enough to flush through the sanitary system. Launching the last three at once should alert Moscow that something out of the ordinary was taking place.

Turning on the seawater valve, he pulled the lever at the side of the steel toilet to rotate the large ball valve at the bottom to the open position. The water washed the metal spheres into the open mouth of the valve. Yuri turned the water to full and continued to let it run.

The officers' toilets connected to the smallest sanitary tank on the ship. When he had reviewed the auxiliaryman forward's log earlier in the evening, it had been nearly full at that time. He let it run a few more minutes.

No use doing this, he thought. He wasn't going to get the tank filled to the top anyway. He shut the flapper valve, let the water run to form a seal around the valve, and then turned the water off. Climbing the ladder to control, he looked around and saw the auxiliaryman forward sitting in a corner of the darkened room, taking a break.

"Let me see your log," he asked.

"You've already looked at it once tonight, Lieutenant Thomas," the auxiliaryman said, handing over the clipboard.

"Just force of habit. I guess I'm new enough to being a division officer that I still enjoy it a little," he said. Looking through the log sheets, he found the reading for sanitary tank one. Not much changed from the last reading, a little bit fuller.

"Better ask the OD for permission to blow the number one sanitary tank."

"I think it can wait until the next watch," the auxiliaryman said. "Then we'll blow all the sanitary tanks."

"This one is closer to the limit than the rest, and several of the officers have taken showers in the last hour. I want you to get permission and blow that now. We should be shallow enough."

"Yes, sir."

Russian Federation Ship Rostov

CAPTAIN First Rank Stavros surfaced from a deep slumber, shedding sleep like water as he woke. The knot of fear that clutched his stomach was due to too little sleep, too much caffeine, compounded by the alarm that rang in his ears.

The knot loosened a little as he reoriented himself on coming fully awake and realized the ringing was the telephone line to the bridge, not the collision alarm. He reached out, knowing where the phone was from long habit, even in the complete dark that is only known in deep mine shafts and in sealed metal cylinders hundreds of feet below the surface of the ocean.

"Speak," he said, putting the phone to his ear.

"Captain, XO here. We have located the American sub."

"I'll be right there," he said, smiling, as he returned the phone to its cradle.

Stavros turned on the small light above his bed. It pushed back the night to the edges of the small stateroom, though shadows still lurked in the corners. He swung his feet out of the bed and paused to let his blood find its new course through his body. It was a lot harder getting out of the rack these days than when he started making patrols twenty years ago.

He slipped on his shoes and checked his watch. He held it at arm's length to see the dial. He was not yet ready to surrender to glasses, but soon. More than three hours since he had laid down in his trousers to rest for a few minutes. He pulled on his jacket and buttoned it as he walked forward to the control room.

"What is the position of the American sub?" Stavros said, entering the control room. Everyone stood straighter at his watch station.

"The American submarine is on a bearing ten degrees off the starboard bow," the executive officer said, looking

up from the plotting table. "Our sonar operator estimates
the range to be no more than three kilometers, perhaps
half that. We detected him blowing sanitary tanks. He
made a mistake and blew some air over the side." The XO
smiled.

Stavros also smiled, elation washing away the last of
the sleep. We got lucky," he said putting his arm on the
XO's shoulder. "We have them now."

"Come right to two zero zero," Stavros said, his voice
resonant with the confidence of command, even at the re-
duced level used when hunting other submarines. "Make
your speed five knots."

The officer of the deck acknowledged the order. The
deck tilted down to the right as the submarine banked
into the turn.

"Executive Officer," Stavros said, his voice barely
above a whisper, "assume the American is on course one
hundred and eighty-five degrees and making a speed of
three knots, that would be his standard operational patrol
speed. Plot a course to put me a hundred yards astern."

"Aye, aye, sir."

"Also, pass a message by word of mouth to the crew
that we are tracking the American submarine. There is to
be no unnecessary movement. All personnel not actually
on watch are to remain in their bunks." The American
sonar was so good that even loud voices could be detected.

The executive officer started to move away to comply
with the order. Stavros grabbed his arm. "Check the intelligence publications and see at what depth the Americans
blow sanitary tanks. Pass the word that everyone has done
his job well."

"Yes, sir," said the executive officer, excitement in his
voice. The excitement was contagious. Stavros knew it
would spread by word of mouth through the crew. They
would all be more alert for the end of the hunt.

15. A LITTLE LUCK

USS **Martin Luther King**

SENIOR Chief Joshua Clark stood in front of the small group of enlisted men that made up the Auxiliary Division. He smiled as they found seats on lockers and deck plates, wedging themselves into the narrow spaces between the humming equipment. They drank coffee, grumbled at each other, and gradually settled down. They were a lot like any other all-male group, roughhousing and digging at each other with verbal jibes. Except for the four-letter expletives they managed to insert between every other word, it could have been a group of big boys at a scout meeting, rude and crude and playful.

No one sat next to Spanos, but that was not unexpected. He stood out like a skunk even among these earthy-smelling men. Spanos never showered unless physically forced into it. He would sometimes make it through the entire three-month patrol without taking soap to skin or water to soap. His shipmates, however, often took matters and Spanos into their own hands.

Recently, Spanos had blown the sanitaries on himself. He had used the toilet when he got off the mid-watch, disregarding the warning sign on the door that the sanitary tank was pressurized to blow the contents overboard. In his sleepy stupor, he had pulled the flush handle when he was finished and had blown the sanitaries not outboard, but inboard. The gusher that had erupted out of the toilet pinned him against the door until the pressure had been completely vented, along with a good portion of the sewage in the tanks. Spanos being Spanos, he had picked the biggest chunks of detritus off of himself and climbed into his bunk. His bunkmates had dragged him out of his rack and scrubbed him down in the shower with bristle brushes.

That was several weeks ago, but judging by the empty space around Spanos, it might be time for another shower party. It was not the kind of discipline that the captain would have awarded at captain's mast, but it was one of those kinds of things that Chief Clark, and even the officers, would quietly choose to ignore unless they were forced to consider it. *A motley crew,* Clark thought, shaking his head, *but they are all mine.*

Clark tapped the butt of his pipe on the counter to get their attention. "For our divisional lecture today, we'll be reviewing the use of the OBA, the oxygen breathing apparatus."

"Ah, Senior Chief," one of the men interrupted. We're auxiliarymen. We know all about that. We give the lectures on this to the rest of the crew."

"That's true, but there are some new men in the division this patrol, and they haven't heard the lecture before. Besides, it's on the lesson plan.

"Also, practice makes perfect. So if you want to be like me, you'll practice a lot," Clark said. A smile sneaked around the stem of the pipe he held in the corner of his mouth. A couple of the men answered him with raspberries.

"Senior Chief," Gates said, raising his hand. "Why in hell are we having our divisional lecture at this ungodly hour? It's almost twenty-two-fucking-hundred at night."

"It is not at all strange, Gates. We had battle stations missile drill on our normal lecture day and a field day yesterday. Tomorrow the engineer wants to review our training records. If he finds that the training was not done, he will chew Lieutenant Thomas's ass. The lieutenant will then chew my ass, and when he is done, I will kick your butt. So I guess you could say I'm saving your ass."

Clark smiled as the man laughed. Leadership at the enlisted level was not something you learned at school; you tried stuff, and when it worked you used it again. Humor worked. "First thing, no smoking during the lecture." Clark took the pipe out of his mouth and tapped the ash out into an ashtray.

"We are dealing with oxygen, and anything burns given enough oxygen and a hot enough temperature," Clark said, his voice serious. "Even steel will burn in a pure oxygen atmosphere. Even though we are using just a small amount of oxygen, your cigarettes could catch on fire, and your face along with it."

"Looking at some of these guys' faces, that might be an improvement," Gates interjected. He poked Wilson in the ribs.

Wilson scowled and moved away from Gates. Clark watched Wilson as he waited for the laughter to die out. Wilson had hit the rack after the evening meal and had to be dragged out of bed for the lecture. Wilson wasn't much of a morning person, but then, he wasn't much of an afternoon, evening, or night person either. Clark shook his head.

"This is an oxygen breathing apparatus, more commonly known as an OBA." Clark lifted a small, back-packlike object with wide web carrying straps. Attached to one end of the backpack by a hose was a face mask with straps.

"The OBA is a self-contained unit capable of providing oxygen to the user for periods of up to one hour, depending on the activity level of the person wearing the unit. It is not suitable for underwater use, but inside a smoke-filled environment, it provides freedom of movement without the limited range of travel associated with using a mask with an air hose attached.

"We have the OOD's permission to light off several canisters, so I'm going to go through the procedure, and then we'll have a couple of you men put on OBAs for practice."

Clark pulled the crossed straps over his head, holding the cloth-covered black box against his chest with one hand. He attached the strap hanging down behind him on one side, did the same on the other side, and then pulled it, adjusting the strap on each shoulder loop tight.

"When the OBA is properly stowed, it can be donned in less than a minute by an experienced operator. Proper stowage is important, and we will come back to it later. An important point to remember is that if the unit is not put away properly and there is an emergency, the next person to use the OBA may not get it on in time. That next person sucking smoke rather than oxygen may be you.

"All that remains at this point is to attach the face mask and insert the canister into the bottom of the generator," he said, pointing to the cavity at the bottom of the chest pack. He slid a canister into the slot. "You then fasten the clamp and pull the igniter cord on the candle starter." Clark omitted the last step.

"OK, Wilson, you try it," Senior Chief Clark said, pointing to another OBA unit. Wilson was the most junior man in the division and would benefit most from the training.

Wilson looked away as if he hadn't heard the chief. He sat on the deck, legs crossed, arms resting on his knees.

He just can't bring himself to take orders from a black man, Clark thought. Clark had not intended this to be a contest of wills, but by God, Wilson was going to obey orders. This was the Navy, and there was going to be discipline, even if it meant taking Wilson to captain's mast.

None of the other auxiliarymen said anything. The hum of the CO_2 scrubber, which had previously been background noise, suddenly sounded loud. Everyone seemed to find something interesting to look at on the bulkhead, overhead, or deck plates. The tableau lasted only a few seconds but seemed as long as hours to the frozen actors.

Honeybear stood up and picked up an OBA from the stack at Clark's feet. "Let me help you with that, Wilson," he said in his slow, quiet voice.

The tension drained out of the air as if it had been shorted to the metal deck plates. Even Wilson seemed relieved to be given the opportunity to get out of the situation he had created. Wilson smiled, but it looked more like a nervous tic than smugness.

Clark was so angry he wasn't sure if he could speak if he tried. Wilson would learn to take orders from a United States Navy senior chief whether he liked it or not.

YURI looked into the crew's mess. Twenty-two hundred hours, one of the few times that the crew's mess was almost deserted. The afternoon shift had finished with their after-watch movie, and the mess cooks had not yet started preparing the midnight snack for the mid-watch.

Yuri tugged at the dial-x telephone. It was stuck again.

There was no chance that a depth charge would accidentally take the receiver off the hook. As usual, the problem was getting it out of the cradle when you wanted to remove it. He put both hands on the stubborn receiver, yanked it out of its cradle, and dialed the bridge.

"Bridge, Chief of the Watch," the voice at the other end of the line answered.

"Chief, this is Lieutenant Thomas," Yuri said. He looked around to make sure he was still alone in the crew's mess. "I'd like permission to go into the fan room to trace out some ventilation lines for qualification." Yuri waited as the chief checked with the officer of the deck. He knew there wouldn't be a problem. All of the officers on board would love to get him qualified and have one more man on the watch bill. That would give them more time off duty between their shifts.

"Lieutenant Thomas, Chief of the Watch. Go in the fan room."

"Go in the fan room, aye. Thanks, Chief."

Yuri pushed the phone into its cradle until a snap indicated the receiver was locked into place.

He walked out of the crew's mess and across the passageway. He stopped at the door to the fan room. After looking up and down the passageway to make sure he was not observed, he reached behind the transformers bolted to the floor just outside the fan room door and lifted the canvas bag he had placed there earlier.

Air whistled around the rubber seal as he unfastened the dogs on the fan room door. Air from the passageway rushed past him into the fan room with the door fully open. Stepping into the dimly lit interior, he stooped to avoid the return-from-aft ventilation duct as he closed and sealed the door. Turning sideways, he slipped around the foreword supply duct and continued forward until he was out of sight of the observation window in the door.

Yuri rubbed perspiration from his forehead with the

back of his sleeve, his body oblivious to the cool and constant wind tugging at his shirt. He opened the gray canvas bag, removed an OBA, quickly strapped it to his chest, donned the face mask, and started the ignition candle. Moving rapidly, he took a glass beaker and a bottle of hydrochloric acid from the bag. Fortunately, the theft from the nucleonics lab had not been noticed. There were always more reagent chemicals on board the ship than could be used during a patrol. By the time there was an inventory, it would be too late.

He sat back on his heels and willed his breathing to be slower, and he slowed his pounding heart. There was no reason to rush, this close to the final step in the complicated dance, and spill acid on himself. He allowed himself to feel the coolness of the rushing wind and thought of springtime and a park in Moscow. He shivered as the thunder of his heart subsided. He slowly poured the acid into the large glass beaker. Yuri took pellets from a sealed plastic package and dropped them into the beaker.

The fan room is unusual, even for a high-tech, space-age submarine. It is tucked out of the way in a corner of the operations compartment. The pressure in the fan room is lower than the pressure in the operations compartment, by design, and air is drawn by the pressure differential into the fan room through a metal grill in the door. The amount of air drawn into the fan room through the door, several cubic feet per minute, is small only when compared to the total volume of air that is processed through the fan room.

To insure proper mixing of air in the submarine, air from various parts of the ship is dumped into the fan room by return air ventilation ducts. Air is drawn from the fan room and carried forward by a large conduit to the front end of the operations compartment. Another major air supply line extends aft to the engine room. Air pickups in various parts of the operations compartment return the air to the fan room, and similar air pickups in the missile compartment and the engine room return the air from aft. Some air from the engine room is drawn through the reactor compartment tunnel and picked up in the missile compartment.

The fan room was, if not the heart of the submarine, at least its lungs, and it circulated life-giving oxygen to all parts of the ship. Carbon dioxide was removed as the air passed through the auxiliary machinery room.

The high-pressure fans created a constant, ear-numbing whine not unlike the roar of a jet at full throttle, which was felt full-body as well as through the normal auditory channels. The overtones and undertones would have made dogs sing in harmony, if there had been any of the canine kind aboard. The gale-force winds tugged at Yuri's clothes. The smoky haze that bubbled from the beaker swirled up around his gas mask. Fumes from the witches' brew he had concocted were swiftly drawn into the supply forward and the supply aft ducts.

THE air supply vent for the operations compartment upper level opened above and behind the diving officer.

The diving officer, seated between and to the rear of the planesman and the helmsman, made a routine scan of the instruments; trim angle, angle on the stern planes, angle on the sailplanes, and speed. He checked the angle on the sailplanes again. The buoyancy of the submarine was almost neutral. He had been fine-tuning it for subtle changes of water temperature, but now it was right on. He looked over his shoulder. "Secure pumping, Chief. We are within a gnat's hair of being trimmed out."

"Secure pumping, aye." The chief of the watch leaned foreward and flipped the toggle switch for the trim pump to the off position. He extended both hands, one toward the forward trim tank and one toward the after trim tank hydraulic valve toggle switches. He stretched, inhaling as he hoisted his ample belly over the ballast control panel to reach the switches. The air, reflected from the ballast control panel, blew in his face. He made a choking, snorting sound and doubled over violently in his seat. His face smashed into the apron of the panel.

All around the control room, heads turned toward the chief of the watch, except for the helmsman, who had doubled over unnoticed. Air from the overhead blower ruffled the helmsman's hair. The officer of the deck stepped down from the conning stand and moved to help the chief of the watch. The OD's knees buckled as his step down turned into a headlong crash to the floor. No one noticed. By this time, everyone in the control room was busy with their own anguish, either doubled over, thrashing violently, or unconscious.

IN maneuvering, the panel operators lounged in various states of repose. The electric plant control panel operator had a reactor plant manual opened in his lap, casually thumbing through the pages, periodically glancing up at the steady-state dials on his panel. Everything was "copacetic," the latest in-word, discovered by one of the enlisted men in the dictionary, someone who had not brought enough reading material to make it through the cruise.

The reactor plant control panel operator slouched in his chair with his knees on the edge of the panel. He appeared to be in the terminal stages of boredom as he stared mesmerized at the unmoving instruments through half-closed eyes. Next to him, the throttleman had his feet on the rear bulkhead, facing away from the steam plant control panel. He was still awake, or at least his eyes were open, also his mouth. Fortunately, there were no flies on board.

Chief Dietz, the engineering watch supervisor for the section, leaned his head inside maneuvering and looked at the status board. He took a drag on a cigarette and said, "Only thirty-nine more days to go." It was a standard opening line, used to strike up conversation.

There were no takers. The engineering officer of the watch didn't even look up from his logbook, spread out on the small desk behind the panel operators. He continued recording the pumping of the engine room bilge. This was the only exciting event, in fact the only event, in what had been a routine watch.

Finally, the reactor operator relented, and grunted out a tired "Yeah," albeit with great effort. After all, Chief Dietz was the Reactor Controls Division leading chief petty officer, and would eventually write his enlisted evaluation. It never hurt to suck up to the boss.

Not to be deterred, Chief Dietz continued. "Yup, I have been on patrol so long, when I get home to the wife, I don't remember whether you fuck it first or eat it first." He laughed, but he was the only one. They had all heard the line before, many times.

"Maybe Gates can let you borrow one of his *Playboy* tech manuals, Chief," the throttleman said. "At least you'll be able to review what all the parts look like." The throttleman looked around to see if anyone was going to laugh. Chief Dietz was the only one who did.

"Gates has probably eaten half of the pictures out of the magazine by now." Chief Dietz poked the throttleman on the arm.

"Engineering Watch Supervisor," Lieutenant Rogers said, looking up briefly from his logbook. "If the engineer or captain decides to take a tour of the engineering spaces and catches you talking through the maneuvering room door, they are going to have your ass. Then you'll have to worry about how to 'do it' with your ass nailed to the wall. You know the rules: no eating, no drinking, and no informal chitchat in the maneuvering room.

"So, either come in or go away," Lieutenant Rogers said and continued writing.

"OK for you, sir," Chief Dietz said. "I'm on my way. You just better hope the relief valve on your bladder doesn't blow. If you need a break for a head call for the rest of the watch, you just blew it. For the rest of the watch, I'm going to be very hard to find," he said with a twinkle in his eye and turned to leave.

Chief Dietz froze as Lieutenant Rogers doubled up over the logbook. The maneuvering room air supply blew the loose-leaf pages in his face. Before Chief Dietz could say anything, the other panel operators slumped in their chairs like dominoes. Without thinking, Chief Dietz lifted the chain that hung across the entrance and took a step into maneuvering. A step was all he had time for before he, too, collapsed with the rest of them.

WILSON held the OBA against his chest as Honeybear helped him snug up the shoulder carrying straps. Wilson pulled the cord to light the candle to start the oxygen generator. He slipped the mask over his face and started to tighten the straps on one side.

"Here," said Honeybear, reaching to help him, his voice surprisingly quiet for a man his size. "Tighten the straps on the top first to get it centered front to back. Then you pull the two side straps by your chin at the same time, to draw the mask up snug. That way it stays centered on both sides and gives you a good seal against your face."

Honeybear took a step back to visually check that the face mask was centered. The air vent flattened his hair. He gasped as the cyanide gas reached his lungs. He fell to his knees with a thud, his fingers scratching at his throat. Everyone was frozen in place as he toppled over, face-first, on the deck plates. Gates was the first to react and was on his feet in one quick motion. As he stepped toward Honeybear, he started gasping with a sound like a growl.

Chief Clark, standing off to one side, held his breath as the members of the Auxiliary Division fell to the floor in rapid succession. He quickly drew the OBA mask over his head and pulled the straps tight. The rest of the division, with the exception of Wilson, convulsed on the deck plates or had stopped moving completely.

Wilson knelt by Honeybear and started to take his mask off over his head. Chief Clark grabbed his wrist.

"Leave the mask on," Chief Clark said.

"Keep your fucking hands off me," said Wilson, flipping his hand back to shake off Clark's grasp. Wilson stood quickly, fists balled at his side. "Honeybear is hurt," he said reaching up again with both hands to take his mask off.

Clark stepped forward and punched Wilson in the stomach. He put his shoulder into it and felt the shock of it in his own shoulder. This was definitely a nonregulation way to get an enlisted man's attention, but he needed Wilson to focus completely and immediately, and this was something Wilson would understand.

Wilson's hands came down from his face mask, and he clutched his stomach. Clark wrapped both of his arms around Wilson to hold Wilson's arms at his sides until he was sure he had Wilson's undivided attention. Wilson twisted from side to side in a vain effort to free himself.

"Think, Wilson. Honeybear is not sick. All the men are down, all the men without an OBA. You and I have our masks on, and we are the only ones standing. That is what is keeping us from being just as unconscious as they are." Clark suspected worse.

"You black son of a bitch. You're going to wish you were dead," said Wilson behind clenched teeth, voice muffled by his face mask as he continued to struggle.

"We can talk about that later. In the meantime, don't move and don't take your face mask off. That's an order. I'm going to pass the word."

Clark released him and raced up the ladder to the upper level. He grabbed the emergency microphone off its hook and shouted to make his voice heard through the mask. "This is Senior Chief Clark, machinery one, upper level. There are contaminants in the air system. All personnel don emergency breathing apparatus."

He knew the message was broadcast over the speakers in maneuvering and control. It would be up to them to pass the word to the rest of the ship over the 1-MC.

"Maneuvering, request you pass this on the 1-MC," Clark said, pressing the microphone to the voice connection on his face mask a second time. He released the button and waited.

"Control, request you pass this on the 1-MC." He struggled to keep the growing sense of panic out of his voice.

"Maneuvering, con, acknowledge."

Clark knelt on the deck and stuck his head down the hatch to the middle level. "Wilson, get up here, now!" His voice was loud and urgent, even though muffled by the face mask.

Clark got no answer from below and climbed halfway down the ladder. Wilson was kneeling next to Honeybear and was struggling to put an OBA on him.

Clark climbed the rest of the way down the ladder. Crouching beside Wilson, he put his hand lightly on Wilson's arm and said, "Wait." Clark's voice was patient. Clark put his index and middle finger on Honeybear's neck next to the windpipe. He looked at Wilson and shook his head.

"He's dead, Wilson. That OBA is not going to help him one bit. I'm getting no answer from maneuvering or con, so we've got bigger problems than a dead man or even an entire dead division.

"You go back to the engine room, and if you find anyone still breathing, put him into an OBA, or get an EAB and hook him into the emergency air supply.

"Do you understand?" Clark said. Wilson rocked back and forth on his heels, head hung. He nodded but didn't say anything. Clark hesitated.

"Unqualified or not, we've got an emergency to handle. If I come back here and you are still sitting on your heels, I'm going to kick your ass all the way into next week." Clark's voice was firm. He wanted to get Wilson moving, but without getting him angry and unproductive. Give the men something to do and don't let them hear the panic in your voice.

Clark scrambled up the ladder and headed toward the missile compartment upper level. His feet pounded out a hollow, ringing rhythm as he ran past the huge cylinders that contained the missiles. He slowed his pace as he ducked his head and high-stepped through the watertight door into the operations compartment. Running again, he followed the passageway to the right as it bypassed the ship's inertial navigation equipment. He stepped through the door to the control room and stopped suddenly. The tangle of bodies was like something from a nightmare.

"Damn," he whispered to himself. It seemed inadequate, but it was all he could get past his suddenly dry mouth.

The officer of the deck was crumpled by the diving officer's chair where he had crash-landed headfirst, after coming off the conning stand. The chief of the watch lay across the ballast control panel. The helmsman and the diving officer were on the floor where they had fallen. The planesman was slouched across his control stick, which was held forward in the full-dive position.

Clark pulled the planesman off the stick and checked the depth gauge and rate of depth change. Rock solid, steady on depth. Thank God the controls had been set to automatic.

Clark checked for a pulse in the diving officer's neck. Looking at the open, staring eyes, and the grimace frozen on the diving officer's face, he knew it would be useless. It was.

He picked up the microphone and punched the circuit for maneuvering. "Maneuvering, con. Acknowledge." Clark scanned the diving panel to reassure himself that the angle on the ship was steady. The USS *Martin Luther King* stayed steady on course and depth.

Wilson's voice came over the engine room speaker. "They are all dead back here, Senior Chief, every last one of them. God, everybody's dead," Wilson said, his voice too loud and colored with panic around the edges.

"Settle down, Wilson. Just settle down," Clark said, keying his microphone, keeping his voice calm and slow.

"Settle down? You stupid motherfucker, don't you understand? They are all dead. Every last one of them as dead as flies."

Clark punched the override and cut him off in his best parade ground voice. "Wilson, does that mean we have to die, too? We will surface the ship and get help as soon as we can. Some of the men may still be alive, only unconscious." Clark didn't believe that, but it might help get Wilson moving again.

"You get up here to control and stand by the ballast control panel. If anything happens, we can blow the main ballast tanks and surface the ship. I'll release the emergency buoy, and with any luck we'll have some rescue vessels on the way before we surface."

Charleston

SWEET Jane sat up suddenly in bed, the sheets cascading down around her naked hips. She made the transition from completely asleep to bolt upright in the wink of an eye, in the beat of a heart. Her heart raced furiously toward some unknown goal, each beat shaking her small rib cage. Perspiration sheened her skin.

She slowly pulled a double fistful of sheet up around her small, firm breasts, inching it up over her body, almost afraid to move. The silence was loud in her ears, despite the pounding of her pulse. What sound there was, was clear and distinct. The clock ticked out each second in a measured manner, Big Ben in a bedside box.

She could clearly see everything in the small bedroom, in the pale, silvery moonlight shining through the single window, from crown molding to the intricate pattern of the paper on the wall. All senses were sharp, a knife edge of sensory perception. The soft, shallow breathing of Alex Pendergast sleeping beside her was clearly audible.

She thought about waking Alex, but what would she tell him? That she thought someone was looking at her? No, she knew someone had been watching her. Alex would insist on going outside to check around the house. But she knew that it wasn't someone outside. Someone had looked into her mind for one awful second, and she had caught him at it.

She turned her head slowly and looked out the window. The white cotton curtains framed a section of small backyard. The manicured patch of grass was empty. There was no one there. She had known there would be no one there, but she had to look.

She sat in bed wet with fear in the cool, air-conditioned room. How could she explain to Alex that there had been someone there momentarily, not an apparition, not a dream, not a real person, but that someone had looked in on her, or through her, with the most clear, penetrating, blue eyes she had ever seen. There had been a presence in the room.

She wanted desperately to reach out for a cigarette, but she was afraid to move. She slowly eased herself back into a reclining position against the headboard, pulling the balled-up sheet with her.

It certainly hadn't been as easy to end it with Alex as she thought it would be when he had first come back from patrol. She looked over at his face, completely relaxed in sleep. One of the few times he wasn't smiling was when he was asleep, but even then there was a hint of a smile in the laugh lines around the eyes.

They could always end it after this off-crew. *After this off-crew, no more,* she thought firmly. Mark could get a transfer to another ship, maybe another home port. That would certainly end it. Telling Mark would also end it, but she was no longer certain that was the best thing to do. She eased down farther in the bed, hoping that sleep would overtake her soon.

ACROSS town, on impulse, Sarah looked in on Nicole. It was still Baby most of the time, even though she was somewhere between a baby and a little girl. Sometimes it was Bug, or Princess, or Sweet Pea, and once in a while, even her real name, Nicole.

Until Baby had come, it was hard to understand why their friends had always referred to their children as "rug rats" or "curtain climbers." They did, and were, all those cute little things and more. She had slipped easily into use of all those fuzzy-feeling names for children, those little creatures that were attached to the heart by emotional strings too strong to explain to those without children.

Biological bonding had been something in a textbook

until Nicole had been born. Looking across the delivery room when the obstetrician held her up, something had happened, a transference, a connection was made that was at once as insubstantial as air and as strong as steel. A love that was as whole and complete and substantial as a part of her body had been born with that look.

Sarah went all the way into Nicole's room. Eggshell-white walls sported large paste-on pictures of bears, birds, and clowns. The sun, the moon, and the stars watched from blue curtains.

Sarah knelt down by the side of the crib so that her face was only inches from Nicole's face on the other side of the wooden bars of the crib. She loved the smell of Baby's breath better than any perfume, or even the flower by the same name, if it had a smell at all.

She looked at the little body with her knees drawn up under her tummy and her hands by her head. Just like a frog. A bundle of energy caught in a still shot, ready to take off. She wanted so much to reach out and touch her, to squeeze that pudgy little arm, but she settled for pulling the blanket up around Baby's shoulders.

Come home soon Josh, she thought as she watched a moment longer.

THE nurse pulled the starched, white sheets up around Dee's shoulders. Dee stirred uneasily in her tranquilized, if not tranquil, sleep. The nurse thought about putting up the short, metal side rails on the bed. The patient was restless tonight, but she should be okay. The drugs that sedated her and cables on the cast would keep her from going anywhere. The nurse hesitated a moment longer, decided against the bed rail, and tucked the sheets in tighter.

The nurse checked the record on the clipboard again. The patient had been here a long time. Maybe the day shift could wash her hair. That would make her feel better. The nurse put the clipboard back and left.

Dee twisted against the restraining sheets as shadows chased her through her dreams and emotions raced across her face. Sometimes the shadows followed her husband, Neil, unsubstantial but sinister, as he jogged unconcerned down a tree-lined street. She tried to yell to warn him, but nothing came out except a low groan that jumped across the veil that separates dreams from reality. Then again, something was after her, but her legs refused to move, though her heart ran at full gallop.

As she pushed at some unseen thing, the weights and pulleys attached to the cast covering her arm followed her movements in a grotesque pantomime. She relaxed, and gravity, weights, and pulleys moved her arm back into proper position, the real-life version of the molasses that slowed her in her dreams, pulled her down.

16. THEN THERE WERE THREE

USS **Martin Luther King**

YURI looked up and down the passageway as he left the fan room. The beige-colored passageway was empty, from the officers' wardroom to where it turned the corner around the crew's mess. No need to call the chief of the watch to report the fan room clear. They should all be sleeping peacefully by this time.

Yuri started toward the forward end of the ship. As he passed the half-open door to the small galley adjacent to the wardroom, he stepped around an arm sticking partway out into the passageway. Yuri pushed the door the rest of the way open and looked at the enlisted man lying faceup on the floor of the galley. It was Lee Hang, a Cambodian who had joined the Navy after coming to the United States with the large influx of refugees in the early 1980s. Yuri hardly knew him. He was a pleasant, hardworking, quiet, industrious fellow who kept mainly to himself. Most of the officers were excited about the native dishes he cooked. With a few extra spices, he could turn routine meat and rice into something exotic. Food was one of the only ways to break the sustained monotony of the cruise, and anyone who could do that was highly valued.

Yuri continued forward, but stopped abruptly with a sudden sinking feeling in his stomach. The mess cook's eyes were open and fixed, unusual for someone unconscious or asleep. When you were anesthetized, did your eyes stay open? Yuri didn't think so.

Yuri turned back and knelt beside the mess cook. He put his hand on the carotid artery. There was no pulse. Had Lee Hang had an allergic reaction to the gas? Perhaps he had banged his head as he had fallen. Yuri stepped back into the passageway and climbed the ladder toward the operations compartment upper level. It was regrettable, but in military operations sometimes there were casualties.

The first order of business was to check that all systems were in a static condition. Yuri shifted his mind into a lower gear. Certain things must be done and done now. There was no time to dwell on an accidental death. First, he must make sure the ballasting systems were all aligned properly and that the nuclear reactor was in a stable condition. Then he would signal the fleet and bring the submarine to the surface. Yet he felt a certain reluctance to walk into the control room. The air felt thick as he forced himself forward.

He hesitated before stepping into the control room. Lee Hang's death had left a copper taste in his mouth. Yuri had only known the crew of the *Martin Luther King* for a short time, but some of these men had become friends during his time on board. Yuri had betrayed their trust. Well, the good part was that they would get to go home early. The story they would be given when they revived on a merchant ship is that they had been rescued at sea.

Yuri stepped into the control room, steeling himself

against the sight of his shipmates. The OOD lay face-down; a pool of blood surrounded his head. Yuri knelt beside the OOD and checked for a pulse. There was none. Yuri could still smell the aftershave on the man's face, but the life had left him, evaporated. The first two people he had encountered were dead. Surely they all could not be dead? He felt nausea rising in his throat.

"Mr. Thomas?"

Yuri jumped to his feet so quickly that his feet actually left the deck. He whirled around in a half crouch, bringing a pistol out of his pocket. The hairs on his head and the back of his neck stood at attention.

Wilson stepped around the edge of the periscope stand where he had been sitting beside the ballast control panel. "Everybody is dead, Mr. Thomas," he said. "Do you know what happened? It's a good thing you had on your OBA—" Wilson stopped as he noticed the pistol in Yuri's hand.

"What's the pistol for, sir?" He said, pointing at the gun.

"No talking," Yuri said curtly, giving the pistol a wave. He felt numb. Everyone dead except Wilson. Wilson was sitting in the control room in an oxygen-breathing apparatus, fat, dumb, and happy.

"But I don't understand, sir."

"What are you doing in an OBA?"

"We were having our divisional lecture. I had the OBA on for practice when something happened to the air system. Senior Chief Clark and I thought we were the only ones left alive. Everyone else is dead."

"Everyone is dead? That can't be right," Yuri said.

"Yes, sir. That is, everyone except me and the senior chief. Senior chief also had his OBA on."

"Where's Chief Clark now?"

"He went aft to release the emergency buoy." Wilson pointed toward the stern of the ship with his thumb.

Conflicting emotions coursed through Yuri. He had

killed everyone on board the submarine. It would be easy to shoot Wilson, right here, right now. With so many other people dead, would it matter? Yet he could not quite bring himself to do it. Borzov had said the chemicals were an anesthetizing agent, which would render everyone unconscious. Yuri now realized Borzov had never had any intention of letting the American sailors live. They were all dead by Yuri's hand, and here he was, ready to shoot one more. Was he any better than Borzov?

Also, a shot might alert Chief Clark. That was the deciding factor. Clark must be prevented from releasing the emergency buoy. Borzov had put him in this position, but the only way out was to go forward.

Yuri motioned with the pistol. "Walk in front of me. We'll go back to the missile compartment and talk to Senior Chief Clark." Yuri waved the pistol again. "Don't say anything. I don't want to answer any of your questions."

Yuri followed Wilson aft. The chief of the watch slid slowly off the ballast control panel and crashed unnoticed to the deck as they left the control room.

SENIOR Chief Clark stood in front of a gray metal electrical box. The cover hung open, and rheostats and switches covered the inside of the panel. Clark pushed the three-pronged plug of a large drill into a bulkhead receptacle. In a metal ship everything had to be grounded.

A humorous variation of one of the electric safety rules inexplicably and inappropriately surfaced in his mind. The safety rule required a second person as backup during electric work to rescue you if you accidentally touched a hot wire. Sailors, always anxious to add a humorous twist to any given subject, stated it differently. If you touched a live wire, you would cook slowly in your own juices until God saw fit to take you away. The corollary to the rule stated that your shipmates would console your widow after your death in ways that you would deem inappropriate, which always drove the point home.

There was, of course, no backup available, just him and redneck Wilson. Safety, however, had become a habit. Clark started to pull a pair of safety goggles over his head when he remembered he was wearing an OBA. How could he forget? Wearing the rubbery-smelling old thing was like having a gym bag over your head. The Plexiglas eyepieces in the face mask would serve the same function as safety goggles anyway. *Lifelong habits are hard to break,* he thought, as he ground the hasp of the padlock off the manual release switch for the emergency buoy. *It certainly won't help blinding myself with metal slivers after surviving poisonous gas. It would be a bitch to get off the submarine and be blind.*

The captain or the weapons officer probably had a key to the emergency buoy padlock, or at least a key to the key locker. But it would be easier to grind off the hasp than to check dead men's pockets for keys. First you would have to search the ship to find the right dead man, not something he was anxious to do. Once in the key locker you would still have to search through the hundreds of keys to find the one for the padlock. Sometimes brute force was the correct choice.

The high-pitched whine from the grinder changed tone as the abrasive grinding wheel bit through the last of the hasp. Clark put the drill down and opened the safety cover for the eject switch. He checked the settings for the buoy, armed it, and pressed the manual release. There was a satisfying, solid *thunk* that vibrated through the ship as the buoy doors swung back on the outer hull of the submarine. The submarine rocked slightly as the buoy ejected through the open doors.

Clark picked up the drill and stopped in midmotion. He was on a ship full of dead men, several hundred feet

below the surface of the ocean, and he was getting ready
to restow a drill. He shook his head. Keeping things ship-
shape was the least of his worries. He bent to put the drill
down. He still could not bring himself to toss it on the
deck. Out of the corner of his eye, he saw some movement. Clark turned to see Wilson coming around the end
of the missile tubes with his hands behind his head, followed by Lieutenant Thomas.

Clark cocked his head to one side, puzzled, but only
for a moment. Then all of the pieces fell into place: Lieutenant Thomas's lack of knowledge about the Navy football team, Davis's suspicions, and everyone on the ship
dead. He understood, yet he felt like a statue with his feet
welded to the deck plates as Wilson and Thomas marched
up to him.

Yuri shifted the muzzle of his pistol to cover Clark.
"Put your hands up," he said.

"Who are you?" Clark said, keeping his hands by his
side. Yuri didn't answer.

"Your name isn't Thomas, is it? What should we call
you?"

Clark noticed Yuri had removed his face mask. Clark
shifted the grinder to his left hand and pulled off his face
mask with his right hand. He tossed it on the deck plates.

"You can take off your mask, Wilson. If Lieutenant
Thomas is not wearing one, it's safe."

Wilson slowly took off his face mask, hesitant now
about giving it up.

"Did you have to kill them all?" Clark asked, his voice
harsh and grating in his throat.

"They weren't supposed to die. You must believe me."
Yuri's voice was plaintive, and his face twisted at the corners of his mouth. "They were only supposed to be re-
duced to unconsciousness for the duration."

"Duration of what?"

"No more questions, please." Yuri's voice was now hard and flat. "Put your hands above your head."

"You mean he killed everyone?" Wilson said, looking first at Clark, then at Yuri, then back to Clark.

"No talking," Yuri said, shifting his pistol toward Wilson.

"You killed everyone? You killed Honeybear?" Wilson said, his voice rising. His arms started coming down of their own volition.

Clark watched as Wilson's face slowly turned red. It started with a crimson flush at his neck, which crept up his chin, cheeks, and forehead. Clark could see what was going to happen. Wilson was building up a head of steam like a boiler. He would charge like a bull, and Thomas would shoot him dead. Thomas took a small, almost imperceptible step back. Thomas sensed it, too. Watching Wilson was like observing a force of nature, like a tremble in the ground before a volcano erupts.

They wouldn't have a better opportunity, Clark thought and acted on the impulse. He felt adrenaline flowing through his body like electricity and was elated with the sudden surge of energy. Clark stepped forward, flicking the trigger switch of the heavy-duty grinder to the on position. The tool swung up in a smooth arc as Clark accelerated, trying to get the drill between himself and Yuri. He rushed to close the several feet that separated them. The distance halved with the first full step, and halved again with his foot in midair on the second step.

Yuri's pistol moved from Wilson toward Chief Clark, but it seemed to be moving in slow motion. Yuri stepped back as he swung the pistol, instinctively trying to give himself extra seconds. Yuri's left arm came up to block the grinder. He hesitated just a little too long before firing, and the projectile struck the grinding wheel that Clark had been aiming toward the muzzle of the gun. The grinding wheel shattered about the same time that the

drill reached the end of the electric cord. The plug held
fast in the socket long enough to pull the drill into a vicious, slashing arc, whipping the shattered edge of the
grinding wheel across Yuri's arm. The pistol dropped to
the floor with a clatter and slid along the deck plates.

The taut electric cord pulled Clark off balance, bouncing him off the side of a missile tube and onto the floor.
Clark recovered from his acrobatics and struggled to his
feet, ears ringing from the sound of the shot echoing in
his head. His nose burned with the smell of the gunpow-
der in his face. Like days hunting with his dad down
home, except this time he had been on the receiving end
of the gun.

Yuri crab-crawled after his gun, his forearm spurting
blood in a brilliant stream. His hand hit the gun, and it
skittered on ahead.

Clark didn't hesitate. Wilson had gotten tangled in the
cord and fallen to the floor during the encounter. Clark
pulled him to his feet, and they struggled through the
hatch, arms, legs, and the electrical cord tangled together
and the grinder bouncing along the floor behind them.
Clark pulled the cord loose and half dragged, half pushed
Wilson into the reactor compartment tunnel, then on to
the engine room.

"Run, damn you, run," Clark shouted. *When words
fail, curse.* Wilson was slow to start but took off like a
bull when he got going, all 180 pounds of him.

Behind them, Yuri finally got the gun in hand and fired
several shots into the engineering spaces after the two es-
capees. A bullet struck a lighting distribution panel with a
solid sound. A shower of sparks was accompanied by a
deep-throated buzz as a high-voltage current arced across
the wires. The fireworks were accompanied by brightening and dimming of the overhead lights. Then the engineering spaces became dark as a breaker opened loudly.

Chief Clark pulled Wilson to the side, out of the line

of sight of the watertight door. He held Wilson by the meaty part of his upper arm as he said, "Douse that light by maneuvering." Clark pointed toward a pale, battery-operated emergency light. The light had blinked on above the maneuvering room door when the fluorescent lights went out. The battery-operated lights came on automatically on loss of electrical power to the lighting bus.

Not waiting for an answer, Clark jumped to the other side of the passageway, minimizing the time he spent passing in front of the watertight door. Taking out his utility knife, he used the butt end to smash the front of the emergency light at that location. The light made a popping sound as it went out, followed by the tinkling sound of glass hitting the floor.

Clark sucked at his fist where it had been cut by flying glass. He turned in time to see Wilson bodily ripping the emergency light near maneuvering from its bracket. Wilson smashed it facedown on the floor. Clark smiled in the sudden darkness. Wilson was not very imaginative, but sometimes he could be highly effective.

Clark did not wait for his eyes to adjust to the dim light coming through the door from the missile compartment. As he ran back toward maneuvering, he brushed one hand along the switchboard to guide him. He called softly to Wilson as he passed him.

"Follow me. Put your hand on my shoulder and stay close. The first thing we need to do is to get our hands on a couple of blunt instruments."

Clark felt Wilson's hand firmly on his shoulder. Turning the corner after maneuvering, he said, "Wait here. Keep your eyes on the watertight door and let me know if Thomas, or whoever he is, comes through the door." There was just enough light coming from the tunnel to see Wilson nod his head.

Clark continued along the wall behind maneuvering. He stopped when he reached a metal toolbox bolted to the deck plates near the outer hull. In the near darkness, he rummaged through the tangle of tools and removed several large crescent wrenches and a ball-peen hammer. He slapped one of the crescent wrenches against his free hand. The meaty smack it made felt good against his palm.

Retracing his steps, he asked Wilson, "How's your accuracy with a hammer?"

"I don't know, Senior Chief, but I sure would like to try. I played quarterback on the football team in high school," he said, as if that said it all. There was excitement, even eagerness, in Wilson's voice. Clark clapped his shoulder. Pitching iron was something Wilson could probably do, and do well.

Clark was face-to-face with Wilson, whispering in the dark. Wilson's breath smelled like he had been eating dog turds, and he smelled almost as bad as Spanos. It appeared that among Wilson's many other negative attributes, he was a sweat hog. Clark smiled, high on endorphins and adrenaline. He had never liked Wilson as much as he did at that minute.

"You take the hammer," Clark said, handing it to him like a prize. "If he comes through that hatch, do your best."

"My pleasure, Senior Chief," Wilson said as he hit the hammer against his palm to show he had understood.

"Good." Clark patted him on the shoulder. Stranger bedfellows never plotted mischief in the dark. Clark had moved from something less than waterboy in Wilson's eyes, to captain of the team. "In the meantime," Clark said, "I'll be over at the high-pressure air manifold. I think we can rig a trap for him."

Clark worked his way toward the high-pressure air manifold located on the port side, aft of maneuvering.

"Senior Chief," Wilson called in a stage whisper as Yuri appeared in front of the door. Silhouetted against the lights in the missile compartment, Yuri looked cautiously into the engine room, a pistol in one hand and a flashlight in the other. A tourniquet bound his pistol arm.

Wilson let the hammer fly without preamble. It would have been a touchdown pass. Out of the darkness the hammer flew, straight and true, headfirst, hitting Yuri squarely on the shoulder. He half jumped, half fell to the side of the door, out of sight once again. Clark would have to give Wilson a 4.0 on hammer pitching on his next evaluation, provided either of them lived long enough to write about it.

"Thomas, or whoever you are," Clark shouted. He was at Wilson's side in time to see Yuri tumble out of view. "That pistol is not going to do you much good in the dark. If you can't see it, you can't shoot it." Yuri didn't answer.

"It looks like we have a stalemate," Clark continued loudly. If he could get him talking, they might work something out. Isn't that what the police did in hostage situations?

"In case you are thinking of doing anything foolish in the forward part of the ship to annoy us, just remember we can stop the main engines. That means that the ship sinks and us with it." Clark spoke to the oval of light and waited for an answer.

"We will do that rather than let you get your hands on the ship," Clark said. "I have also shut the hull valves for the aft main ballast tanks, so don't even think about surfacing the ship."

"All we want is the submarine," Yuri's sullen voice came through the hatch. "You will be released safely if you come out with your hands up."

"Released safely just like the rest of the crew?" Wilson bellowed. "Is that what you mean by *safely*?" Clark put his hand on Wilson's arm. Those were the most words Clark had heard Wilson speak in one coherent sentence during the entire cruise.

"They weren't supposed to die. I had nothing to do

with that. I told you that." Their voices carried back and forth easily despite the ever-present rumble of machinery.

"Perhaps not," Clark said, "but they are just as dead. The people you are working for could never let it be known that they had captured, or stolen, a United States submarine. Who are they? Terrorists? Russians? They cannot afford to have survivors. Even if you meant what you said, they would never let us live. If we give up, we will never get out of this alive. I would be surprised if they let you live; you know too much.

"I suggest you give yourself up. I've released the emergency buoy, and there will be U.S. ships on the surface waiting for us. Give up, and we can all get out of this alive."

"What better treatment could I expect at the hands of the Americans?" Yuri said, bitterness lacing his voice. "Intentionally or accidentally, a lot of people have died because of me. What better treatment can I expect from you?"

Clark could not answer that question without spinning a seine of lies. He knew he should give Yuri some reassurance that nothing would happen to him, but he couldn't make himself do it.

"I perceive by your silence that you agree with me, Senior Chief. You see? My position has become untenable. I have no other choice but to go forward."

Clark waited, but Yuri said nothing else. There wasn't much else to negotiate. Clark certainly wasn't giving up. Clark touched Wilson's shoulder. "I'll be at the high-pressure air manifold," he whispered.

Back at the air manifold, Clark removed the locking pins from several valves. In the semidarkness, working by sense of touch, he shifted valve positions, opening some, closing others. The plastic-covered handles were barely visible in the dim light from the emergency lamps, but Clark knew where each valve was and what it did. This was his system. The Auxiliary Division was responsible for maintaining the system and making sure everyone on board was qualified to operate the system. He knew it by heart.

Clark attached a crescent wrench to the handle of a ball valve. The ball valve ended in a short pipe, which vented into a muffler. Ball valves are larger than the pipes that they are part of. They have a cylindrical opening in the center that is the same diameter as the pipe. Ball valves are highly efficient, because when rotated ninety degrees, the ball valve goes from fully shut to fully open. Clark attached a piece of light rope to the end of the wrench and returned to wait by Wilson. He played out the rope behind him.

"We've got him now, Wilson. If he steps through that watertight door, I will dump the air pressure from the header, and that emergency watertight door will slam shut like a meat cleaver."

"Sounds good to me, Senior Chief."

"If we miss him, it's going to be you and me and crescent wrenches against Thomas somebody and a pistol. By now he has probably located a flashlight, which will even the odds. If anything happens to me, and you're still OK, you'll have to hand-crank the watertight door open and go forward. If you get to the control room, blow the main ballast tanks and surface the ship."

USS Nimitz

ADMIRAL Armstrong paced restlessly back and forth, oblivious to the other men on the bridge. *I suppose I should be in my bunk,* he thought. The task force would enter the submarine operating area for the *King* in the early morning hours, and then he would have to be available on a minute's notice. Still, he doubted he would sleep if he did lie down.

Armstrong stopped pacing, balancing against the slow, very slow, roll of the ship. Not like the destroyers he had commanded in his younger days. In those days, in the rough North Atlantic, thirty-degree rolls were nothing. On an aircraft carrier, especially one this size, a couple of degrees of roll or pitch was a big event. That was not merely because it was unexpected, given the size of the ship. More than a few degrees, and the aircraft on the flight deck and other equipment not tied down would roll off the deck into the ocean. It would be embarrassing, to say the least, to explain how he had lost several $30 million airplanes over the side.

He looked out of the bridge windows at the points of light that comprised his armada, bobbing in the darkness around him. From his vantage point Armstrong could see the green starboard running lights of the ships on the port side of the aircraft carrier. His old memory trick for keeping port and starboard lights straight sprang unexpectedly to mind; port, like wine, is red.

Admiral Armstrong always felt better to see for himself. The task force units were searching the area for hundreds of miles around the task force, both above and below the sea, with sound waves, radar waves, infrared detectors, and night-seeing optical sensors. What good was another pair of eyes on the bridge? Yet he had to see for himself. He was responsible for these men and their ships in every sense of the word.

He had seen what he needed to see, yet he still put off going to bed. There was a tension in the air that wouldn't let him sleep. There was an assigned task, a job to do, a mission. This high-priority evolution was more worthwhile than cruising on station with the battle group performing the standard exercises and making port calls to show the flag. This was a chance to do something important, something meaningful. This was what he had trained for during the long thirty years of his career.

The satellite intelligence and the long-range reconnaissance aircraft launched from the aircraft carrier gave Armstrong a clear picture of the Russian units. They had altered course in the general direction of the same ocean area toward which his task force was steaming. Normally, the Russian and American units would avoid operations in the same area to reduce the possibility of any confrontation. There was too great a chance that a Russian ship and a U.S. ship would collide, or that action taken by one side might be considered aggressive and lead to an outbreak of hostilities, even in this new age of détente.

What were those damn Russians up to? They had kept most of their fleet in port since the breakup of the Soviet Union. Now they were confronting Ukrainians at every opportunity and making belligerent noises at the United States again. Their military policies seemed to change as frequently as their leaders.

Armstrong's orders, however, were quite clear. Proceed to operating area Sierra, and stand by to render assistance to a U.S. submarine. Avoid contact with Russian naval units, if possible, while remaining in the operating area. Damn hard to do, especially with most of the Russian Black Sea fleet moving into the same operating area.

Admiral Armstrong could see the officer of the deck watching him surreptitiously. Armstrong continued staring out to sea. The OOD no doubt wished he would go below or go up to the flag bridge or just go away. Armstrong rolled his head to the left, right, back, and the rest of the way around. It made a satisfying click as it reached the different cardinal points. There was an extra knot of tension in the muscles at the back of his neck that built up as they approached the submarine operating area.

The bridge phone squawked twice. The OOD picked it up and said, "Officer of the Deck." He listened for a moment and hung up.

"Messenger of the Watch," the OOD said to a watch

stander. "Inform the captain that the officer of the deck sends his respects and wishes to report that radio is receiving a sub sunk message from approximately seventy degrees off the port bow. Combat information center is attempting to get a geographic fix on the signal with directional ranging from the other ships."

The messenger of the watch said, "Aye, aye, sir." He saluted smartly and left.

"Admiral . . ." the officer of the deck said, stepping up to Armstrong and saluting.

"Thank you," Armstrong interrupted. "I overheard your message to the captain. I'll be back in flag plots. You may expect orders to change course to port. We will follow a line of bearing to the emergency signal."

The admiral left the bridge, barely ahead of the officer of the deck's "Aye, aye, sir."

Entering flag plot, Admiral Armstrong started issuing orders to the flag watch officer before he was completely in the room. "Send a message to Supreme Allied Commander, Europe, with copies to CINCLANTFLEET, and the National Command Authority. 'In receipt of a submarine emergency message. I am ordering a change of course to investigate. Request amplified rules of engagement and weapons release authority.' " The duty radioman scribbled frantically to keep up.

"That's the end of the first message." He turned to the duty officer. "What's our present course?"

"Zero eighty-five degrees true, sir."

"Very well. Order task force units to alter course to zero fifteen true. Can the carrier launch aircraft on that course?"

"I believe so, sir."

"Don't guess; find out! I want two additional aircraft in the air as soon as possible. How far ahead of the task force is the submarine screen?"

"Approximately eighty miles, sir," the watch officer

said without looking up, still jotting notes. Armstrong paused to let him catch up.

"Order my staff to come to flag plot immediately." He stopped to think. Was there anything else?

The admiral sat down to wait for his staff. A yeoman brought a cup of hot, black coffee. Armstrong knew that while the fleet ran on fuel oil, the sailors, including Armstrong, ran on coffee. He smiled. "Thanks." Never forget the troops, especially when things were busy. It was easy to be nice when the tempo was easy. It was tough, but more important, when things got rough. You set the tone by how you reacted.

Armstrong wondered if he had forgotten anything. Should the task force speed be increased? No, the slower units couldn't keep up. The throttles were already to the firewall on the escorts. Any faster, and the frigates, with their special underwater submarine-sensing equipment, would fall behind, leaving the carrier exposed. The carrier was too valuable to leave uncovered. Losing her could very well mean losing the Mediterranean in the event of war. While the submarines operating ahead provided some early detection capabilities, they had to slow down periodically in order to effectively use their sensors, and then sprint ahead. There was a limit to even the high-speed capability of the fast, nuclear-powered submarines.

No, best to maintain speed, getting aircraft launched and out along the line of bearing to provide further information.

Damn, he thought. He pounded his fist on the plotting table. The coffee bounced but didn't spill. Everyone in flag plot watched him from the corner of their eye, waiting to see if they had screwed up. There weren't enough detailed instructions. In many ways it was nice to be given the opportunity to react to unfolding events as he saw fit, and no one could foresee all possible situations, but there were those back in the States who would cheerfully hang him if things turned out badly. There was a five-sided building by the Potamac back in Washington, full of Monday-morning quarterbacks. Each of them would have done it differently, could have done it better, after watching the replay. Well, this was what he had trained for since that first day at the Academy. *I just hope it's not a hot war.*

USS Phoenix

COMMANDER James Hammer, commanding officer of the USS *Phoenix*, sat in the captain's chair on the conning tower. He was doing his best to relax. He pressed his hands on the armrest to raise his hips off the chair. It was pretty bad when your ass went to sleep, but pacing was worse. It made him more nervous rather than less, but this sitting was going to give him hemorrhoids.

His submarine was essentially blind while running at high speed, which is what he was doing now. The sonar array couldn't pick up anything over the ship's own self-generated noise at this speed. Most of the equipment ran at high speed during a sprint, and quiet as the 688-class ship was, its pumps, motors, and generators still made noise. The faster they ran, the more noise.

But to maintain the ship's position relative to the battle group, it was necessary to sprint ahead. Then the sub would slow to the best listening speed and search the ocean for thousands of feet in all directions. Meanwhile, the battle group would close in on them, and they would have to sprint ahead again. Armstrong had been driving them awful fast over the last few days.

"All ahead, one-third," he ordered.

"Ahead one-third, aye," the diving officer repeated.

Not able to stand the suspense any longer, he jumped up and walked over to look at the computer-generated maneuvering board showing the ship's position relative to the symbol for the theoretical position of the battle group. The computer solution still showed the position of the carrier group based on the projected course and speed from the last sonar fix. It would take a few minutes for the ship to coast to a good listening speed and positively locate all of the U.S. forces. And then sort out foreign forces if there were any in the area.

"Captain," said the phone talker. "Sonar reports air noise twenty degrees off the starboard bow." The phone talker lifted one of the earphones to listen for the captain's response.

Hammer picked up the handheld unit, bypassing the phone talker in his rush to get the information. "Sonar, this is the captain. Do you detect high-speed screw noises?" His voice was tight, and he clipped the words off precisely but under control, no panic. The sound of air propelling a torpedo out of a submarine's torpedo tube was one of the worst sounds a submariner could hear. The other was the high-speed whine of the torpedo's propeller.

"Captain, sonar. No high-speed screw noise. Repeat, negative high-speed screw noise. We believe this to be a buoy launch of some type."

"Do you have a fix on distance?" His voice relaxed, a little more lazy, a touch of New York creeping back in.

"No sir." The response from sonar over the handheld phone was clearly audible around the conning stand. "We'll need a longer baseline. If you can change course perpendicular to the target, we can get a triangulation from the towed array. Also there was another noise—"

"Wait," the captain cut him off. "Officer of the deck, come left, steer course north." It would take a few minutes to steady on the new course.

"What was the other noise?" he asked, returning his attention to the handset without waiting for the officer of the deck's reply.

"When we heard the buoy launch, we detected what appeared to be an echo. It's like the noise from the buoy launch bounced off something else nearby. It was very faint. There may be another submarine out there, and close. We're not sure; we are just starting to pick up some equipment noise from the first contact."

"Very well, sonar. Let me know when you have something."

"Captain, there is something else." Hammer could hear the hesitancy in the man's voice, even over the phone set.

"Spit it out, sailor." Impatience colored Hammer's voice. This was no time to pussyfoot around.

"It sounded like a gunshot. I can't believe anyone would fire a gun in a sub, Captain, but that's what it sounded like."

"Sonar, conn, aye." Hammer hung up the phone.

"Officer of the Deck, when sonar has enough data to calculate distance to the contact, bring the towed array shallow so that we can get a depth fix on the contact."

"Aye, aye, sir," said the officer of the deck.

"XO, what do you make of this?" Hammer said, drawing the executive officer to the side and lowering his voice to a whisper.

"Our instructions on the situation are pretty vague, sir. Possible interference with a U.S. submarine could mean almost anything. If we are getting an echo from another submarine out there, it's not one of ours, and it is not one of the NATO submarines. That means it is probably Russian. The Ukrainians didn't get any subs with their small part of the Black Sea fleet."

Hammer nodded. "That's my thought, XO. You relieve as officer of the deck. Go to battle stations. Have the word passed by word of mouth and sound-powered phone. I don't want to have our own public address system give us away." He said.

He put his hand on the XO's arm as he started to turn

away. "I'm pretty sure that's the *King*. It's at the right place, at the right time. When we have established her course, load the mini-sub in the tube. Set it to swim out parallel the course of the *King*. Get it set up to simulate 688 noise." Hammer hunched over to talk to his executive officer. It seemed he was always stooping over to keep his six-foot-tall body from beating his head against the overhead, while talking to the shorter people you usually found on submarines.

"Set up only, XO. Don't activate the simulator until I give the orders. Run all checks on the decoy active sonar. We may want the decoy to go active on sonar while we hide in the background." Hammer ran his hand through his long black hair while he considered whether he had missed anything. The XO waited patiently. Hammer was still shaken up by what he had thought was a torpedo launch. If anyone did fire a torpedo, he wanted the mini-sub out there drawing fire away from his submarine.

"I'm going to be on the horn with radio. I want to float a communication buoy to keep the admiral informed of what we are doing."

As the captain picked up the telephone, the executive officer turned to the officer of the deck. "Lieutenant Smith, I relieve you as officer of the deck. Report to your battle station."

"I stand relieved sir," Lieutenant Smith said, handing over the keys to the weapons access panel. "Attention in control. The XO has the conn." The quartermaster entered the change in ship log.

Lieutenant Smith walked the few feet from the conning stand to the weapons control panel. As weapons officer, his battle station was supervising the fire control panel in control, which handled the targeting for the torpedo and cruise missiles.

"So we're finally going to get to fire up the baby sub," Lieutenant Smith said quietly to the XO as he rigged the sound-powered phones around his neck. He unwound the cord and plugged it into a phone jack.

"I thought you had launched the mini-sub before," the XO said, crouching down on the raised conning stand to bring his face level with Smith.

"No, sir. The only time this ship has launched the mini-sub was during sea trials out of the shipyard. That was before I reported aboard. At five million bucks each, the Navy lets you launch these things only under certain meteorological conditions, like during the blue phase of the moon, or when the temperature of the sea in hell is less than thirty-two degrees Fahrenheit."

"I get your point." The XO chuckled. "Without a re-covery vessel standing by to recover Baby, it's gone. There's no way to get Baby back into the torpedo tube, after it is flushed out with the bathwater."

"This isn't the time to bullshit!" said the captain, hanging up the phone to radio. "I want reports on man-ning battle stations, and I want them now."

"Aye aye, sir," the XO and weapons officer said in uni-son. The captain ran a good ship but he had a hair trigger. When the pressure was on, you didn't want to be on the firing line in his crosshairs.

THE radio supervisor for the watch section, a tall, black, muscular first class petty officer, hung up the phone from control. His teeth, showing through his broad smile, would have made Colgate proud.

Sandburg, a third class petty officer, looked over and asked, "What are you smiling about Bailey?"

"We're going to send a message," Bailey said, slap-ping his thigh.

"You mean we're going to surface?" Sandburg said hopefully. This was his first patrol, and he was standing an under instruction watch. Anything to break up the routine would be nice, but a look at the sun would be best. Well, best after women. After women and a drink.

"No, I don't mean we're going to surface," Bailey said, exasperation in his voice. "We're going to battle stations, we're playing hide-and-seek with the Russians, so the last thing we want to do is surface and send a message. You surface and send a message, and everyone will know where you are.

"Now think about it, Sandburg. I know you're not qualified on subs yet, but you've been to Radio School and you've been to Sub School. How do you send a message from a submarine without surfacing and raising the radio mast?"

"You send it on sonar," Sandburg said, his face brightening.

"No! Come on, think. We're eight miles in front of the task force." Bailey stood and pulled the operating procedures out of the bookrack. "Those surface pukes couldn't hear us if we detonated a good-sized bomb under water, let alone sent a sonar message. However, any Russian submarines nearby would sure hear us and know right where we are."

Sandburg's pale, freckled face screwed up with concentration as he worked on the problem. Bailey shook his head as he watched him. What did they teach these kids in Sub School these days? He coded the message the captain had given him.

Rolling his eyes, the supervisor patted a heavy metal pipe that disappeared into the hull overhead and said, "Sandburg, what is this thing you bump your head on several times a day?"

Sandburg's face lit up. "You're going to float a radio buoy."

"Of course, we're going to float a radio buoy. We get the message coded, feed it into the buoy, and pop the buoy up. It floats to the surface while we clear the area, shoots out a brief radio message to the battle group updating them on our situation, and sinks. It's new technology, but not that new.

"If the Russians have surface ships out there, we'll be long gone. And the buoy message is so short, they can't get a fix on it. Plus, we put in a time delay on the broadcast and we're even farther away from the scene of the crime when it sends the signal. One-way communication, sure, but slicker than snake shit.

"Get a buoy out of the locker, and let's input the message."

17. SUB V. CHOPPER

Russian Hormone Helicopter

IGOR Petrov watched the black shape of the *Moskva* grow smaller in the predawn darkness. He twisted the collective in his left hand, increasing the pitch of the rotor on the Hormone II helicopter. As he tilted the cyclic, the helicopter moved ahead, up, and away with his right forward hand.

The *Moskva* became a black shadow on the dark, night-shrouded sea as he gained altitude. The faint phosphorescence from her bow wake was soon lost among the waves.

What foolishness. Every military ship, plane, and satellite has radar, and here we are pretending that we can't be seen if we turn off the lights. He shook his head, angry that he would have to spend a good part of the night trying to keep from crashing into the almost invisible ocean. *Half of the U.S. Sixth Fleet sailing into the eastern Mediterranean, and I am flying right at them to track submarines. How better to start a war?*

Petrov flew west at 200 knots, receiving course corrections from the *Moskva*. After reaching the assigned search area, he dropped a string of sonar buoys on an east-west line. Any submarine traveling south would have to pass close to one of the buoys. He would be standing by when the buoy radioed the information to his helicopter. The buoy array was a completely passive system, and the submarine wouldn't even know it had been detected. That is, unless the helicopter launched a homing torpedo at it, he thought, smiling. The Americans would know then that they had been detected. For a few minutes before their sub blew up. This was starting to look like the good old days, when the Russian military was a force to be reckoned with.

Petrov adjusted his earphones to a more comfortable position and adjusted his controls to fly east and west along the buoy line to conserve fuel. The streamlined shape of the helicopter as it flew forward provided lift over the rotor, which kept the helicopter in the air with less fuel than hovering. Nothing more to do at this point, unless the submarine stumbled through his snare. Even then, the orders were to report to the *Moskva*, which would report to Moscow. With all decision-making centralized in Moscow, he couldn't shit without permission from headquarters.

USS Phoenix

THE XO of the *Phoenix* leaned over the shoulder of the weapons officer. "Have you got a fix on him yet, Bob?" He sneezed. He had accidentally used so much aftershave he could barely stand the smell. Old Spice, the same as when he started shaving about eighteen years ago. At least it would keep him awake.

"No, sir. If you can't hear him, you can't track him."

"The U.S. Navy buys you the most sophisticated, not to mention most expensive, integrated, computerized sonar system in the world, and you can't hear anything?" The XO knew he was demanding more than the weapons officer could give, but it gave him something for which to strive. He had high expectations of his men, but that made them perform. It was how the captain would do it. And, of course, the captain would want to know soon, anyway.

"We can hear plenty," the weapons officer said defensively. "We can hear shrimp talking, whales whistling, dolphins mating, fish farting, and once in a while a Russian sub."

The weapons officer pointed at the computerized tracking display mounted like a television set in a metal frame. The console had the smell of hot electrical equipment, almost as if electrons had an aroma. "It's just that the Russian sub is trailing the *King* and probably rigged for quiet and is just not making any noise. A shadow in the ocean."

The XO squinted at him patiently, face and forehead wrinkling upward into a balding scalp. He knew if he were patient enough the weapons officer would say more, usually more than he intended. He drew it out of him with extended pauses.

"Besides," the weapons officer continued. "We just use the input from sonar for targeting. If you want to bitch at someone, with all due respect, sir, talk to the sonar officer."

One of the enlisted men called out, "Captain in control," as the commanding officer entered. All around the darkened control room, red-light shadows stood a little straighter, and the idle conversation died out.

"Good morning, Captain," the executive officer said.

"Any changes in status, XO?" The XO could see the captain hadn't had a caffeine fix yet.

"No, sir. We are still getting intermittent detection on the Russian sub, but not enough to identify her or to run a fire control solution. We are basically tracking the *King*, and it looks like the Russian is in trail several hundred yards back and several hundred feet below. It's embarrassing to be able to track our own sub but not the Russian. We are supposed to be quieter than the Soviets."

"Right. U.S. subs are quieter. But the *King* is rigged for patrol, which means she has normal equipment running. The Russian is probably rigged for quiet, with every nonessential piece of equipment turned off, everyone not on watch in their bunk, and all housekeeping functions like serving hot meals suspended. I'm not surprised we can't hear them. The new Soviet subs are very sophisticated." He smiled. "After all, they stole the very best technology from us they could get."

"Captain," the weapons officer said, "why don't we ping them with active sonar and get a fix on them?"

"That would get a fix on them, all right, but it would also tell them we were here. It would tell them right where we are. Also it could very well be interpreted as a hostile act, preparatory to firing torpedoes." The XO was surprised, the captain could be vicious in the morning. Today he was in a pedantic mood, no pressure, training the junior officers. "I don't want to start World War III," the captain said. "Our orders are to prevent interference with the *King*. Trailing the *King* is not interference.

"However, we do need to know exactly where the Russians are, so I guess its time to stop screwing around. XO, launch the mini-sub. We will either be heroes or scapegoats."

"Launch the mini-sub, aye." The XO was not above being excited about an evolution so far out of the ordinary. The mini-sub was barely past the prototype stage. As far as he knew, this was its first operational use.

The executive officer turned to face the weapons officer. "Weapons officer, launch the mini-sub."

"Launch the mini-sub, aye," said the weapons officer,

repeating the order back in the traditional Navy manner so that there would be no mistake, the order had beeen heard and understood and would be carried out. The XO could hear the satisfaction in the weapons officer's voice as he relayed the order through the sound-powered mike at his neck. This was his equipment. It was his chance to do it right.

IN the torpedo room, the chief torpedoman repeated the order back just as carefully when he received it over the sound-powered phones. In a less formal manner, he announced to the enlisted men manning their battle stations in the torpedo room, "We're going to launch Baby."

He detached a laminated checklist from a metal-bound book mounted on the bulkhead. He gave detailed orders, referring frequently to the torpedo firing checklist he held in his hand. He knew the procedure better than anyone on the ship, perhaps better than anyone else in the world, but there was a right way, a wrong way, and the Navy way of doing things. Nobody was going to forget a critical step in the launch sequence and hot run a torpedo in the tube of his ship, by God.

The mini-sub was already tube loaded, standard practice on the subs equipped to run them. He made a check mark on the sheet with a black grease pencil to signify each completed step.

"Flood torpedo tube number eight," the chief called out.

"Flood tube eight, aye," the watch stander responded. He punched a sequence of electronic control pads that opened electrically operated valves in sequence to admit seawater to the tube. The chief knew that each component had been designed for quiet operation and machined to tolerances measured in thousandths of an inch. Nothing was left to chance on this equipment. Each part was mounted with rubber grommets to insure no noise would be transmitted to the hull and to the water. The submarine was the original stealth machine. You were quiet, or you were dead.

The chief made sure each operation was performed carefully and methodically, as it had been practiced a hundred times before. The pressure in the tube was equalized with sea pressure outside the submarine. Additional continuity checks were run to insure that the submarine could command the mini-sub through the umbilical wire that connected them, and the mini-sub could relay information back to the mother sub.

It was time for the next to the last step. The chief ordered the outer door to tube number eight rolled open, and Baby was ready. The trim pump was lined up to the tube, and the mini-sub was flushed out without a sound. The chief missed the loud *thunk* that shook the ship when the old impulse torpedoes were launched, but that sound could be heard for miles. The electric motor on the mini energized as it left the tube. No high-speed whine that was characteristic of the Mark 48 and other warshot torpedoes. This was a stealth torpedo, designed to gather information above the soundproof thermocline, while the noisier, parent submarine lurked below. Baby's purpose was to listen and not be heard, except when set for active sonar; then it was a decoy. Then it would call attention to itself and away from the mother sub. Baby was expendable.

Trailing wire, the mini-sub moved slowly and silently away from the *Phoenix.*

Russian Hormone Helicopter

IGOR Petrov rubbed his hip. His legs hurt, his whole body hurt. Flying a helicopter with a tail rotor out of balance was a lot like riding a jackhammer. Soon even your bones began to rattle under your skin and your organs turned to jelly. As the helicopter blade passed over the tail surface, the pressure on the blade was different than when it was in the open air surrounding three-quarters of the craft. As each blade passed over the tail rotor, there was another bump. Four blades times hundreds of revolutions per minute added up to a lot of bumps.

"The mechanics that fix these machines should have to ride them," Igor snorted, "preferably strapped to the tail rotor." The air in the cabin of the helicopter burned his nose. It smelled of sweat, hot engine oil, and a trace of urine. The sanitation was primitive to say the least. It was a smell Igor often hated but often came back to him in his dreams when he was away too long.

Even the brightening eastern sky could do nothing to distract him. The transformation from black to purple blue and orange pink were not high on his pyramid of primal needs. Coffee and food in any form filled his mind.

Igor Petrov often suspected that his brain had started to turn to jelly from the constant vibration. But how would you know for sure? If your mental abilities start to deteriorate, would you have the mental acuity to detect the change? It was something to think about.

Hovering over the dark, cold ocean provided too much time to think, provided his brain had not already jelled. Flying was hundreds of hours of sheer boredom punctuated by a few seconds of sheer terror. Your mind wandered, and then the terror came. A helicopter was, after all, 10,000 parts flying in close formation. If one broke formation for independent maneuvers, the rest might not all land in the same country.

Igor's introspection was interrupted by the sonar officer shaking his shoulder to draw his attention to the sonar console. Number three sonar buoy was picking up a submarine transiting. The sonar officer listened with his shoulders hunched and with both hands on the earphones to shut out external noise. The noise in the chopper was a universal constant. It permeated your body. It shook you to your soul. The sonar officer turned toward Igor with a smile and gave a thumbs-up signal.

Good. They had finally found the American submarine. Now it was time to go home and fill the fuel tank and empty the bladder. Someone else could come out and play tag with the American submarine.

As Igor reported the contact to the *Moskva*, the sonar operator again shook his shoulder to report another contact. What, another submarine? Did intelligence know of this and just forget to give the operator in the field the information needed to do a thorough job? That was like them. Trust no one.

Igor keyed the microphone to report the new information. The sonar operator again interrupted him. Number four sonar buoy picking up a contact. What is this, a parade? A contact trailing a contact trailing a contact?

Igor made his report. Let someone else worry about this; he had done his duty. It was a job.

Moscow

COLONEL Borzov watched as the data came in from the *Moskva* and was plotted on the status board. The best-laid plans had certainly gone astray this time. The three radio locator beacons all popping up at the same time had blown the game. There was no way to interpret the data that would place the *King* anywhere else but under the beacons. Now, the *King* had been located, and a Soviet submarine was in trail. Worse, there was another submarine following the Russian submarine.

It had been a near letter-perfect operation up to this point. The plan was great, and the execution was excellent. Creating an opening in the officer ranks on board the *King*, getting Yuri substituted for the officer, tracking the *King* across the Mediterranean until it was in the right position, all letter perfect. Now the Russians knew where the *King* was located. There was no way to get Ukrainians aboard. And what was this other submarine in the operating area? It had to be American. Perhaps all was not lost. It was still possible, even likely, that the Russians and the United States would be at each other's throats. The Ukraine could still get mileage out of that.

"What will you do, Borzov?"

Borzov jumped, startled to find Admiral Tikhonov standing beside him. The admiral had crept up on him unaware while he brooded.

"What do you mean, Comrade Admiral?" Borzov asked.

"Doing nothing would be the prudent thing. Whatever is happening, Russia is not yet involved. There is no international incident; we are just conducting operations in the eastern Mediterranean."

"Doing nothing would be the same as letting them go, Admiral!" Borzov almost yelled. He must convince the admiral to proceed with the plan. His face turned red as he struggled to calm himself.

"If we do nothing," Borzov said, forcing his voice to a slower pace, "the third submarine, if it is a U.S. submarine, may interfere with us putting a crew aboard when Yuri Amelko surfaces the *King*."

"So what will you do, Borzov, sink the second American submarine? The Americans can't fail to notice. Their carrier battle group is only ninety kilometers away now, and steaming in the direction of the *Moskva*."

"You know we don't have that authority, Admiral. We can, however, frighten the American submarine away,"

Borzov said. His eyes lit up as he thought of a solution. "We can go active with the helicopter dipping sonar. Once the American submarine knows he has been detected, he will depart."

"We will see," said Admiral Tikhonov. "Either you will be a hero, or the AFB will wish to disassociate itself from your plans." Borzov didn't like the way the Admiral smiled when he said it.

Russian Hormone Helicopter

"HELO one, go active on the dipping sonar."

Igor Petrov sat in stunned disbelief, forgetting for the moment to acknowledge the order he had received on the radio. Could they really be thinking of chasing the United States submarine, with the American fleet almost on top of him? He took off his earphones and looked at them before putting them back on.

"*Moskva*, say again your last radio message," he said, keying the mike.

"Helo one, go active on the dipping sonar," the radio ordered. "Locate and identify submerged contact number three."

Igor repeated the order. He was careful that the muttering he was doing under his breath did not go out over the open radio channel. He tilted the cyclic forward to move the helicopter ahead and pressed on the foot pedals to turn the tail rotor around, pointing the craft in a southerly direction. Left foot to turn right, just opposite the controls on American helicopters.

He flew the helicopter to a point ahead of where he thought the third submarine would be. He brought his craft to a standstill, hovering twenty feet above the pale sea, which was becoming visible with the approaching dawn. With two-foot rollers, the ocean was relatively calm. The breeze was steady at five knots. Good weather to maintain a steady position.

"Lower the dipping sonar," he ordered the sonar operator when the helicopter was at the proper height above the water. The sonar operator lowered the sonar to 350 meters to get below the layer, nearly the full length of its cable. Flipping switches, the operator energized the sonar transducer. Below the surface of the water, a sound pulse churned outward. On the cathode ray tube in the helicopter a green ring of light expanded outward from the center of the screen. A blip on the screen marked a point on the expanding ring, showing the direction and distance to the first submarine contact. The first blip was soon followed by a second, then a third.

Igor checked the sonar screen over his shoulder. *Now everyone knows we are here.* The sonar operator had the amplifier on, and Igor could just hear the ping of the sonar return over the ear-numbing noise of the helicopter. Igor nodded his approval.

"Recover the sonar module," he ordered. "We will fly to a new position and triangulate all three targets."

USS Phoenix

"CAPTAIN Hammer, sonar reports active sonar off the starboard bow," the sound-powered phone talker reported.

Hammer picked up the sound-powered handset, bypassing the phone talker. "Give me some details on the active sonar." Not proper phone procedure, but he was feeling impatient.

"Captain, we had a single ping. It was not from the *King* or the Russian submarine. Repeat, not from the Russian submarine. The frequency indicates it was probably a Russian helicopter. This ties in with what might have been rotor noise right before the active ping. If the helicopter is hovering low enough when using its dipping sonar, we can pick up blade noise in the water. We're going to play the tape back and check."

"Sonar, Captain, aye. Report when you have confirmed that it is a helicopter."

"XO," the captain said as he hung up the handset. "We have a helicopter topside. When he pinged us, the Russians may have picked up an echo return off us. We have to assume they know we're here."

"Do you think they're targeting us, Captain?" the XO asked.

"I don't think so. We're not at war, and relations with Russia are supposed to be OK. However, I don't know exactly what they're up to with the *King*.

"Better change course," the captain continued. "Come left thirty degrees. We'll make it hard for them to plot a course.

"Left thirty degrees, aye," the XO repeated. "Diving Officer, left standard rudder steer new course one five zero degrees."

"Captain," the phone talker said. "Sonar reports positive identification of the active sonar as a Russian helicopter-mounted sonar. Blade noises have disappeared, helicopter may be moving to a new location to triangulate our position and plot our course."

"Captain, aye." The CO turned to the executive officer. "XO, what do you think?" Hammer knew he was not the only one with good ideas. Also, it was good training for the XO. One day the XO would command his own ship, and this practice would make him better.

"Captain, I think the active ping by the helicopter may be a hostile act under the rules of engagement."

"I hope you are not implying that active sonar ranging gives us the right to fire on the Russians. We will not fire unless fired on. Is that clear, XO?" An aggressive attitude was good in a naval officer, but Hammer made a mental note that the executive officer may be a little too aggressive, especially under stress. Hammer tilted his head left, back, right, to free the tension in his neck.

"What we will do, XO, is ping him back. If he goes active again, we will put a sound pulse in the water that will blow his socks off. If the helicopter fires a torpedo at us, that is another story. We will launch an antiaircraft missile in search mode and take him out. Do we have a tube loaded?"

"Yes, sir. Tube number one."

"Captain," the phone talker reported. "Sonar reports helicopter blade noises directly ahead."

"Phone talker, Sonar," the captain ordered. "If the Russian helicopter goes active, put a high-energy sonar pulse in the water. Boil some water."

Russian Hormone Helicopter

IGOR brought his craft to a hover above the water, to the left of what he thought the track of the American submarine would be. "Lower the sonar and go active," he ordered.

The dipping sonar again slipped out of its housing and slid into the water on its steel tether. The sonar operator continued lowering the sonar to its full length below the surface of the water. He energized the transducer, generating a sound pulse.

Below the surface, the wave of sound spread out in an expanding sphere. The sound pulse reached the *Phoenix* and reflected back. The sound of the sonar could be clearly heard by the crew inside the hollow metal submarine.

In the sonar room, the chief sonarman flipped a switch on the panel to the active mode. He pushed another button. The submarine generated a full-power sound pulse from her hull-mounted sonar. The sound pulse was so strong that it literally boiled the water in the immediate vicinity of the sonar dome.

On board the helicopter, Igor watched as the return echo from the helicopter marked the position of the American submarine. The return echo was immediately followed by the high-energy pulse generated by the *Phoenix*.

Sound, if the intensity level is high enough, can cause excruciating pain. This sound level was more than sufficient. The sonar operator shrieked and tore his earphones off his head. Igor had switched his headphones to receive input from the sonar panel. Unfortunately, he had his hands on the controls. His hands jerked back in a reflex action, causing the helicopter to strain upwards. Below the surface, the sonar, held to the helicopter by a steel cable, acted as a sea anchor. The cable was strong, but not designed to tie down a helicopter under full power. It parted with a snap.

As the helicopter jumped upward, released from its tether, a torpedo mounted below the fuselage dislodged from its mounting. Falling into the ocean, the salt water activated its motor. Not programmed, it was essentially operating blind. But the helicopter was pointed toward the *Phoenix*, so the torpedo ran straight and true toward the submarine.

USS Phoenix

"**CONN,** Sonar. High-speed screw noises! Sounds like torpedo. From the general direction of the active helicopter sonar."

"Left full rudder, ahead full. Come to a reciprocal course." Without waiting for a reply, the CO turned to the weapons officer. "Activate the mini-sub and snap shoot torpedo tube number one."

"Activate the mini-sub, aye," the weapons officer repeated as he reached over the operator's head and flipped the proper toggle switch.

"All ahead full," the executive officer acknowledged.

"Fire one," the weapons officer ordered the weapons panel operator. He repeated the order over the sound-powered phones, passing the information to his people in the torpedo room. "Snap shot, tube number one."

As the team in the torpedo room rushed to carry out their assignment, signals were transmitted to the mini-sub over the electronic umbilical that connected it to the mother submarine. Prerecorded sounds in the mini-sub's computer were transmitted to its sonar transducer, amplified, and broadcast into the water. To anyone listening on nearby sonar, the mini-sub sounded just like a 688-class submarine that had appeared out of nowhere. Pump noises were present, screw noises, and other sounds associated with a full-sized submarine.

On board the *Phoenix*, the muzzle door to torpedo tube number one rolled open, and a canister was impulsed out. No need for quiet now. As the canister left the tube, buoyancy carried it upward toward the surface. At fifty feet below the surface, pressure-sensitive switches detonated explosive bolts, which separated the two halves of the canister. Other switches closed to transmit an electronic signal to ignite the rocket motor of the modified sea sparrow missile inside. The missile rose from the water on a column of fire.

As the missile left the water, it climbed to five hundred feet and started a preprogrammed, circular search pattern. Its infrared detector scanned the air in front of it. It had made almost one full circle when its heat sensor picked up the hot motor exhaust from the Hormone helicopter against the cold ocean background.

Igor had seen the missile leave the water. He knew immediately what it was and banked the helicopter sharply. He knew what his chances were. The missile had an airspeed more than three times that of the Hormone. He barely had time to start a turn away and tilt the craft forward to gather speed before the missile hit. The helicopter disintegrated when the missile detonated, its thousands of parts and pieces flying apart.

Below the surface, the torpedo launched by the helicopter passed by the mini-sub and continued past the *Phoenix*. The fall from the helicopter into the water was enough to activate the motor, but the warhead wasn't armed.

18. LAST ONE OUT

USS **Martin Luther King**

YURI leaned against the circuit breaker panels and closed his eyes. The warm heat from the electric current, lifeblood of the ship, soaked into his back. The pain in his arm from the jagged cut of the grinding wheel was like an electric shock, jolting him in time to his pulse. He sat quietly and could hear his heartbeat in his ears, still well over a hundred times a minute. Some silly song from his childhood kept flirting with the corners of his mind, a fragment that toyed with his vocal cords and was gone.

What was Illya doing now? He tried to picture a proper map in his mind, but he couldn't concentrate. Maybe she was on her way home. He walked through the route she would take. Was she at work? He pictured her in the tight skirt and loose sweater she preferred. What time was it in Moscow? Is the longitude in the eastern Mediterranean the same as Moscow? It must be morning in Moscow. He couldn't keep it straight.

He imagined her walking to work with her ready bag

on her arm, like all the women. Ready for a bargain,
something in stock at the store for a change. *Glasnost*
filled the souls of the people with hope but left their stom-
achs empty. Capitalism was fine, but people had to eat.

Does she think of me? Perhaps there was telepathy
when two people were so much in tune. *Maybe she will
know I am thinking of her. Perhaps there is someone else*,
he thought with a sudden empty feeling. He regretted that
he had never married Illya. It didn't seem important at the
time; now it was everything.

Yuri looked at the gaping, black hatch leading to the
engine room. They were waiting for him, of course. A
standoff was no good. That was as good as a loss. He
would have to surface the ship, which meant that he would
have to eliminate these two men who stood between him
and success. Would killing two more matter after murder-
ing one hundred? Borzov had lied to him, of course, but
was there anything else left except to go forward? There
was no way to go back.

He tightened the tourniquet on his arm, letting his
breath escape slowly. It was time.

JOSHUA Clark crouched next to Wilson in the semidarkness. They both watched the small section of the missile
compartment visible through the open hatch. The light
from the missile compartment faded into the blackness
that surrounded them and filled the engine room. The familiar hum of machinery was strangely comforting. It
was a touch of normalcy in a world that had spun off its
pivot.

Clark held the line from the valve in his hand, ready to
shut the watertight door at the first sign of movement. He
wiped his hands on his trousers and looped the nylon
rope in his hand.

Beside him, Wilson held the wrench, eager to improve

his pitching record if Thomas showed himself again. Wilson seemed more focused and more alive than he had ever been. He continually shifted back and forth on his feet, unable to remain still. He was like a tiger whose tail will twitch as he lies in the bush, with the rest of his body completely motionless.

There had been no activity for twenty minutes, and "Thomas" hadn't answered any of their attempts to restart the conversation. The constant alertness was starting to wear on Clark.

"What do you think he's doing, Senior Chief?" Wilson whispered. "Do you suppose he's gone forward?"

"No, I think he's waiting. Waiting for one of us to get impatient and stick his head through that door. Waiting for us to relax."

"What are we going to do?"

"We are going to outwait him." Clark said, looking at Wilson's dim outline in the dark beside him. Wilson had come a long way. "I don't know if there is anything else we can do. We can't surface the ship from the engineering space because there's no way to blow the forward ballast tanks. He can't surface the ship from forward without us, because he thinks we have the lines to the after ballast tanks closed."

Clark looked back toward the hatch. "He'll have to move before we do. My guess is that he will want to surface the ship during the nighttime, and since its almost daylight on the surface—"

He was cut off in midsentence as Yuri stepped in front of the door and fired several shots at random into the darkened space, left, right, center. Yuri jumped rapidly to the other side of the entrance, out of sight. The bullets made a high-pitched whine as they glanced off steel-cased machinery. A shower of sparks cascaded down a motor breaker panel.

Clark and Wilson ducked their heads down behind the

workbench, not that it would stop a bullet. The sound damping tiles on the hull of the submarine cut short what should have been a hell of an echo. Yuri stepped back in front of the door and fired again.

The sound of the pistol left a loud ringing in Clark's head. He put his hand on Wilson's shoulder and shouted, "Get ready, he'll be coming through now." His other hand tightened on the rope to the valve.

Still firing, Yuri jumped headfirst through the hatch. Joshua pulled the rope tight, opening the air valve, as Yuri's head passed through the hatch. The scream of high-pressure air from the header, venting into the bilge, sounded like a Boeing 747 ready for takeoff.

The air-operated watertight door to the engine room snapped shut, catching Yuri just below the hips, crushing his legs between the watertight door and the bulkhead. The door hesitated momentarily with the meaty part of Yuri's legs caught in it now, and closed part of the remaining distance, leaving the compartment in almost complete darkness. The sound of venting air, added to the high-pitched whine of the turbines, the generators, pumps, and motors, was loud enough to cause physical pain. Clark clamped his hands over his ears. He could still hear Yuri's scream above all the other noises.

Wilson hefted his wrench. "Come on, Senior Chief," he shouted. "We've got that sucker now." He started forward.

Clark reluctantly took his hands off his head. He restrained Wilson with his hand on his shoulder.

"Wait," he said.

The scream still echoed in his head. He had a rabbit named Patches when he was growing up. One day he had been horsing around with his sisters, and he had stepped on Patches and broken his back. The rabbit had screamed, something he didn't know rabbits could do. It took a long time for the rabbit to die.

Yuri's flashlight had gone out when his upper body

flopped on the floor, legs held in place by the door. It suddenly came on and flashed back and forth across the passageway. He fired another shot, and Clark and Wilson pulled their heads back behind the bench.

"Listen up, Thomas," Clark yelled, keeping his head down. No way he was going to call him Mister. "I know you're wedged in the door. That's where you're going to stay until we let you out. Now throw down your pistol, and we'll override the door controls and release you."

Yuri fired another shot. The bullet passed through the sheet metal locker near Clark's shoulder. Clark hurriedly moved behind a heavy trim pump.

"This is foolish," Clark shouted, anger in his voice. "You need medical attention. Let us help you. We'll free you, surface the ship, and get help."

"You don't want to surface the ship. You don't know what's waiting for you up there," Yuri said, his voice thick with pain. "They lied to me. I know what they'll do to you."

"Well, we can't stay here. What do you suggest we do? You've got the gun. The evaporators are still turning salt water into fresh water and sending it somewhere. The oxygen generators are turning fresh water into oxygen. The balance of the ship is changing. A submarine can't stay stable forever. We'll go through water of different temperatures, and the hull will contract or expand. We're eventually going to sink."

Yuri was quiet, pondering the situation. The pain was terrible, but worse was the sick feeling, knowing that his legs were crushed. There was no way he would ever be the same. He once saw a legless man begging for change, his body on a dolly with wheels. It was in America, in New York. The sight had been so terrible and surprising he had turned away, pretending he didn't hear. Illya must never see him like that.

"You two can go," Yuri said, reaching a decision. Borzov had put him in this position. He would make sure Borzov got no profit from it.

"Go out the emergency escape trunk. I won't stop you."

"Let us take you with us."

"No, I'll stay here."

"Let us surface the ship, and we can all three get out of this," Clark tried again, keeping his head out of sight as Yuri's flashlight searched the darkness around them.

"No, go now if you're going." Anger edged around his voice.

"How do we know you won't shoot us as we climb the ladder to the escape trunk?" Wilson shouted, hardheaded and practical.

"That's your problem. I don't care. You can go one at a time if you like. When one is safely up, then the next one can go."

"All right, we'll go up one at a time," Clark said. Then in a lower voice to Wilson, "I think he means what he says. I'll go first. When I've entered the escape trunk, and only then, you come on up."

"We aren't going to let him get away with this, are we, Chief? Let's finish him off. I'll go around the evaporator, and we can come at him from both sides."

"No," Joshua said putting his hand on Wilson's shoulder. "Now you're asking us to play judge and jury. Even if he killed every person on board, and I'm sure he did, we can't kill him in cold blood. Then it's murder. And there's always a chance we won't succeed.

"I didn't want to say anything to you before while we were waiting for something to happen, but I heard the hull creak several times," Clark said. Wilson, a shadow in the darkness beside him, looked anxiously at the cylindrical hull of the sub curving above their heads. "I think we are getting deeper, slowly but surely. The deeper we get, the more the hull contracts, the less buoyancy the ship has, and the sub sinks more. The hull contracts again, and the pace of descent accelerates.

"The deeper we are when we start our ascent from the escape trunk, the less chance we have of reaching the surface without nitrogen bubbles coming out of our blood and us getting the bends. So we really can't wait him out."

Wilson kept smacking the crescent wrench in his hand and looked from Clark toward the sliver of light that marked the watertight door into the missile compartment.

"Listen to me, Wilson." Clark grabbed Wilson's shoulders. There was a temptation to shake Wilson to make sure he was paying attention, but Clark let it pass. "Your life depends on this. If something happens to me on the way to the escape trunk, do your best and try to get forward. Blow the main ballast tanks. Contrary to what I have been telling Thomas, they are all operational. I don't think you will be able to get out the escape trunk, submerged, by yourself."

Without waiting for an answer from Wilson, Clark called to Yuri, "I'm going now."

He started forward, moving slowly in the nearly pitch-black compartment. Yuri flashed the light in Clark's face, then moved it to the area in front of his feet. Clark realized with surprise that he was afraid, terrified. Up until now he had merely been reacting. Now he was out in front of a madman with a pistol. His testicles were pulled so far up inside him they hurt.

He stifled a laugh as it bubbled to his lips. If he started laughing, he might not be able to stop. But it was funny. He was on the verge of being shot, and he was worried about his balls. Sarah would have some choice comment about that. He hoped they would be able to laugh about it later.

Forward of maneuvering, Joshua started up the ladder leading to the escape trunk. Yuri followed him with the flashlight. Clark never realized the ladder was so long. He noticed as if for the first time the no-skid coating on the riser treads, how the joint between the vertical rails and the steps had been buttered in by the welder. Moving cautiously, careful not to make any rapid moves, he rotated the large, stainless steel handwheel to undo the lower hatch to the escape trunk. He pushed it upward and inward and climbed up after it.

Wilson followed him more rapidly, crab-walking near the wall to present a small profile. Yuri followed him with the light.

Clark flipped on the waterproof battle lantern in the escape trunk as Wilson climbed in. Together they dogged the lower watertight door behind them.

"We're deeper than I thought." Clark said. He checked the external pressure gauge. "So we are going to have to move rapidly once we start flooding the trunk, in order to minimize the amount of time we are breathing high-pressure air. Otherwise, we will have the bends when we reach the surface no matter what we do. The bends, nitrogen bubbles in the blood, depend on the pressure and on the time spent at that pressure." His voice echoed, hollow and metallic in the four-foot-diameter, vertical metal tube. The sickly yellow light from the battery-operated lamp barely filled the space.

"Put on this life vest, and we'll inflate it when we get to the surface," Joshua said, handing Wilson a yellow rubberized vest.

"We're going to leave the inflatable raft here," Clark said. He grabbed the cylinder of rolled-up, vulcanized yellow rubber that filled the Y-shaped tube that sloped upward from the main hatch, and pulled it down. "There's too much of a danger of it getting caught accidentally in the escape trunk. I've heard of that happening, and we just don't have time to fool around with it at this pressure." He pulled on his inflatable life jacket as he talked.

"I've already checked that the drain valves to the escape trunk are shut. I'm going to have you operate this valve." Clark put his hand on the valve marked Air Supply. "This will help pressurize the escape trunk while I'm flooding. Normally we would flood first and then pressurize, but we want to minimize our time at this pressure as much as possible. Pressurize to this mark," Clark said. He pointed to a mark on an internal pressure gauge.

Wilson's eyes, large and ringed with white, darted back and forth to gauges and valves in the dim, closet-sized, circular room. Clark took the wrench from Wilson's hand. He didn't seem to notice.

"We don't want to overpressurize," Clark continued. "Then we would have trouble undogging the upper hatch. We don't want to underpressurize either, for the same reason." He noticed Wilson's increasing nervousness. He was talking now as much to relax Wilson as he was to prepare the escape trunk.

"Don't worry about the water coming in over your head, there's a built-in air pocket here between the escape trunk hatch and the regular, operational hatch. The water should only flood up to our chests with you adding air as we go. Are there any questions? Do you understand?"

Wilson nodded and said, "Yes, Senior Chief." His eyes never stopped flitting around the small, enclosed space, like trapped birds.

"Good man," Clark said putting his arm on Wilson's shoulder. "Once we start pressurizing, we won't be able to talk because of the air noise. If you have any questions, ask now." Wilson nodded, his mouth hanging open.

"As we flood the trunk, that's going to add even more weight to the submarine and cause it to sink a little bit faster. Act rapidly, but don't get rushed. We should have enough time.

"Remember your training from Sub School. When we get pressurized, I'm going to let you go out first. You'll hold your breath until you get out of the escape trunk, and then you'll pucker your lips and start blowing air out on the way up. I'm going to be right behind you. Don't forget to blow out air."

"Right, Senior Chief." Wilson said, but his eyes had a dazed look.

Clark hesitated, considering whether to repeat everything again.

He decided against it.

"All right, start now." Clark opened the flood valves and cold sea water cascaded in about their ankles and swirled rapidly to their knees. It was unbelievableably cold. At this depth the water temperature must be forty degrees Fahrenheit. His body went numb as the sea water rose around him.

Wilson stood unmoving. Clark pushed him out of the way and opened the air valves. The rush of air into the small, enclosed space was deafening. The smell was like old rubber shoes that had been put away wet. Watching the internal pressure and the external pressure gauge, Joshua throttled back on the air. As the water reached their shoulders, Joshua again opened the air valve full.

Wilson clung to the ladder, climbing higher as the water rose. Joshua watched as the internal pressure gauge climbed to above indicated sea pressure and then settled back to match the external pressure. He cut off the air. After the near-deafening rush of air, the silence in the small, enclosed air pocket in the trunk was awesome.

"Now is the time for all good men to save their ass," Clark said, cranking open the escape trunk outer hatch, the one to the Y branch. "Let's get out while the getting is good."

Wilson nodded, his knuckles white as he gripped the ladder with all his strength.

"There's no way I can wrestle you out of this trunk, Wilson. You are going to have to go on your own." Wilson nodded but still didn't move. His face quivered, and he swallowed repeatedly.

"We're going to change the game plan, Wilson," Clark said, pulling Wilson around behind him. "I'm going to go first, but I want you to hold onto my belt and go out with me." Wilson's head bobbed up and down.

"On the way out, blow air out all the way up, just like you practiced in the tower at Sub School. If you're not blowing out air, I'm going to have to hit you in the stomach to make you blow out. Are you ready?"

"Yes, Senior Chief." This was now his standard reply. He did well with yes and no answers, Clark thought. He would have made a good witness.

"Take a deep breath and follow me," Clark said. "Wait until we are out of the trunk before you start blowing. Blow out like you are blowing through a tube. Purse your lips so you get some resistance. Grab my belt. Ready? One . . . two . . . three . . ."

Clark took a deep breath and ducked his head under water. He started up the long, slippery, side tube that connected the engine room hatch to the escape trunk. He pulled himself along the sides of the trunk on the ladder. He breathed a mental sigh of relief when he reached the hatch to the escape trunk, finding it was not fouled or blocked.

Releasing his grip on the edge of the hatch, he starting floating upward at a faster and faster pace. He could feel Wilson's hands tightly gripping his belt.

Reaching for Wilson's hand, he realized it was too dark to see if Wilson was blowing out any air or not. It was too late to do anything now if he wasn't. They had been in high pressure an awful long time anyway. Either they were going to get the bends when they got to the surface, or they weren't.

The trip to the surface seemed to be taking forever. The seconds telescoped outward like hours. How long could the human body go without air? The cold water at that depth would slow the metabolism, but the high state of near panic had made his heart beat like a sprinter in the escape trunk. Even blowing out air, which seemed to be in endless supply as the air in the lungs and blood expanded, didn't seem to end the desperate, claustrophobic feeling of the ascent through hundreds and hundreds of feet of water.

The surface above looked like a translucent mirror in the early morning light. It looked like you could almost reach your hand out and touch it, but it seemed to get no closer. It was just out of reach, no matter how fast you ran.

His body floated upward faster and faster, like a balloon released by a small child, until it reached terminal velocity. *Terminal* seemed an appropriate choice of words. He could not go any faster if he kicked his feet, but he did anyway, careful of Wilson.

His lungs ached, and there was no more air to blow out. Still he rose. Long after he thought he could wait no longer, he waited. His head broke through the surface. He sucked air that never had tasted so sweet. It was intoxicating. Wilson's head bobbed out of the water, his face inches from Clark.

Clark started laughing. "Good work, old buddy, we made it."

Wilson seemed a little dazed, still holding onto Clark's belt. Finally he gave a hesitant laugh as if trying it on for size, and then laughed again. Soon they were both laughing with total abandon, with near hysteria, hugging each other and treading water.

Clark sobered up first. "Get your life vest inflated," he said, pulling the release toggle on the self-inflator for his vest.

The rubber-reinforced vest and collar puffed up to its full size, enough to carry a 250 pound man and then some. Wilson inflated his vest. Soon they were riding with their heads comfortably out of the water tilted back. The water at the surface was warmer, but still cool.

"Looks like our problems are not quite over," Clark said pointing at a large warship headed toward them, about two miles distant. They could see it clearly each time a wave lifted them to its crest. "I can't be sure, but that doesn't look like a U.S. vessel. We don't have any ships with half a flight deck."

"What do you mean? Is it a Russian ship? I thought you got off the emergency submarine buoy?"

"I did, and it's around here somewhere. Any U.S. warships in the area should be converging on us shortly; that is, if there are any in the immediate vicinity.

"My guess is that's the *Moskva* or one of her sister ships. We had some classes on ship identification during the off-crew. We may have jumped from the fire into the frying pan. Those must be Thomas's cohorts waiting to put men on board the submarine."

"What do we do, Senior Chief?"

"There's not much we can do. We wait. They may not see us. We're a couple of miles away and pretty small. If they do pick us up, however, they are not going to want to leave any witnesses around.

"Look at the bright side. This is a chance to get some sun. I've been waiting many years for swim call in mid-patrol."

Clark lay back, his arms folded across his chest. Already the sun was starting to warm his face and dry his hair. A seagull circled overhead. Clark looked up at the clear, blue Mediterranean sky. It was one of those days when you could almost see forever.

"Senior Chief! Take a look over there," Wilson said, pointing at a periscope poking though the water about thirty degrees off the line of sight between the two men and the warship bearing down on them. "Someone is checking us over. Think its one of ours?"

Clark looked over as the submarine followed the periscope up, white water washing off its jet-black sail and sail planes as it broke the surface. It was a beautiful sight.

"Looks like one of ours," Clark said. "It's a 688 class."

A head appeared at the sail. Cupping hands around his mouth, Captain Hammer hollered, "Hey, would you guys like a lift?"

Clark cupped his hands around his mouth. "I don't know. Which way are you going?"

EPILOGUE

USS Martin Luther King

THE submarine slipped lower in the water. A large, black marine creature as silent as those within her.

A gunshot rang out in the engine room. The sound-damping tiles on the hull stifled the sound quickly in the now-lifeless ship.

The depth gauges in the control room proclaimed the depth to unseeing eyes. A light winked coyly on the ballast control panel; a portable water tank was full.

On the steam plant control panel in maneuvering, a red warning light signaled a high temperature on a main turbine bearing. No one noticed.

The small down angle on the ship caused water to flow from the aft trim tank to the forward trim tank with the valves on the ballast control panel lined up in the open position. The automatic depth control system compensated for the increased angle by increasing the rise on the stern planes.

The evaporator continued to make fresh water out of

sca watcr. Thcrc was still room in portablc watcr tank number two. The small increase in weight was compensated for by the automatic depth control system by increasing the rise on the fair water planes. Everything still operated within limits.

The main seawater pump continued to leak, but it was less than a gallon per hour. The engine room bilges were quite large. There was nothing to worry about. No one worried.

A stray current pushed the submarine slightly off course. Or was it the almost imperceptible list to the port which turned it to the side? The automatic control system brought the ship back to almost the correct heading. The gyro that provided an input signal to the control system for ship's heading had drifted slightly so that the ship's true heading no longer matched the gyro heading.

The ship's speed was slightly under three knots. The flux pattern in the nuclear reactor had changed ever so slightly as the reactor continued to provide power to the main turbines and the turbine generators. Withdrawing the rods from the reactor a small distance would have put everything in spec. No one lifted a hand.

The newer Navy submarines had sufficient uranium in their core to cruise several times around the world without refueling. With the power still available in its almost new core, the *King* would be able to cruise just a few days short of forever, silent and virtually undetectable.